If Kaiden can kill his master, he can become a vampire lord in his own right, beholden to no one and free of a thrall's overpowering bloodlust. Or at least Johann says so. To kill his master, Kaiden will have to learn how to fight against a powerful vampire lord who's preyed on the countryside of Kaiden's old home for centuries. The tools of the vampire hunters are weak, and the holy magic of the fallen empire has long faded. But the true problem is Kaiden's own nature. If a thrall drinks human blood, they become mindless killers. Kaiden can survive on animal blood, but his hunger for humans is always there. And Johann, handsome and kind, is especially tempting.

If Kaiden can resist his own bloodlust, he can live as he chooses and be a beacon of hope for a civilization fallen to vampires. If he fails, he will fall to the fangs of his master or to the stake of the man he's learning to love.

This book was previously published.

Thrall
Copyright © 2020 Ravon Silvius
ISBN: 978-1-4874-3102-0
Cover art by Martine Jardin

Published by eXtasy Books Inc or
Devine Destinies, an imprint of eXtasy Books Inc

Look for us online at:
www.eXtasybooks.com or www.devinedestinies.com

THRALL
FALLEN EMPIRE TRILOGY BOOK 1

BY

RAVON SILVIUS

CHAPTER ONE

The man my master had commanded us to kill stood on the other side of the river. His wagon creaked as the wooden wheels rolled over the bridge. The man was a mere shadow, even to my enhanced eyesight, silhouetted against the rising moon.

To my left, another of us chattered her teeth, her fangs emerging from her lips. My own stomach growled at the thought of the warm blood that would gush from the man's veins and feed us. Until now, Master had forbidden us human blood. This would be the ultimate prize. So much better than the deer and other forest creatures I'd been feeding from.

The wagon moved slowly, the horses straining to pull it across the arched bridge. There were two, both with dark-colored coats. One wore a frayed blanket across its back, and the other limped as though its shoes fitted improperly. This man was clearly no wealthy merchant.

One of us hissed, a sibilant, high-pitched sound that only those like us could hear. An answering hiss came from the bushes near the river. Our master had given us the plan, and we would follow it.

The lead horse flicked an ear. The man in the wagon seat shifted his weight.

As soon as the first horse set hoof on the grassy bank, the one to my left attacked. Four others joined her, dark shapes against the light of the moon, swarming toward the animals and their pumping, flowing blood.

I cursed in my mind. I had been turned too recently, and

compared to them I was slow. I swallowed saliva, my fangs pricking my lower lip, and leaped forward, dashing through the forest.

Then light flooded the trees.

The four who'd run ahead screamed, their hissing drowned out by the sizzling of bodies exposed to solar light. I ducked behind a tree, screwing my eyes shut. Heat from the light prickled on my skin.

This was no weak man the master had sent us to eat, a gift to us. This was a vampire hunter.

And I was just a thrall.

The light died, fading to a dull orange glow over the horizon. A solar flare would work only once. I knew that from . . . somewhere. My life before, I supposed.

My muscles tensed when the man spoke—a word to his horses, or perhaps just a comment to himself. The man was mine. The other servants were dead. I would kill the hunter, take all his blood for myself. Me, the newest, weakest servant, able to take human blood. The command tightened my muscles further and pounded in my head. My master's order—*Kill.*

I peered out from the edge of the trees, my vision sharpening with bloodlust. The man's heart beat in a slow, steady rhythm. The light from the wagon made my eyes water, even used up as it was, but it couldn't hurt me. Not any longer.

The hunter sat in the wagon seat, a weapon of some sort across his lap. He wore tight leather trousers, and my gaze lingered over his muscular thighs. For a moment I imagined taking more than just blood.

The thought died quickly. Since my master had turned me, any lust but that for blood never lasted.

The man had light brown hair, though it appeared red in the fading light of the solar flare. Dark eyes scanned the forest and then settled on me.

I froze, my own thoughts tangled, my body screaming for

me to take his blood. His scent—human and sweat mixed with woodsmoke and the bouquet from the village over the river—filled my nostrils.

He raised the weapon. I now saw it was a crossbow outfitted with a wooden stake. His heartbeat was steady. In that moment, I knew I would die.

My master's orders still screamed in my brain, in my very being—*Kill*. I was a servant. I obeyed. I was a weak vampire servant, nothing more. But I knew I would die if I attacked.

I didn't want to die.

His horse snorted. The hunter held his crossbow trained on my heart. The sharp wooden stake that it would fire jutted from the barrel. A servant like me would never survive that.

I could attack. I wanted to leap, to try to sink my teeth into his veins, to obey the orders of the one who'd made me what I was. My teeth ground against each other, and my fangs drew blood from my lower lip.

Instead I turned and fled without truly knowing why. No shot came from the forest.

The unusual silence in the forest as I ran back distracted me from my hunger, and it took me a moment to remember that every other servant was dead. I was truly alone.

I hadn't known them. It shouldn't matter. We hadn't even spoken, only interacting when we fought during our nightly hunts for deer or other animal blood. Without them, there would be more for me. I should be glad.

But happiness, like anything else, faded quickly. I fought to keep running, to ignore the command in my mind that told me to turn back and kill the man I'd been ordered to kill. Doing so would be suicide. He was a hunter. He killed things like me for a living.

It was only when I entered the castle grounds that I wondered if my master would be angry with me.

The gates soared over my head, carvings of wolves seated atop iron bars. The castle blocked the view of the mountain that both overlooked it and kept it hidden from curious on-lookers. Gray stone and old rotted wood melded against dead trees.

I took my usual path, through dusty hallways on the fringes of the main keep. Inside, thousands of scents mingled, mold mixing with cold stone and dead leaves and the sharp scents of the other thralls. Their scents would fade. The scent of blood wound through it all, and saliva filled my mouth.

I followed the scent, my bare feet silent on the cold stones, and found my master where the stone became plush rugs. A shiver of fear went down my spine but faded quickly, just like every other emotion or feeling I had.

"What are you doing here?" My master's voice chased away everything else. "I still sense that man on my territory."

The vampire who had made me strode closer. His blond hair was tied back with a blue ribbon, and deep blue eyes met mine. He frowned, and I ducked my head, curling in on myself like a cur. I should have attacked the hunter and been done with it.

"Where are the others?" my master said, his voice fainter, the presence of his power decreased on my shoulders and chest.

"Dead," I managed. "The man was a hunter."

"Hm." My master turned on his heel, striding down the hallway. With a whisper of his power, I was compelled to follow. He always paced when he thought.

My master's shoes clicked on the stone floors, the sound loud and echoing down the halls. I heard tiny hearts beating from creatures racing along the floor and outside the open windows, the blazing fast pulse of mice, and once the slower beat of a cat that must be hunting them.

"Why did you return?" my master asked. I tore my gaze

away from the bare stone walls.

"I . . . I could not kill him."

"I ordered you to kill him." My master stopped walking, pivoting on his heel like a dancer. He was far more graceful than a human dancer would be, though. "I'm surprised you returned. Why?"

I blinked, mind racing. My master stared at me, blue eyes steady, his mouth a firm line. His shoulders were thrown back and square.

"I thought you might like to know that he's a hunter," I said, my fangs snapping on the words. "He's likely hunting you."

"I feed only on the unwanted, the criminals and the freaks of the village. I am a boon to those humans. Why did they send a hunter?"

The words brought a strange stabbing pain in my chest that it took me a moment to place. Distant, hazy memories, ones that used to matter, played through my mind.

I had been unwanted. Penniless, homeless, a slave to drink who everyone always taunted. The son of a whore, never amounting to anything. I remembered little of my life, fits and flashes, but I knew that much.

But not anymore. My master had made me strong. Nearly two months ago, he'd given me new life.

"Well?" my master snapped, bringing me back to the present and to the drafty halls of the castle. "Did the hunter speak to you, make demands, or any such thing?"

"No." I had not heard his voice. "He killed the others with a solar weapon. He was going to kill me with a stake, but I ran."

"A solar weapon." My master's words were cold. "A relic of the old Empire. Foolish to waste it on thralls, but he may have more of them. Hunters tend to know more history than I'd like."

I didn't respond. There weren't many things that could kill a vampire lord like my master. I supposed a flare was one of them.

"And now you are my only servant." My master frowned. "A disobedient servant." I ducked my head.

"Go and feed on a deer in the forest. Do not enter the city. And stay very, very far from that hunter. I have nothing to fear from him, but you do." My master waved a hand. "Dismissed."

Before I could move, my master vanished the way he always did when he was done with me. His command thrummed in my brain. I headed toward the end of the hallway, out through a door of rotting wood and mold.

The soft wind rushing and the chirps and chitters from the forest quieted the clamor in my mind that competed with my master's order. I had every intention of following his command — my fangs lengthened, saliva filling my mouth at the thought of a meal, even if it was just animal blood. I had yet to taste a human.

But another part of me wondered, even as I crouched into a hunter's stance and listened for my prey, about the hunter and what my master was going to do. He had used his solar weapon, but he might have more. He might be hunting my master.

Of course, my master wasn't stupid enough to charge a hunter as we had. He was no mindless servant.

Then again, I supposed as I picked up the gamey scent of deer, I wasn't mindless either — I'd survived.

I wondered if my awareness, my mind, would last. The others had been older, had served Master for far longer than I. It had been a mere two months since master had drained my blood and made me what I was now. They had been turned years ago, I think, and the only words they'd ever spoken to me with any routine had been "move, weakling," or "wait your turn." They always took the largest share of any animal kills we made. And they had leaped mindlessly to their deaths.

Once, weeks into my turning, they'd told me about a servant who'd taken a human from the village, who had crossed the river to work on the roads. He hadn't had Master's permission. He had been the oldest, according to the female among us, and finally he'd lost his mind completely. It happened to all of us eventually — we turned into animals.

Master had killed him. I supposed that was fitting. He would kill me, too, if I didn't obey.

A strange fear froze me in place at the thought, and a gust of wind scattered the scent of the deer I'd been tracking. I wondered if all vampire servants feared death the way I did. The others had rushed to their demise without thought. And I'd already died once, in a way, hadn't I?

I remembered very little of that. My master had stood over me, his blond hair a halo in the light of the streetlamps. The cloying scent of alcohol and my own vomit, along with the trash that had littered that alley, still singed my nose in my memory.

"What are you doing here?" he'd asked, his fangs sharp and long. I had thought he was beautiful.

When I'd opened my eyes again, it was to the stone wall of the castle hallways and to a hunger that never left.

The scent of the deer blew with the breeze again, thicker and more pungent. Prey was close. My memories scattered like leaves as I broke into a silent, loping run.

The deer stood out in my enhanced vision, standing like a fool in the light of the stars. I leaped, closing my hands around its neck.

Its hooves drew fiery trails down my sides. A lucky kick caught my knee. Bone popped, but I held on, sharp fingernails digging into the fur of its neck. My jaw clenched, my fangs puncturing the skin of my lip. If I bit now, I would miss the vein and spill precious blood on the leaves.

Vertebrae cracked, and the animal went limp. My vision fuzzed. Drool dripped from my mouth as I leaned down to finally sink my fangs into my prize. It was strange not to have others fighting me for it.

I quickly sucked the animal dry, my mouth filled with the coppery taste of life. It infused my body, filling me with energy and power. My knee cracked once more as the kneecap slid back into place, and the pain of the torn skin faded as it mended itself.

I stood, the dark night a little brighter with the energy of the deer's blood within me.

"Hold there," a voice demanded, and I whirled.

The hunter emerged from the tree line, his stake-loaded crossbow in one hand. In his other he held a lantern, and it took me only a moment to realize it was another solar flare. He'd come prepared.

"You," he said. "Servant. *Stop right there.*"

CHAPTER TWO

My muscles thrummed with power from the deer. If he hadn't been holding two weapons, and if my stomach wasn't full, I would have killed him by now.

He stood upwind of me, and I wished I could scent him. He stood without a trace of fear, his hands steady. I was probably faster, but I couldn't be sure. All I knew was if he wanted me dead immediately, he would have fired by now.

Wind gusted, and the scent of death from the deer wafted back into my nostrils. Something flew overhead in near silence — a hunting owl. I studied the man before me, his well-formed features, tight slacks, and short, dark hair.

"You are very . . . controlled for a vampire's servant," the hunter said. "No desire for human blood?"

I tensed. "I am not permitted human blood." Not anymore. I had failed tonight. Saliva filled my mouth at the thought. Of course, if I killed this man, I would have it. But that would mean disobeying my master again.

"Are there others like you?" the hunter asked. He hadn't moved an inch. "Other servants, aside from the friends of yours I killed?"

I tilted my head. "You think I'd tell you?"

"How long have you served your master?"

I took a step back, some part of my brain firing a warning. I opened my mouth, showing my fangs like a dog snarling. "Don't press your luck, human. You won't kill me."

The hunter did something then that I didn't expect in the least.

9

He relaxed, dropping his guard. The crossbow lowered, and he took his thumb off the switch to the flare. He stood straight, facing me like a man. "I am Johann Malire, a hunter of the fifth order. I was sent here to make the vampire lord in this area answer for his crimes in the village of Penthorn."

I blinked, and for a moment I anticipated killing him. My legs tensed, my mouth opened, and my hands curled into claws.

A gust of wind brought his scent. Masculine sweat. Pine. A spice that was probably something he chewed. And underneath it all, a tinge of fear.

He was afraid, and yet still he addressed me as an equal. No one had ever spoken to me like that before.

Tension left my muscles. If he was afraid, then why? Why had he dropped his guard like that, if he didn't have some sort of trick?

"So, servant," Johann said. If he was aware of how close he'd come to death, he didn't show it, his voice light. "How about you tell me your name?"

I opened my mouth, then froze.

My master never referred to me by name. People and places danced through my head from my time as a human, fleeting images of other people taunting me, my time drinking in bars and in alleys, and an old woman's face. There was a cat.

I didn't have a name. I had one. But it was gone.

"No name, servant?" Johann said. He had the audacity to smirk. "I know it."

"Tell me," I snapped.

"No."

I stepped forward. "Tell me!" Something filled me, a need that for once had nothing to do with hunger for blood. Memories of the cat and the old woman wouldn't leave my head, and there was more, blocked by a haze of alcohol and the image of my master in the alley.

"You're not a human any longer," Johann said. "Chasing human memories may only hurt you, you know."

"Then why did you ask me my name?" I growled.

"Because there's a way for you to be more than what you are. To reclaim who you were, in a way."

I backed up, lifting my head as though he'd slapped me.

"Why are you telling me this?" I growled. "Why would I want that?" The memories began to fade, as they always did, in a haze of indifference, but this time they left edges behind. I should have killed him back with the others. I probably would have died. Why had I even cared then?

"Maybe you don't." He shrugged, turning to leave. "But if you do, come find me. You have my scent now. If you want something more than to die a mindless, blood-crazed servant, that is."

I blinked. "You think you can just go, and I'll *let* you?"

"If you kill me, you'll never know."

"I could bring you to my master."

"And he'd kill me." He began walking away, leaving me alone with only the deer I had killed for company. "It's your choice, servant. Probably the most important one of your short afterlife."

I could have chased after him. I could overpower him, force him to reveal whatever he knew.

My name. Who I had been. Who I was.

Instead, I stayed put until the moon shone directly overhead. I waited for the apathy to return, subsumed by the return of the hunger.

The hunger returned, but the apathy didn't.

I hadn't been to the village since my master had turned me.

The night turned cold as the hours went on, the cold that permeated the air just before the morning began. I shouldn't be here, darting through the trees close the to the village borders, just over the river that separated me from them, the bridge mere yards away. The sun would be up soon.

The village of Penthorn blended with the woods, the houses made of the same pale bark. No fires burned in the town square. Winding alleys radiated from the bell in the center of town, framed by thatched houses that looked small and cramped from my spot in the tree above the river. Most had been abandoned over the past three centuries, but at this hour even the well-kept houses were dim, silent, the only sound the quiet clucking of chickens in someone's front yard. Beyond the houses, fields stretched into the distance. Many lay fallow, but small dots marked sheep that grazed overnight.

The small village was familiar. The bell in the center of the square had marked every morning and evening. I could still hear the sound every night, ringing even to the castle. No one slept in the alley I'd once lain in, although maybe I was unable to see them amid the various twists and turns of the walkways and paths between old buildings.

Part of me wanted to enter, immerse myself in a life I'd had once but could not remember.

I also wanted the blood. Hunting in the middle of a village, surrounded by the beating hearts and scents of living people, would be torturous bliss until I sank my fangs into one of them. Then it would just be bliss. I licked my lips, the deer I'd hunted earlier already forgotten. I couldn't cross running water, not like my master, but the thought of all that blood in the village almost made me want to try.

As I watched, a light flickered to life in the window of one of the houses. I leaned forward, straining to see through the trees.

The light traveled, the spark of a candle held by someone inside. The window dimmed, and then the front door swung open.

"Out you go, Whisk," a reedy voice spoke. "Out, out. Go and hunt."

That voice struck me hard.

"Hey there," a woman said. She was blurry in my vision, and I stumbled when I tried to stand. "You can't sleep here. It's too cold. Come on, let's go back."

"I'm fine."

"No. You want to freeze to death? Holy Laurel may no longer have any power, but I know the holiness of hospitality. Follow me. Come on, now. You know the way. You'll catch your death if you stay here." Matilda turned on her heel, and like a child, not a twenty-year-old man, I followed. Matilda always talked about Holy Laurel. A god that meant nothing anymore, her power gone for centuries no matter how many old women like Matilda used her name to do good.

Her house had been warm, and upon lying down on her couch, I was asleep in minutes. Her cat had slept on my stomach. I left in the morning before she woke, my head pounding.

I blinked, the memory and sensations of warmth and something deeper fading. This time, though, they left something behind. A hollowness that had nothing to do with hunger for blood. I watched, unmoving, as the door closed and a cat prowled away into the night, its ears twitching for the sound of rapid heartbeats and tiny feet. That wasn't the cat I remembered.

At the sound of wheels on wood, I turned.

"Picking out your targets, thrall?" The hunter's voice was loud in my ears after the silence of the river and the village. The lantern he held illuminated the planes of his face and the red highlights in his brown hair. A gorgeous color in the firelight. "Or have I pegged you wrong, servant?" He shifted the lantern from one hand to the other, displaying the crossbow strapped to his back as he rolled his shoulders. "Have you given up, and are you here for me to kill you?"

I frowned. "You can't kill me with that at this range," I said.

"You can't lift it to fire quickly enough."

Johann raised both eyebrows. "Smart, for a servant."

My eyes narrowed. "Why are you following me? Bothering me, if I am just . . . mindless. Like the ones you murdered."

He huffed. "I didn't murder them. I put them to rest. They didn't know it, but that was what they wanted."

I opened my mouth to protest, but the words stilled on my tongue. "How can you know that?" I asked instead.

"I've killed creatures like you for over a decade."

I reappraised him. He was youthful-looking, but his jaw was firm and his eyes held wisdom and a good deal of wariness. Thirty, at least. Older than I had been. "I've seen more vampires, and more of their servants, than you can imagine. All of the servants are mindless drones, intent on fulfilling their master's orders and filling their stomachs with blood, and nothing else."

If he was trying to offend me, it wasn't working.

"Now, servant. You came to this village. Why?" He shifted his weight, the wooden bridge creaking. His horse snorted, the air cold enough to make the beast's breath visible. It wasn't the same horse as either of the two old ones that had pulled the wagon. "Tell me," Johann urged, and he met my eyes.

My gaze instantly shifted away, as it always did when my master looked at me, trained submission. This was just a hunter, not my master, but it was strange to have someone other than my master acknowledge me.

"You really aren't like other servants I've met," Johann said, breaking the silence. "So, depending on your answer, I may not kill you." He flashed flat teeth at me in a grin.

Wariness, not fear, flashed through me. "You can't kill me," I said. "And no, I didn't come here for blood." Saying it brought saliva to my mouth, but it was true. "I fed already. And my master forbid it."

14

"Human blood will make you powerful, you know," Johann said.

My fangs pricked my bottom lip. His scent blew on the wind, filling my nostrils, and his heart beat loud in my ears.

I turned and darted into the forest, putting the man and the village at my back. I had fed. It was time to return to my master.

"I'll see you again, strange servant," Johann said. He didn't raise his voice. He knew I could hear him, no matter how quickly I moved away.

CHAPTER THREE

The farther I ran from the village, the more the memories — and the strange sensations they evoked — faded. By the time I reached the castle, I allowed my mind to wander, letting my senses inform me. Birds flying overhead, the soft gusts of wind against my skin, and the ever-present pattering of paws and claws on stone.

And moaning. My master had found another source of entertainment before retiring for the morning.

I knew I wouldn't escape the sounds. The woman's moans, slow and slurred, permeated every inch of the castle. My master, of course, was silent. Or perhaps it was only because his fangs were probably in her neck while he took her.

He would drain her completely before the sun rose, another lady of the evening lost to the night. Perhaps that was why a hunter was here.

It had taken them long enough. My master took a meal every week.

I navigated the winding halls, passing empty stone. Scuffs marked where a painting had hung once, and in one place letters I could barely read that began with *curse the* were scrawled near the floor. Dust caked the walls. Had I been human, it would have cloyed my nose and lungs.

The moaning slowed and then was cut off with a gasp. In my mind, I imagined the form of my master, crouched over a writhing woman, his body tense.

The image became Johann, the hunter's dark eyes smoldering as he grappled with me. His breath would be hot against my cold skin, his blood delicious.

I stopped, the strongest flash yet of lust going through my body all at once. I steadied myself against the wall.

Fighting confusion, I brought up the image again. Johann, naked, his body warm and powerful, his skin soft in my hands. His strong shoulders, his wide, muscular thighs, how his body would feel against mine. How his blood would taste, coppery and thick.

Warmth I hadn't felt since being turned filled my body. My mind, not my senses, began to sharpen with something I wanted, not something my master had ordered me to want. My fingers curled against the stone. I replayed the sound of Johann's voice in my head.

Then my master's voice boomed in my head, in my being, the way it did every morning. "Sleep."

The sun was rising.

I gritted my teeth as the heat and pleasure faded, swallowed by the command. I hoped, as I lay down on the pallet in the windowless room of the castle with four empty pallets next to me, that I would dream this time.

"Servant." For a moment, I thought I heard the hunter's voice, but then the heavy presence of my master made itself known. My eyes shot open, adjusting immediately to the darkness of the room. No light glowed anywhere, but I didn't need light to be aware of my master standing over me.

"That hunter is still in my forest. I order you to kill him. Drink his blood when you succeed. *Go.*" The words pounded in my head, imprinting me with the command. My master ordered, and I had to obey.

The only way I could tell he left was the absence of his weight on my mind. I followed after him for a short time, turning down the halls and leaving the castle, the order erasing everything inside me except for a burning hunger for blood. The hunter's blood. *Johann's* blood.

The air outside had grown even colder than last night, my skin prickling in a way that told me hunting would be bad, most animals having taken shelter. But my prey tonight was human. And I would not be bringing a body back for my master. The blood would be mine. Hunger roared in my stomach.

But first I had to find him.

I stopped, listening, sniffing the air. The chill brought a clean scent, one that deadened my own and made it harder to pick up others.

I had to think. If I were a hunter, where would I be?

His words from last night replayed in my mind. *I will see you again.*

My ardor for blood ebbed slightly at the memory. He would find me. He wanted to talk to me. Or perhaps he would try to kill me. He knew something important.

But my master's orders made my stomach growl and my mouth fill with saliva. The hunter was prey; that was all. Despite his words, his appearance, and a scent that was delicious in more ways than one, he was human. And I *had* to kill him.

He was human. I turned, darting through the forest toward the village.

The night was young, and lights still burned over the river that separated me from the village. The steady glow of fires in homes and from lampposts burned my eyes as I grew close. People still milled in the town square, and others hurried to their homes. I froze by the water's edge, staying close to the trees. The scents of humans traveled, mingling with the water, a mixture of sweat, stale skin, and alcohol, along with the heavy scent of the riverbank.

The hunter was there, talking to two people. One swayed where she stood, a woman with torn stockings and ruby red lips.

"Taken, last night," she slurred. "I didn't see it. But she

always checks in with me."

I remembered the other woman's moans, drawn out of a lazy throat by my master's fangs. Now I knew where he had gotten her.

"Do you know what time?" Johann asked. I focused on his lips as he spoke, on the powerful way he held his body. Confident, for a human. My master stood the same way often, his movements lending strength to his aura of command.

"Nah. I just know she didn't come back. We stay at the Stuck Pig." She nodded, her body swaying as she did. "You should come by. We girls would like a guy like you." She leaned into him, stroking his arm as she mocked a fall.

My teeth gritted together, my fangs pressing into my gums, and I relaxed my jaw with effort. Memories came back like twinkling stars. The Stuck Pig. The cheapest, dirtiest whorehouse in the village, where I'd been raised and where my mother had worked The madam there had given me a sack of hay once to use as a pillow when I grew older and started sleeping in the streets.

And my master was killing them.

The order burned in my brain once more, erasing something almost painful — a pity for the humans. I couldn't think of pity. Only hunger for the blood of the one my master had ordered me to kill.

I *had* to hunt him, the way he would hunt us.

I watched, silent, as he bid good night to the woman and mounted his wagon. He headed toward the river.

I swallowed a mouthful of saliva, padding on silent feet through the trees. I would not make the mistake the others had last night and charge him as soon as he crossed the river. I would wait. I was alone, and I had to use every instinct my master had gifted me with to make my kill. I could not be ruled by the hunger that cramped my stomach and whetted my mouth. I repeated the thought in my head, even as my senses sharpened, the scent of the hunter thick on the breeze.

Thoughts began to fray. Sweat. Horse. Blood. The sound of his beating heart grew closer, growing louder than rushing water of the river. The scent of him and his horse separated into a unique bouquet, sweet and delicious compared to the stink and refuse of the city.

He paused once he crossed the bridge. I crouched, silent, in the dark of the forest. I would have to be fast, make my ambush perfect. The trail from the river was predictable.

A breeze blew, filling my nose with his scent, more than just blood. My bloodlust faded in the face of something new.

"Damn," he said, and then the crimson, metal scent of blood filled the air. Human blood. The bloodlust returned stronger than before.

I was moving before I could even consider he had cut himself. Blood. My master had commanded me to kill, and I would. Blood erased everything else from my mind.

I wanted the blood. I wanted *Johann's* blood.

His horse reared as I leaped toward the wagon as fast as my muscles could take me. Sharp hooves caught me as I bounded, smashing my foot, but that didn't stop me. I didn't care. Blood was all that mattered.

I met his eyes, a dark gleam.

Then rope erupted from the wagon seat.

My shoulder wrenched from its socket as my leap took me into the net, my momentum stopped completely. I turned. The rope tangled farther, cutting into my skin. My fangs snapped, and I gripped the coarse fibers with both hands.

A dull pang of fear went through me.

"Hold still, servant," Johann said. Ropes tightened around me as I writhed, trying to see him, but I couldn't move enough.

Everything went bright, then dark.

CHAPTER FOUR

The pain of hunger, of bloodlust, woke me first.

"Get up." Johann's voice was second.

My master's command fired through my veins, mingled with my desperate hunger. I lunged toward his voice, my fangs snapping on air as iron shackles clanged against a stone wall and bit into my wrists. Light and heat from the torch in his hand made my eyes water and my skin prickle. Shadows danced around us in the dark stone room, bouncing off the wooden door behind him.

"Listen to me." Johann spoke. I lunged once more, his heartbeat loud in my ears. His scent was maddening. I snapped my teeth again, my fangs cutting my bottom lip. The thoroughly disappointing taste of my own blood tinged my tongue.

"Kaiden!" Johann shouted, and I froze.

"Kaiden, what are you doing here?" My mother's voice was weak, breathy. She looked like a doll as she lay on the straw-filled pallet, wedged in the corner of the small room . . . A broken doll with graying hair among tattered bedclothes. A roach scuttled on the wall behind her, and the scent of sickness and rot filled the room. An actual doll woven of straw lay next to her, a sign of Holy Laurel. "You should go." A rattling breath. "I'll be dead by morning. Go, or you'll get it too. There's nothing left here."

My lungs and throat were already thick with sickness, but I was glad she thought I might have a chance.

21

"That's your name. Kaiden." Johann's voice snapped me back to reality, to the crumbling wall I was chained to. Johann sat across the room, his weapon across his lap. "Are you understanding me, Kaiden?"

Kaiden. Not servant, not thrall. That was my name.

"How?" I asked, my throat dry from hunger and thirst. How had he known my name? I had no idea how long I'd been here, but the lack of complete exhaustion told me it was still night. My weakness and hunger, however, told me it had been hours. I'd never gone this long without some kind of blood before.

"There are some in the village who remember you." Johann's words hammered in my skull. "A young man. A useless drunk whose mother was a whore. They say your love of drink was a weakness of demons, and that she fathered you with the vampire."

"That's not true!" I growled, then stopped, the anger fading as fast as it had come. Why should I care? That was another life. I—no, Kaiden—had been dead for two months, killed in an alley by a vampire. My master.

I was dead. It didn't matter anymore. My master's orders were all that mattered. And he had said to kill—

"Kaiden!" Johann shouted, and I blinked. "Listen to me. I can help you."

Saliva filled my mouth and I swallowed. My fangs still pricked my lower lip. I could *not* find the words I needed and growled instead, the scent of blood filling my nose. His heart beat loud in my head, a steady, calm drumming that inflamed my hunger with every pulse.

"Listen!" His voice cracked in the flatness of the stone room. "Do you want to survive as a man, or die as the demon everyone claims you were?"

My growling stopped. I looked up, meeting his dark eyes.

"Tell me, Kaiden." The sound of my name chased away the

biting, curdling edge of hunger. "Tell me what you think you are."

"I . . ." Saliva and hunger thickened my words. "I am a servant." My master's orders boomed once more. *Kill him!*

"You are *not* just a servant," Johann said, his voice the only thing keeping me from snapping my fangs at him. "You are a thrall. A man turned by a vampire lord, bound by his blood to serve him until you die."

I fell silent. I knew that. I hadn't known the name, the term *thrall*, but I knew what my existence was.

"But . . ." And now Johann stepped closer, his scent overwhelming. His heartbeat steady. "If you truly didn't care about anything but blood, if you were truly the mindless thrall the others were, you would have died with them last night. But you didn't. You ran from me. Why?"

I blinked. He stared at me, his torch burning in his hand. The light hurt, and I looked away.

"Why, Kaiden?" Johann said again. The torch hissed as the wood and pitch burned.

"Why do you even ask?" I said. "I didn't want to . . ." I trailed off. I was already dead. Saying that I hadn't wanted to die would sound foolish.

But it was true. "I don't want to die," I said, a growl entering my voice again. "So if you're going to kill me, I won't let you."

He stood, swiftly for a human but still slow to one like me. He left, the wooden door slamming shut behind him, leaving me in darkness so thick not even my keen senses let me see through it. I closed my eyes.

His light footsteps echoed on stone for at least a hundred paces before fading. A large building, then, but clearly not inside the village. Had it been so, I would have heard familiar sounds. There was also the fact that no sane vampire hunter would imprison a bloodsucker like me in a human village.

I leaned back against the wall. His scent lingered in the room, along with the stench of mold and droppings from small animals. One of the other servants had always complained about her sense of smell. "The whole castle smells like rat crap," she'd growled at us, "except for the main keep, but Master never lets us in there."

Master. Without Johann here, the order had faded, but it was still there. *Kill the hunter.*

I lunged once more against the cuffs, pain flaring down my wrist for a split second. Any harder and my wrist would break.

If I got my fangs in Johann, the break, and any other injuries I had, would heal. I could get out of the cuffs and hunt him if I tried hard enough. That would be what my master would want of me.

I was preparing to lunge again when his footsteps returned. And this time his scent was mixed with something else — fresh blood.

My nostrils flared, hunger cramping my stomach. Deer, just like I had last night.

It wasn't human, but it was better than nothing.

"Here," Johann said as soon as the door swung open. The carcass of a fawn was slung over his shoulders. It hit the ground in front of me with a dull thud. "Have your fill."

I was on it before he finished speaking, my fangs in the animal's neck through the tough, fibrous skin. The blood was cool, not the fresh heart-pumped blood I wanted, but it still filled my stomach, filled my body with strength, and took the edge from my bloodlust.

When I lifted my head, Johann was staring down at me, his expression flat. "Animal blood is all a thrall needs to survive, yes?" he said. "You've never had human blood before."

I nodded, licking my lips. The puncture wound from my fangs was gone.

"Why did you attack me tonight?" Johann asked. "Tell me."

"I don't serve you," I answered back.

"I could kill you, you know," Johann responded, his heart still infuriatingly steady. "You're a bloodsucker, but not a particularly powerful one. A thrall. The lowest of the low. None of them have an ounce of intelligence. They're no more in control of themselves than that animal whose blood you just consumed. So let me guess. Your master ordered you to kill me?"

I stayed silent.

"I thought so." He nodded. "But you, Kaiden" — and when he used my name I paid closer attention — "are different. Slightly, anyway. You ran when you suspected your life was in danger. You planned. You're not mindless." He leaned closer, and if I hadn't just eaten I would have snapped at him again. "And if you listen to me and believe what I have to say, I think I can help you."

I narrowed my eyes. "What could you possibly have that I want, that you'd be willing to give?"

He smiled. "Pretty words for a thrall."

"You're the one who said I was different."

"Yes." He nodded, pausing, the smile fading from his face before he took a breath. "What if I told you that you could become a vampire lord in your own right? A true vampire, beholden to no one. No sire to control you."

I fell silent, awash in the small sounds of vermin scuttling in the stones I was chained to and the steady beat and breathing of the human next to me. A vampire lord. Like my master. The beauty, power, and grace of my master would be mine. I felt no excitement at the prospect.

"You think I want power?" I finally said.

Johann frowned. "Do you want to die instead?" he asked. "Because your only option is death or moving on as you are — a thrall to a vampire. Become one, and you won't be such a slave to your own bloodlust."

I stared at the human, his scent filling my nostrils. With my stomach full, he smelled different, a combination of spice and pine that I found pleasing for a different reason.

I wondered if becoming a vampire lord meant I could bed others the way my master did.

"How would I do this?" I asked.

He shifted his weight, tensing muscles the way I would if I anticipated an attack. "By killing your master," he answered.

Something in me thudded hard. Not my heart. Something deeper, an instinct I didn't know I had that made me bare my teeth and narrow my eyes.

"I knew you would react that way." Johann spoke louder. I was growling, my teeth clenched. "You're a creature of instinct, a dog defending his master. But think, Kaiden!"

My name again. The room grew silent.

Johann moved, turned his back to me, setting a thoughtful pace. A very human thing. "If you kill your master, you will feel again. I mean *really* feel." He leaned closer, sending his scent over me. I didn't think he realized it. "Feel emotion. Feel pleasure beyond slaking your hunger. You will feel ambition. Your life will have meaning!" He met my eyes—his contained a startling gleam. "Don't you want that?"

I dropped my gaze. In my mind I saw the same image, that of a woman dying on a bed. I tasted a hint of alcohol, a bitter tinge on my tongue.

I could remember so little of my life before, but I was sure I'd never wanted anything. I'd never thought my life had meaning. The realization made me feel deader than I already was.

"I had no life before," I said, clinging to those flashes of memories. How strange to do so. I'd been so ready to forget, but now it seemed important that Johann understand. "You know. You spoke to the villagers." I met his eyes this time.

"You said they called me a demon, a useless drunk. I had nothing. Why would you think I—"

"Did you hate them?" Johann snapped. "Do you want to kill them all and take their blood?"

I gritted my teeth and didn't answer.

Johann rocked back on his heels, his gaze fixed on a point above my head. I craned my head up. There was nothing there.

"Do you truly think this is better?" he asked finally. "Do you hate the villagers and want to kill them? Some of them called you a useless drunk, a waste. It's true. I won't lie to you."

The anger I expected didn't come. It was simple nothingness, not sadness the way it had once been.

"I don't feel anger."

"I believe you." Johann met my eyes. "For all the pathetic life you may have lived, the scorn some showed, you don't seem to hold any anger. Thralls don't feel." He sighed. "If you showed viciousness and malice like a vampire, I would have killed you by now."

I leaned my head back, the stone scraping against my hair. Thralls didn't feel. I hadn't felt then, before I'd died. When I'd lain beneath the fangs of my master. I had thought I would die, and it would be over. I still could — if I attacked Johann . . .

No. That wasn't what I wanted.

Regret tried to climb my throat. Regret for the life I once had, thrown away.

"I don't want to hurt anyone from the village," I said.

"Good," Johann said. "Then you will come with me, Kaiden. And if you're good, and I can trust you, then I will help you kill your master."

CHAPTER FIVE

The wagon was loud.

Of course, it wasn't just the wagon. To my ears, *everything* was loud. Stuffed into the interior of the wagon like a sack of grain, I could hear every movement of the creaking wheels, every snort of the horse, and every stomp of its hooves on the ground.

I had chosen to go with Johann, but I was still chained. He wouldn't trust me in any village.

I predicted when it would happen. The wagon was dark, but exhaustion stole over me at once. A command thrummed in my mind, but weakly. My master was leagues away at least. We were far from the village and the old castle.

Then the morning exhaustion stole over me and I closed my eyes. The wagon was like a coffin.

"Get up, Kaiden!" Johann's voice. He had woken before me. "I'm keeping your schedule now."

Pale moonlight stole into my hiding spot from the opened door to the compartment, and the night air drew me the rest of the way from sleep. Hunger cramped my stomach, but before I could lunge for Johann at the scent of him, something warm was thrust at me.

I sank my fangs into the neck of the pig before I knew what I was doing. It was still alive when I bit down, and sharp cloven hooves tore at my chest while it died.

"Good," Johann said when I was done. He raised an eyebrow. "You are very clean for a thrall."

"I don't waste blood," I said. I tossed the dry body to the ground. The horse flicked its ears back when I left the wagon.

Johann held his crossbow ready. Of course he would. I had agreed, yesterday. But now, even far from my master, I knew I could run through the night and make it back to him before sunup.

Either he'd given me up for dead or I was more in control of myself than I realized. I waited, looking to Johann, his scent winding around me. He smelled of sleep-sweat and the forest we'd traveled through.

"We will keep traveling," Johann said. "But while we do, we can talk. I assume you'd prefer keeping pace with the wagon to staying holed up inside, right?"

I raised my eyebrows at his tone. The guarded, careful words were gone. He spoke to me like . . .

Like a human. Like I wasn't a demon, or a pathetic man with no future. Even in my life before, I wasn't used to that.

"I won't run away," I said, and Johann nodded. "But where are we going?"

"To a place close to the merchant road where we study creatures—people—like you." The slip didn't offend me. "A gathering place for vampire hunters."

My jaw tensed, my back teeth grinding. "They'll kill me."

"No." Johann patted his horse, and it began to walk, Johann beside it on foot. I followed. "Hunters are experts at killing your kind, it's true. But me—I'm different. I'd like to study you too. I've captured thralls before—none like you, of course. And hunters exchange information about vampire lords, like your master. We decide what to do when they are as large a threat as he is."

"Is that why you hunt him?"

"Kaiden, your *master*"—and the word twisted in Johann's lips—"has been killing in Penthorn for years."

I nodded. The oldest of the thralls had been turned years

ago.

"Yes, he takes those who he thinks won't be missed. But they are. He, like all vampires, hunts humans the way you hunt your deer."

I closed my eyes, letting my other senses guide me through the forest. My master. Dimresh.

He had paid no attention to us, other than to order us to kill those he wanted killed — like Johann. In the past, before I'd been turned, I knew he'd ordered the others to kill humans. Aside from killing, he told us to watch the castle and make sure people left him alone.

That was an easy order. No one had ever come.

Every week or so he brought a human to the castle, and we would leave when he did. A woman, usually, but sometimes a man. He would go to the village to get them.

I never saw him leave. He could move more silently than I could. He had power, too, a power to make those he took obey him. There was no other explanation for why they never fought. Of course, I hadn't fought either. I frowned.

"Kaiden?" Johann asked, and I opened my eyes to his dark brown ones as he walked beside me. "What do you know of your master?"

An owl flew overhead, silent to everything but me. "Very little, for someone who's served him." I envisioned him in my mind, a tall, beautiful man with blond hair that he kept tied back. His blue eyes always looked down at me, giving him even more of a commanding presence.

I remembered, when I was human, his beauty had held something sexual in it. I had desired him. But I felt nothing when I thought of him now. Johann's scent next to me was more distracting than my master's had ever been once I began my life as a thrall.

"If I can become a vampire lord just by killing him" — Johann's eyes widened at my words — "then does that mean my master became a lord by doing the same?"

"Unlikely." Johann shook his head. A leaf fluttered from a tree, and I tracked it past his neck. Sudden craving flashed through me, my fangs pricking my lip. "If a vampire wants to create another, they will allow the thrall to drink some of their blood before they are turned. That is the typical way, or so we believe. Some say it doesn't work that way, but we haven't figured out the details yet. There's a lot we don't know," he finished with a sigh.

"Oh." I tore my gaze away from his neck, looking instead down toward his tight slacks that hugged muscular thighs. That kind of hunger was more welcome. "So . . ." I fought to focus. "So how do you *know* it is possible for me to kill him and become a vampire? And . . . *why*? Why not just kill him yourself and be done with it?"

"The more you speak to me, the more human you sound," Johann said with a laugh.

I blinked.

"Your master is powerful. One of the most powerful vampires we know of. That's how he's held his own territory for so long — you've never met another vampire like him, yes?"

I nodded.

"None would risk entering his territory. He's ruthless as well. Believe it or not, not every vampire in the world stakes a claim to a territory and kills as many as he has."

"Thralls kill," I said.

"That's true." Johann eyed me. "But they're different. Thralls are mindless."

"My master isn't mindless. He takes blood . . . slowly." I thought of the women he'd brought back.

"I'm sure he does." Johann held up a hand as if waving away something foul. "Vampires have control. The control a thrall does not have and does not hope to have. You are a strange one, and not something I've seen before, but I guarantee you—if I pricked my finger now, like I did last night, you would be on me in a heartbeat, eh?"

I swallowed a mouthful of saliva at the thought. "Faster than," I said.

Johann tilted his head, eyeing me carefully, tension entering his shoulders and hips. "Are you hungry again already? How much blood do you take a night?"

Talking about it only made the hunger worse. I swallowed hard. "I will hunt now," I said. "I will come back."

"Kaiden!" Johann snapped, but I was gone before he could continue whatever he was going to say.

This was not the kind of hunger that cramped my stomach, fueling desperation. It was more a craving. A craving for the blood of the man in front of me. Maybe if I stuffed myself, erased any hunger at all, I wouldn't feel it so keenly.

I was a thrall, a mindless thing, like Johann said. Or I was supposed to be. Instead I'd become something strange, something never seen before, if Johann was right.

I didn't understand what was happening. I didn't understand *myself*. But I didn't need to think about that right now.

Johann's wagon and horse had scared away most of the big game. Only a few miles out—mere minutes away at my silent speed—I scented prey. Another hunter. A big cat, resting fitfully after what must have been an unsuccessful dusk hunt.

I struck before it had the chance to sense me. For all their power, other predators were easier prey—they never expected it.

The cat's claws lashed at me in its death throes, but after a few mouthfuls of its blood, it ceased, and the blood healed the wounds the animal had inflicted. I drank deeply, more than I needed, reducing the cat to a husk of its former self. I felt fuller than ever, almost bloated on strength and blood.

I could go back now. I didn't crave Johann any longer.

I darted back through the trees, pausing when I saw him.

He'd followed me, tracking my trail, his crossbow in one hand and the solar lantern in the other. He moved like a predator, even more effectively than the panther I'd just killed.

He'd thought I would run. I frowned, the cat's blood still tingling on my tongue. I had told him I would come back.

"Johann," I called out. He whipped the crossbow up, pointing it directly at me. Despite his gesture, his eyes weren't focused on me at all. He couldn't see me.

"So our plan ends here then?" I called out. "I said I would come back." Something flashed through me — regret, maybe. Then it faded.

He moved the crossbow, the tip of the sharp wooden stake now pointing directly at my throat. "Come out," Johann demanded, his voice a whip. "Come out now and we'll talk."

My jaw tensed. For all his words, he didn't trust me.

Of course he didn't. I was a thrall.

I stepped out of the brush. I got within ten feet before he saw me, holding up the solar lantern. I squinted, my eyes tearing, and prepared to run.

"Kaiden, damnit. What did you feed on?" Johann asked. The glow faded when he covered the lantern once more. His heart pounded.

"A big cat." I bared my fangs. "I told you I would return." I pointed to the remains of my kill. Johann moved past me, his scent filling my nostrils while he investigated. But my plan had worked. The craving for his blood didn't return. The craving for his body was still there, though, a rippling current that flared and faded.

"And for all I know, your hunger could have caused you to return to the village and feed on someone," Johann said. "I was a fool for letting you go untied. You have to obey me, or I'll have to kill you."

I tensed my legs. "I won't let you kill me."

"I'm not going to kill you now," Johann said. "But before

we get to the gathering place, you must agree to be tied down."

Tied down. Because he didn't trust me. Because my hunger could, *would,* control me, and I would seek human blood. *A mindless thrall.*

"It's that or I hunt you normally," Johann said. "I know you don't want to be a monster."

"But I am one," I said. My fangs pricked my lower lip. Johann's scent surrounded me, a constant miasma of temptation that would grow stronger with every kind of hunger. "I will agree to be tied."

I wanted to live, after all. Really *live.* He had said I could be more than . . . whatever I was.

"Does my blood still smell good to you, even after your meal?" Johann walked back toward the wagon, his steps clumsy and loud on the brittle twigs underfoot. "You keep moving your head to get my scent." Tension corded his shoulders. I imagined it wouldn't leave him until I was safely restrained.

"All of you smells good." That was the wrong thing to say, but it was too late to take my words back. I was getting hard, a frustrating hardness brought about by his musky, masculine scent, but Johann hadn't noticed. It was worse now that my hunger for blood was completely gone. I wanted to indulge it and see if I could still feel pleasure the way I had when I was human.

Being near Johann made me feel more alive than I had since becoming the monster I was now.

"Now, Kaiden," Johann said once we'd arrived. "Wrists out. Just so you know, this might hurt."

The rope burned. He'd done something to it, some sort of vampire hunter magic—it stole the strength from my arms. I hissed, my fangs flashing, but I quelled the anger even as he reached for his crossbow.

"It hurts," I growled.

"I did warn you." Johann reached for more rope. "Lie down in the wagon. I'll use the chains from before on your legs." Regret tinged his voice.

The wood of the wagon bit into my back. Small creatures burrowed inside with the sound of grinding.

Johann's hands moved over the restraints on my legs and ankles, tying the chain in place. I could break it if I wished, but the time it took to do so would be time enough for Johann to prepare, I was sure. He would kill me if I fought.

I didn't want to fight. I relished Johann's scent surrounding me again as I lay back, drawing out the same hunger for his body. Fear laced his scent, but I focused on the baser parts — the musky scent of his maleness, the tang of his sweat, and the bouquet that was him. I wondered what his touch would be like.

Lust pulsed through me, and I met Johann's eyes in the dark of the wagon. My wrists and legs were bound, but it didn't matter. My hardness jutted through the ragged clothes I wore. His gaze flicked down to it, once, then back up.

"I will travel through the night and day and we should arrive before morning tomorrow night. I will keep you fed." With that, he shut me in the dark.

I had wanted to ease my hunger, but that had been a mistake. I wouldn't be trusted, not as a thrall.

This time I dreamed as soon as the exhaustion of the day came over me.

The acrid taste of wine stained my mouth. It had gone mostly to vinegar, but it was still enough to ease my craving. I'd been desperate for it, my body shaking with weakness. I stood in the alley behind the bar, voices and laughter faint from inside.

"Don't let him have that," a voice said, and I saw Ronaldo. His stained apron rustled as the skinny man came toward me. "Get out

of here, whoreson."

*"He's not hurting anything, and no one else's gonna drink it."
Another man, a younger one, turned big eyes to the barkeeper.*

"It'll keep him coming back. He can go bother James at the distillery if he wants it that bad, but he's an eyesore here." The man moved fast, knocking the cup from my hand. Wine splashed to the ground, the pewter cracking at the same moment he shoved me. I stumbled backward, the world around me spinning.

I jolted awake, my eyes opening to the pitch dark of the wooden interior of Johann's wagon. The hunger for wine faded with the memory of the dream. I was reminded of my hunger for blood.

I had traded one hunger for another.

"Food," Johann called. At his voice, I turned and bared my fangs. He still smelled so good.

I lunged as soon as he opened the hatch, sinking my teeth into the stiffening meat of a full-grown deer. Johann was taking no chances on my appetite.

I couldn't miss the expression on his face when I lifted my head. His brows were narrowed, his mouth turned down. It was the same look Ronaldo had given me.

I swallowed the last mouthful. I didn't recognize the area, although the same scents filled my nose, the same species of trees and animals nearby.

Ahead, though, a faint light glowed through the trees. I narrowed my eyes.

"In only a few hours' time, we'll arrive," Johann said. "Stay there. Be on your best behavior. If you aren't, there's a strong chance you'll be killed regardless of what I say."

"I won't hurt anyone," I said. Johann didn't respond. I took one last look at the forest before Johann shut me inside again.

We hadn't spoken at all since I'd begun riding like this. Some part of me hoped we would once we arrived.

It was that or fall back into nothingness and fragments of

memories that should matter but didn't. I wondered what wine would taste like now.

The creak of the wagon and the quiet breathing of the horses, and of Johann, wound in my ears as we rode on for what must have been hours. The horses' breath was soft and slow, and their gait lighter. Perhaps they knew they were coming home.

Johann's heart beat slightly faster than usual. He was nervous.

I ground my teeth together, then loosened my jaw when the tension just brought the memory of craving. I would be good. I might be a vampire servant—a thrall—but I didn't want to die.

Not anymore.

I was wondering what my master thought of my not returning, or if he simply thought I was dead, when I heard the clumsy sound of human footsteps up the path. Two of them.

"Ahoy there!" A voice rang out, low-pitched through the wood of the wagon. "Who's there?"

"Cursed Samuel still thinks he's a river captain . . . ," Johann muttered under his breath. Then "Johann, returning! I bear important information but would rather not approach yet—send out Susana!"

Leaves crunched under their feet, and then the night was silent save for the faint sounds of life around me.

"Stay calm," Johann said. "I'm going to take you out of there now while they're fetching one of our finest hunters. When she gets here, I want you to look as much in control as possible." While he spoke, the wagon opened. Moonlight shone into my small prison, outlining Johann's form.

I uncoiled myself, snarling but not growling when he tightened chains around my wrists. I met his eyes, a memory of other people in my past always looking away going through my mind. The only person who always held my gaze had been my master.

Johann's brown eyes smoldered in the light from the lantern on his wagon. "Good," he said. "They may want you locked up—in fact, I'm sure they will. We have to keep you under control. But I will stay in contact with you. And—"

The breath whooshed out of me all at once. A force hit me in the side, and my blood sprayed the ground. Weakness went through me, the forest spinning in dim circles. The urge to fight back sped through my body, but I couldn't twist my neck to bite, no target in sight. The energy faded fast as blood dripped from the wound.

"Relax, Susana!" Johann shouted. "He's no threat! Don't shoot again!"

Hunger made me snap my fangs, but weakness threatened to pull me into a sleep that would be different from the sleep of the day. I fought to stay awake, meeting the eyes of a woman who held a crossbow to my face.

CHAPTER SIX

The woman staring back at me narrowed her blue eyes into slits. I focused on the weapon, growling, but I knew better than to fight. With the injury to my side, I couldn't have tried to bite if I wanted to.

"His name is Kaiden," Johann said, his voice sharp. "He agreed to come here. For now, he's under my protection." For all his words, he sounded more afraid than he ever had when talking to me. "Don't kill him, Susana. He's tied to the wagon, see!"

"He's a thrall," the woman called Susana said with a sneer. "I know you've brought thralls here before for your little studies, but not loose like this one. There are hunters, Johann, injured ones. Are you a fool?" Her gaze left my face, focused on what must be Johann.

"He's not like other thralls. He's not mindless. Let him speak and you'll see." Johann's eyes met mine, a silent plea.

I had enough blood in me still that my wound was knitting together, if slower than usual.

I blinked hard, letting the soothing scents of the night wash away anything else. The air was overlaid with the scent of Johann, his maleness and a tinge of his fear, and the anger and fear scent of the woman in front of me. Another hunter. I twitched my nose.

"Scenting me, thrall?" she said with a snarl. "*Now.* Speak up. Did you really agree to follow Johann here? Why, for easy kills?"

I narrowed my eyes, ignoring the distant scent of wood

smoke and horse that spoke of just that. "Why are you shooting a bound thrall?" I retorted. "Easy kills?"

Johann actually laughed. I liked that sound.

Susana's widened. "You are truly a thrall?" she asked, the malice in her voice mostly gone.

"You see?" Johann said. "He's unique. A thrall with humanity. I intend to see if we can work with him, perhaps have him help us kill Dimresh."

Dimresh. My master.

The woman eyed me. "We'll see. Take him in — and keep him chained. He may be in control now, but surrounded by people, I doubt it. Your stories are madness, Johann."

"Come on, then, Kaiden. I have much to tell you — and you have much to learn." He nodded at the woman and then slapped the horse's side. It pulled the wagon toward the compound.

Their compound was a castle, but a castle far more modern than my master's. The scent of decay and dust didn't cloy my nose as we approached the iron gate, and the sounds of life hummed from within. A cat leaped past us as we approached. Johann smiled at it.

"You won't be entering here," Johann said as we approached the gate. "I'm sorry, Kaiden."

"The dungeons, then?" I asked.

"I'll take it," Susana said. "I am —"

"No," Johann said. "Let me. Don't worry. I'll keep him tied."

I met his eyes, and a flash of heat went through me.

"You should report to the Master Hunter immediately afterward," Susana said, eyeing me carefully.

Johann untied my legs when she left, but kept his own weapon trained on me as I stood. I pushed down hunger and the frustration from the pain in my side.

"I'm sorry about that," he said. "I didn't think she'd shoot you immediately like that."

"If she's your finest hunter, she's a bad shot," I said.

Johann laughed again, and the sound of his laughter chased away the pain and frustration as we walked along the slate gray wall, heading toward a squat gray stone compound. The dungeons, I supposed.

"So," Johann said. "What do you know of vampires and thralls?"

"I know I am a thrall," I said, my voice soft in the quiet of the night. "A servant." I sniffed the air, catching more of Johann's scent, and walked closer. His heart picked up.

"Hungry?" he said.

I looked away. "I'm fine." It was true, for now.

"Most thralls feel hunger constantly, especially after an injury like yours," Johann said. "And being near a human is torture for them. Do you not feel that?"

"I feel little right now," I said.

"That makes sense," Johann said. "Thralls have no emotions other than hunger. But . . ." I caught the uncertainty in his voice.

"What?" I asked. His words cut, but only for a moment. It was true. I didn't feel much. But the flickering memories of my village, of my past hungers . . . they were real.

"Tell me, Kaiden," Johann said. "What do you feel? Aside from hunger." We approached an iron gate that barred stone steps into the compound, the stairs leading down. The scent of iron and rust emanated from below. "Do you remember your life before?"

"Only a little," I said. My throat felt tight. "My name helps."

"When you were tied before . . . did you feel desire?" Johann said.

The words sent a rush of surprise through me that lasted longer than I thought. He remembered. "I do feel desire," I said. "At times." I wondered if I should feel embarrassed.

Johann shook his head. "Strange," he muttered, and then unlocked the heavy gate, straining as it creaked. If my hands weren't chained, I could have helped. The weight would be nothing to me.

"Come. I'll find you a nice cell. Down here, the scents of others won't bother you. And then we can talk."

Johann's footsteps were loud on the stone floor, and the stench of death filled my nose. It wasn't just rot—the faded scent of other thralls was everywhere, reminding me of my master's other servants. My one-time compatriots.

"What do you keep here?" I asked. "Thralls like me?"

"One like you is too rare," Johann said. "Now it is those touched by madness. People who desire to be turned. These cells are often for the safety of the ones in them as much as they are for the safety of the others in the barracks."

When I listened, I could still hear the faint sounds of people from the barracks. No scent reached me here, but I could imagine the laughter, the voices, and the light.

I don't know if I missed it.

"Here," Johann said. He stopped by an open door. The black iron shone in the light from his torch, free of any rust. When I stepped inside, the door banged shut with no sound of a creak.

As soon as the door locked, Johann relaxed, exhaling a long breath. His shoulders slumped, and his heart slowed.

I still frightened him.

"For now, you will stay here. I will come back tomorrow night to speak with you." He moved more slowly than he had before as he stepped away, his shoulder shaking from the weight of the torch. He moved like an injured animal.

He was exhausted, I realized. In the back of my mind, I thought *easy prey.*

No. This was Johann. This was life—of some kind.

He turned, heading back toward the stairs. "Johann," I called out. He met my eyes once more. A shiver coursed through me.

"When I ran, that first night you saw me. Why didn't you kill me?" That should have been easy for one like him.

"I don't murder those who don't fight me," he said. "I'm not a monster. Now wait here. I'll introduce you to our leader."

When he left, the dungeons were plunged into pitch black that didn't bother me. I slumped against the stone. The bleeding from my wound had stopped.

I still didn't know whether I was a monster or not.

CHAPTER SEVEN

I closed my eyes, but it made no difference. The stone and iron dungeon I sat in was utterly devoid of light, just like the dingy rooms in the dark hallways of my master's castle.

My master. I was a thrall. Shouldn't I be loyal to him? But no emotion came to me when I thought of him. Only memories, fleeting things like dying sparks.

"Servant," he had said when I woke. I lay in the alley I'd died in, but I no longer felt weak and sick, and the burning pain that had always festered in my stomach from the drink was gone. In its place was something new, a cramping, overwhelming hunger. "You are mine," the beautiful blond man said. His skin was alabaster, his eyes blue. His fangs were stained with my blood. "From now on, you will serve me. I will reward you. Here."

He held out an animal. A cat. The same cat who'd slept on my stomach when I'd slept at Matilda's house. The animal yowled in pain, its claws catching air.

I snatched it from him, its blood refreshing me like nothing ever had before.

I opened my eyes, a pang of something heavy and cold forming in my chest. For the briefest moment, the ever-present hunger was replaced with nausea.

"Thrall," a voice said. I sprang to my feet in an instant and instinctively turned even before the light from a torch flooded the room, burning my eyes.

Johann had returned, and with him stood an older woman,

her neck covered by a metal gorget. Clever. In her right hand she held a metal weapon. I spotted the sharp edge of a wooden stake.

"You are Kaiden?" she said. "Servant to Dimresh?"

I looked past her, at Johann. He gave me the slightest of nods.

"I am Kaiden," I said. I stayed very still — like a rabbit when a cat is hunting it — very aware of the deadly weapon in the woman's hand. Her heart beat fast, but steady, the pace of someone prepared to attack. "Are you going to kill me?"

She blinked, her heart slowing. "That depends on you. Why did you come here?"

I looked to Johann. His heart beat fast too, but he seemed more afraid of the woman than he was afraid of me. "Johann brought me here. He told me I'd have . . ." I licked my lips, and she tensed when I did. "A chance at life. Beyond . . . what I am now."

There was a pause, the dungeon silent. Johann's gaze sent a shiver down my spine that I couldn't explain. A soft, pleading gaze. One of pity.

"He wants to live, Lesalie." Johann said. Lesalie turned at the sound of his voice. "I know that much about him."

I knew that much about myself. I felt like I'd lost a lot more.

"And you think your best chance is with us, not back with your master?" Lesalie demanded.

My master. My lord, but a man I barely knew. He didn't even know my name. "My master sent me out to die," I said. "He ordered me to kill Johann, a hunter, who he knew would most likely kill me. I ran instead."

A slow smile crept over Lesalie's face. "Are you loyal to your master, then, Kaiden? You disobeyed his orders, after all."

"I . . ." I trailed off, gritting my teeth. I *had* disobeyed his orders. He would kill me, most likely. For a moment, fear flooded me, something I hadn't expected. Another emotion, strange and unwelcome.

Lesalie's hand had moved toward her weapon, and I realized I was baring my fangs. I swallowed hard. "Like Johann said. I just want to live."

The Master Hunter relaxed, her hand moving away from her weapon. "Very well then, Kaiden. And Johann." His heart jumped when she turned to face him. "I think this plan of yours may actually work. Come with me."

She turned her back on me and began heading toward the stone steps. Johann gave me one last glance. Then the door to the dungeons swung shut, leaving me once again in darkness.

But through the door, I could hear their voices.

"How is this possible?" she spoke as soon as the door to the dungeons swung shut. "Are you sure he's a thrall?"

"I notice you did *not* test his bloodlust," Johann said. "But if you had . . ."

"Of course." She sighed. "But still. I've *spoken* to thralls before"—her tone let me know how sarcastic she was—"and they do *not* sound like that."

I knew what most sounded like. Dimresh's other thralls. Angry. Simple. Hungry.

"So what?" Johann said. "You think he's some other sort of bloodsucker?"

"I don't fully know what to think," she said. "But you really want to try this plan of yours? Win his loyalty and have him kill his master and become a vampire who's loyal to us? Or wait for him to do your work, and then kill him yourself before he realizes his power?"

I blinked in the dark. Johann's plan. Me, become a vampire loyal to humans. Another form of servant? Or simply a tool to be discarded?

"You'd rather we do nothing?" Johann said. "Anything is worth doing to try to get rid of vampires like Dimresh."

"There's no guarantee this will work, Johann. You may have to put it down soon. I don't like thralls, and this one's strange. That may not be a good thing."

I growled, the sound low in the darkness, but with their human ears I knew they couldn't hear me.

"It's our only chance," Johann said. "We have to try *some-thing*. The magic of the Empire is long gone, and the old ways work less and less well. We have to try something new. We've lost so much already, and nothing works against vampires like Dimresh."

"For now, get some rest," Lesalie said. "You've earned it, and it's nearly morning. And from now on, this Kaiden is your full responsibility."

"I won't let you down," Johann said.

I waited in the dark, but the last thing I heard was their footsteps moving away.

Johann wouldn't let her down. Maybe he would truly help me. Or maybe he would only use me, the same way Dimresh had.

But this still seemed better than drinking blood every night and being ordered to throw myself against someone who would kill me. It was better than the life of a drunk, treated like trash by the rest of the village. This way, I had a choice. Johann had given me that choice. Maybe it was simply a chance to be a different kind of servant, but it was a choice nonetheless. Maybe he would kill me after I helped him. But if I was good, maybe not.

I had no loyalty to humans or hunters. But for now, I wouldn't let Johann down.

I let the exhaustion of the day wash over me. No light would come through the walls of the stone dungeons. As I fell asleep, I heard an echo of my master's voice.

I woke to a pang of hunger and the sound of something

heavy hitting the stone floor.

My eyes shot open, taking in the sight of the open iron door. Johann stood next to it, a freshly bleeding form on the ground.

I moved before I could think, hunger driving me. The door slammed shut, making my ears ring, but that didn't stop me from sinking my fangs into the creature's neck. The taste was familiar — deer.

"Thank you," I said once the carcass looked as though it had been lying in the sun for days, not killed fresh this evening. I stood and moved away from the bars toward the stone wall of the tiny cell. "I was hungry."

Johann gave the body of the deer a disgusted look. "Will that be enough?" He shoved it lightly with his foot through the bars.

I nodded. "For now."

"Good." He stared at me through the bars, calculating. I stared back. He wore different clothes now and smelled freshly washed. Clean and healthy, and . . . tempting. "Are you otherwise well?" he asked.

I put his delicious scent out of my mind. "Why am I here?" I replied. "You told me I would kill my master. But all I have done is be imprisoned."

He swallowed, and through the scent of soap and maleness, I scented nervousness. "Tell me," he said. "What do you know of vampires? Ones like your master, not thralls like yourself. Have you ever seen any other than your master, before coming here?"

No," I responded. My master was the only vampire I knew.

"There are others," Johann said. "Many of them. They are solitary creatures. Some claim a territory and feed there. Sometimes they are impossible to detect — murdering only the very sick, targeting those on the road, the way bandits would. Disappearances that can be explained away. But we hunters are always trying to flush them out and put them down." His heart slowed as he spoke, confidence weaving into his words. He believed in his duty.

"Dimresh—your master—is one of the worst and most powerful. Do you know when he claimed his territory?"

I tilted my head, licking a tinge of blood from my lips. I found it hard to remember living—somehow painful. There were some who claimed my mother had fathered me with the vampire, but those taunts had come later in life, when I'd already taken to sleeping in alleys and begging for drink. Had I ever had a true life? What had caused me to give up so quickly? I hadn't been old. How old had I been?

"Kaiden?" Johann pressed.

I refocused on him. "I don't know," I said.

"We don't know for certain either," Johann said. "But we assume he is very old, like most vampires with his level of power. Centuries. Your master has been targeting messengers and merchants of late, along with undesirables in the village, and making dangerous thralls. I was sent to see if I could prevent more killings, and I brought along powerful weapons from the old Empire."

He must mean the solar flares. "That was why he wanted us to kill you," I said.

Johann nodded. "I imagine so."

"Others would have come if we had killed you, wouldn't they?" I asked. I narrowed my eyes, a thought flashing into my mind. "If you hunters knew about him long ago . . . why did you not kill him then?" My muscles tensed, and in my mind I saw the alley I'd died in.

"Do you feel angry at me for not killing him before he could turn you?" Johann asked quietly.

I stopped baring my fangs at his question. Emotion was strange to me, and memories brought pain. But Johann kept bringing out these fleeting feelings. "I am but recently turned," I said in answer. That much was true. The voices of the others echoed in my mind. *Wait your turn, whelp.*

"I'm sorry for that," Johann said.

At his tone, I growled, some sort of emotion welling in me that I didn't understand. I would have once. "So why didn't you kill him?" I snapped. He took a step back. Fear, I understood. "Why did you take *me*, and not kill *him* as you were ordered to do?"

Johann took a deep breath, like the rushing of wind. In here, that was the closest sound to nature I would get. "Do you know how powerful your master is?"

I stared at the hunter in front of me, protected by iron bars. He'd killed the rest of us effortlessly, using weapons charged by the sun. I had seen his crossbows, with wooden stakes as ammunition. "You're a hunter," I said. "Or do you only kill thralls?"

He gave me a weak smile. "I am always impressed by you," he said. "I hope one day you will realize how unique you are."

"You didn't answer me," I growled.

"Vampire lords have abilities thralls do not," he said. "Powers that rival the magic of the fallen Empire, but dark. Hypnosis. Transformation. Auras of fear. Strength and speed that would put even you to shame. Some have more power than others. And Dimresh uses these powers in fearsome ways. Every hunter who has approached his castle has died. I was sent there to test the solar flares, to see if they could break the fear aura he placed around his castle. They couldn't, not even in the light of day." He sighed. "But when that plan didn't work, I wanted to see if I could establish a new plan to take down a vampire lord who seems unbeatable. And . . . I did find one."

I took a step back, listening to the beat of his heart. It never wavered.

"I'm your new plan," I said. He nodded. He'd been honest

with me throughout. "And . . . what happens to me afterward? Once I become a vampire?"

He raised an eyebrow and laughed, the sound echoing off the stone. "Already so confident that you'll succeed?"

"It's that or die," I said. My master would never let me live if I turned on him. A vampire more powerful than this hunter. Than most other vampires, if Johann was right. Something in me recoiled at the thought of killing him, a loyalty I shouldn't have that curled my fingers into claws, my fangs nearly cutting into my lower lip. Memories of his commands over the two months since my turning thundered in my mind, then mingled with one that suddenly seemed more real. Not a memory.

He was looking for me.

"Kaiden, listen to me," Johann said. His laughter had stopped. "There's a reason I brought you here, rather than sending you at him immediately."

Return. The command was faint, but it was there, and stronger than the unheard command that hadn't punctured my sleep. *Return, servant!*

"Kaiden!"

I snapped my gaze back up to Johann, focusing on his voice. "You're hearing him, aren't you Kaiden?" Johann said. "He knows you're not dead."

"How?" It came out as a growl, and I struggled to sound normal. "How does he know?"

"Vampire lords can sense their thralls," Johann said. "He knows you're alive, and he knows you haven't returned." His eyes narrowed. "He may even assume you've been captured by a hunter, or guess that you've taken human blood and may be lost to mindlessness."

I gritted my teeth against the compulsion, part of me wanting to throw myself against the iron bars. "He told me to drink your blood and return," I said.

51

"Don't do it," Johann said. His voice was weak compared to my master's. "If you take human blood, you will be as mindless as the rest."

I wished he'd stop reminding me. "I don't want it," I said, but that was a lie. Johann smelled like life, like freshness. I could hear his steady heart pound blood through his body. But right now, it was the command to return that I had to fight more than the hunger. I took a step toward the bars, my teeth bared.

"What is he telling you, Kaiden?" Johann said.

Return.

The bars were iron. I couldn't bite through them, but maybe I could bend them. Growling, I put my hands around them, the metal cold and —

Johann threw something, and I hissed, drawing back at the burning pain in my hands. I snarled, and it was all I could do to prevent myself from leaping and snapping at him. He had thrown some sort of burning water on the bars.

"I will sever your link to Dimresh," Johann said. "But you must come with me." Lower, under his breath, he muttered, "I shouldn't have waited this long."

Return.

I sagged. I couldn't keep fighting this command. This was different than the hunger, than the other commands to kill Johann, which had been driven in part by my own bloodlust. My refusal was pain, every second I didn't seek to fulfill his command agony. I could almost feel his will continually fighting mine. His previous commands blended with it, a violent promise. *Kill the hunter. Take his blood. Return.*

"I . . . Johann," I said. My fangs were bared, and I grabbed the iron bars, ignoring the pain. "Do it," I demanded. The room grew less dark, my night vision sharpening. "Hurry."

Johann nodded, his face grim. Then he raised something that flashed, impossibly bright, and pain exploded in my chest.

I hit the wall from the force of it, lights exploding behind my eyes when my head struck stone. Weakness dragged my body down, my eyes falling shut of their own accord.

Johann had killed me. It was all a lie.

But then he stood over me, the weakness stopping just on the edge of taking me into unconsciousness as I blinked. I growled, baring my teeth, but Johann took no notice of me. My arms were wrenched behind my back, chains rattling as he bolted cuffs shut. I wasn't sure where he'd gotten those and wondered how much time it had taken for the weakness to take hold. To me, it had felt like a blink.

"Will this hold him?" I fought to lift my head at the sound of the stranger's voice.

"It did before," Johann answered. "Affix the leg cuffs. Hurry."

At that moment, he drew his hand close to my face, a chain trailing from his grip. My vision was filled with the veins on his wrist, and I could hear his heart pounding in my ears. His blood was right there. One snap and I'd have it.

My mouth filled with saliva, my fangs pricking my lips. Johann's head was turned, watching as the other person tied my feet.

Bloodlust filled me, my master's commands loud in my head.

But there was also Johann's scent, over and above the blood. The scent of sweat and maleness, a scent I craved too. And biting him would ruin that. It would ruin everything.

I turned my head at the last second as the bloodlust overtook me, and instead of latching onto skin and flesh, my fangs fastened hard around the chain links he held, the taste of iron wholly unsatisfying as my fangs scored into it.

Johann yelled aloud, and my head was slammed back against the stone once more, driven by the chain in my teeth. He held it on either side, the metal cutting into the sides of my mouth.

I met his eyes, saliva pooling and running down my chin. I wanted blood, needed blood, to heal from whatever he'd done to me, whatever he'd shot me with. I gnawed on the chain, anger warring with hunger. He was foolish for coming so close, for not paying attention.

"Should I kill it?"

I flicked my gaze to the other person. He held a crossbow loaded with a wooden stake, aimed at my heart. With my legs and arms chained, killing me would be easy for him.

"No," Johann said. "I can tie the chain into his mouth."

"He'll bite you if you try," the other man said. "He almost just did."

No, I tried to say, but it came out as a muffled growl against the chain.

"No, you won't," Johann said, meeting my gaze again. "Right, Kaiden?" He shook the chain in my mouth and hit my head against the stone, a show of force.

I didn't know if he'd seen me go for the chain over his wrist. Or maybe he just trusted me. But I doubted it.

His scent was strange. Animals were easy — they were either afraid or not. I hadn't been around humans since being turned, but fear was an easy scent. The other man was full of it. But Johann's scent held something else, wariness and aggression that combined were more complicated. A fear, to be sure, but almost a desperate one, mixed with excitement.

He needed me. And I needed him.

I tried to nod, chewing the chain. I wouldn't bite him. I would be, I *could* be, good.

"Hold still." He drew one hand back, away from the wall, and instinct took over again. I answered it by biting so hard on the chain that my mouth began to bleed. The other man jumped, the click of his weapon being readied loud in my ears.

"Don't fire," Johann warned him. Quickly and efficiently, Johann tied the chain behind my head. With my hands and legs bound, and now the chain in my mouth, I was helpless.

"See?" Johann said. He stood up, leaving me lying on the floor. "Now we can take him. Just relax, Kaiden. Thomas is going to help me."

I hoped he would tell me where they were taking me. But instead, I was lifted like a sack of grain and taken out into the night.

CHAPTER EIGHT

I rode in a small wagon again, unable to move, trusting that I had made the right choice. Other than being relatively sure that Johann was going to somehow sever my link with my master, I had no idea what to expect.

All I could do was listen to him speak to the other man. Thomas.

"I can't believe you talked me into this," Thomas said.

"It's worth a try, isn't it?"

"You and your dreams!" Thomas exclaimed, his deep voice even deeper through the walls of the wagon. "Johann, we *kill* vampires. And we especially kill thralls. Even if we can't take down a vampire like Lasren, isn't that enough?"

"No." I wondered at the pain I heard in Johann's voice. "It's not."

"What happened in the west?" Thomas asked.

"Dimresh is like Lasren."

Lasren must be another vampire.

"Fear aura, hypnotism. We can do nothing. Another region will be lost. Nothing unless my plan works, that is."

Thomas snorted. "And what plan would that be? Enlist a thrall to kill for you? That won't work. That was one of the first things our order tried, after the fall of Tarek, remember? It didn't work then, and that was two centuries ago. Thralls are mindless killers, and they like to kill humans. All they want is blood. Read your actual histories, not legends and stories."

I wondered what legends he was talking about.

"And where, exactly, have our histories gotten us?" Johann asked. "To lands terrorized by vampires and a shrinking organization. If the magic of Holy Laurel was ever real, it's gone now. The old ways have gotten us nowhere."

"The magic may be gone, but our traditions have helped us to survive," Thomas said. "Were it not for us, the bloodsuckers would be raising us like cattle by now. We still have some functioning cities and towns and merchants still travel due to the protection the order offers."

"Our protection is weakening every year," Johann said. "What were once cities have been reduced to towns, what were once towns have been reduced to villages, and what were once villages are dying. We need to find new ways to fight, and Kaiden may be it."

"*It* has a name?" Thomas barked a laugh. "That thing in there would kill us both given half the chance. Hopefully it'll die when we enter the river and that will be the end of it."

Enter the river. My body seized in sudden tension. No. I couldn't do that.

No thrall could. Crossing running water would sap our energy, steal the life-force from our bodies, and leave us blood-dry, too weak to even hunt to gain back the power we lost. My master had told me that. I could sense it. I'd spent enough time just across the river, staring at the village, the knowledge of the running water keeping me from sating my hunger. There was one bridge into the village, and it was drawn up at night. All of us had known the danger of running water, and humans knew well the protection it offered. For the rest of us, the ones Johann had killed, it had been the only thing keeping them from destroying the town in a bloodlust-induced frenzy.

I ground my teeth against the chain, but not even my fangs were strong enough to bite through metal. I hadn't recovered from whatever Johann had shot me with, and hunger warred with weakness in my stomach. I needed blood. More blood would give me energy.

I should have bit Johann.

No, I couldn't think that.

"He won't die," Johann said. I tried to focus on his voice. He called me him, not it, the way other man did. "He will be weakened, and we will give him animal blood. He'll recover, but without the influence of his master. Trust me. I know a lot about thralls."

"I don't envy you that," Thomas said. "Hard-won knowledge is what makes a hunter."

How did he know so much about thralls? Who was Lasren? There was so much about Johann I didn't know. The man who was trusting me.

But did I trust him?

I didn't have time to decide, and I didn't have a choice even if I had the time. The horse's hooves clopped on wood. I smelled the fresh, loamy scent of a riverbank. Water picked up in a soft rush, louder and more persistent than the rush of blood from a beating heart. The wagon stopped, and then I heard the sound of hooves sloshing on water. They were leaving the bridge . . . They were going to ford through the water.

This was it.

I could sense the running water as we approached. The whisper became a roar that echoed the stolen blood flowing through my body. A horse snorted its displeasure at getting wet. My master's lessons replayed in my mind, mingling with the memories of all of his commands. Water seeped through the cracks of the wagon.

Do not cross running water.

Do not take human blood unless I command you.

Never enter my room without permission.

Do you hear the squeaking? Those are mice. Not worth much, but a good snack from time to time.

Go and kill the man by the river.

Kill the hunter.

Return!

Pain made me open my mouth, my fangs jutting from my lips as I screamed. This was pain I hadn't remembered existed, not since being turned.

Being killed.

I sat in the alley. It reeked of trash and vomit, and the spilled wine did little to cover up the stench. My stomach was spinning along with my head, but I'd already sicked up everything I could. Despite the nausea, I wanted more wine. Or beer. Anything, really, to ease the shakes. They were worse every time, and I had no money left.

There was so much pain. Not just in my body. My mother was gone, years ago now. I'd never known my father. There was someone . . .

Pain rebounded in my mind and body, all I could hear the rushing water beneath me. Every second was an eternity, but the pain made my brain fire in ways it hadn't in years.

I had an opportunity, once, in life, but I'd lost it. What had it been? I couldn't remember. But losing it was why I was in the alley. I'd been doing better, given a chance as a child, but turning my back on it left me there. I had lost . . . something.

And that was where he had found me.

"Greetings, young man." He was beautiful. The moon reflected off his face, illuminating long blond hair and blue eyes, and clothes of silk and cotton that weren't stained with the mud and dust of the village. His skin was impossibly pale, milky white, and unmarked by blemishes of age or illness.

He had captivated me immediately, even more than any drink had.

"It seems you've fallen on hard times," he said. His voice wrapped around me like smoke.

Now, etched against the pain, I could see it for what it was.

Vampire magic. Hypnosis.

"Come here," he said. "Tell me what you want, young man."

I had crawled toward him, ignoring the alley wavering around me and the roiling in my stomach. I had fallen in the attempt, lying on the stones. And there I cried, my tears hot. I couldn't even go toward someone showing me kindness.

"You poor thing. Life hasn't been kind, has it?"

I hadn't answered. I couldn't see him. Or maybe I didn't remember what I said.

But I remembered what he had said next.

"Do you want to die?"

I'd agreed. Stupidly, I had agreed.

But as the pain grew, matching the pain of the memory of his fangs sinking into my neck, I remembered. At the last moment, as the blood had drained from my body, as the weakness of the river overwhelmed me and all I could focus on was memories of Dimresh, I knew.

I hadn't really wanted to die. I wanted to live. And maybe now it wasn't too late.

That was my last thought before darkness took me.

CHAPTER NINE

"What do you think's outside the village?" someone asked me once.

I leaned against the wall of the village bakery, the scent of fresh bread heavy in the air. The sun shone overhead, the sky as blue as . . .

As a vampire's eyes. A vampire with blond hair and blue eyes. Like mine, but beautiful, not grungy and covered in dirt like everything else in the village.

"Kaiden," a voice said. It sounded far away. The image of the sun and sky vanished, replaced with a dark, gaping hunger and the scent of blood.

I snapped my eyes open, and even that was difficult. My arms and legs were leaden, though now no chains bound them. I didn't know why the chains were gone, but that concern was lost in the hunger. My body screamed for blood, for sustenance that would bring me the strength to move again.

Without it, I would die. No, without it I *was* dead. Fear thrummed in me, but without the strength to act on it, the feeling passed on like a cloud over the moon. The only thing that remained was the hunger. I could smell blood, animal blood, but I was too weak to get it. I couldn't even turn my head, seeing only the starry sky framed by trees overhead. I was outside, not in the wagon. Why, I didn't know. I wished Johann would have told me what he had planned.

Or maybe he was just going to kill me here. Hearts beat next to me. Living people.

"It really can't move, can it?"

61

"No. Crossing running water leaves them as weak as when they were first turned." Johann's voice, coming from a distance. He'd done this to me. "This is the best spot for it. This used to be a merchant's crossing, years ago."

"So what do we do?" Thomas asked.

Johann sighed. His heart beat fast, as fast as when he'd thought I'd gone back to attack someone in the forest. From the sound of his heart and his voice, I estimated he was at least twenty feet from me. "If he's still lucid and it worked, we tie him back up and give him the boar's blood. If not . . ."

"All I need to hear. It's clearly not lucid. Look at it."

Something clicked, metal on wood.

"No!" Both Johann and I spoke as one.

"C'mon, really?" Thomas snapped.

"Kaiden, can you hear me?" Johann called. "Please, Kaiden, speak to me."

Please, speak to me. Pain came with that memory, my own voice begging someone. I sounded young, childlike.

"Don't kill me," I managed to say, my voice raspy and weak. My tongue scraped against my dry mouth. "Why . . . why did you do this?" The final few words came out as barely a whisper. I didn't know if they could hear me with their weak human ears.

"We'll give it to him," Johann said, and then I heard a crunching noise, footsteps on leaves. The tart scent of blood filled the air — fresh blood, more concentrated than usual. The blood of a boar, collected in some sort of bag. Delicious and easy to eat.

"No."

"Thomas, what are you doing?" The scent got no closer.

"I put up with this because I thought it would die. But this has gone far enough. I'm not going to stop you. But I'm asking you, one last time, to rethink your choice. Thralls are animals. Give it blood and it will turn on you. What do you really think you're going to accomplish?"

"Hope where there is none," Johann snapped.

I fought to stay awake, to hear the argument.

"We can't keep losing ground to vampires too powerful for a hunter to kill."

"So we focus on those we can save!" Thomas shouted back. "You, a talented hunter, need to stop wasting your time on dreams and help those we can!"

"This will help more people."

"You *think* it will. You claim it's intelligent. The Master Hunter's willing to humor you. But think, Johann. The order is shrinking, like you said, and the damn bloodsuckers are winning. So why do you insist on doing something that's only going to get you killed?" His voice dropped. "I care about you, Johann. You're my friend. And I'm telling you, you're making a mistake. Sooner or later, that thing *will* kill you."

The scent of blood, mixed with my frustration, made me hate Thomas. But another scent blew in on the cold night wind, one that made me wrinkle my nose.

Other thralls.

I had no idea where we were or how far we'd come. I knew they didn't serve my master—no, my old master. Dimresh. His commands no longer thundered in my head. I knew so little of the world outside my village, outside the castle.

But I did know there was danger. Other things like me were out in the night.

" —listen to me," Johann was saying. The scent of the boar's blood was strong on the wind. That was what must be drawing the thralls. "Let me show you the legends."

"Legends," Thomas shot back. "It's always legends with you. You said it yourself—the holy magic of the old Empire is gone. So why even bother with history?"

They didn't know. They couldn't scent them, and their argument was distracting them.

Humans were so weak. I'd thought hunters would be smarter.

I had no energy. If Johann wanted a weapon, he should have told me what to expect, not weakened me without telling me anything.

Maybe I really was just a tool for him. An unpredictable weapon like those strange stake-shooting crossbows hunters held, a weapon he thought would misfire.

But I wasn't about to prove him right.

I summoned up all the strength I could as the sickly, rotting scent of the thralls grew closer. "Watch out," I managed to croak. "Thralls!"

Their argument abruptly stopped. Then I heard a growl from the trees.

At that moment something clicked, and pain exploded in my leg. Someone had shot me. I growled, the pain not leaving. A wooden stake. Without blood, I couldn't heal.

Snarling burst from the trees, and Thomas screamed. Another click of his weapon. Two more. More screaming.

The stench of the other thralls was strong. And then one stood over me, staring straight at me.

He looked nothing like the other thralls Dimresh had made. They'd been able to speak, even if it was just about their desire for blood, for comfort, for things they wanted. But this thrall—this creature—had nothing behind his dark eyes. He glanced at me with less concern than a cat would show, and I could almost see his thoughts behind dead black eyes and greasy hair, what he thought of me.

Not food. *Nothing.*

The air around me was filled with a strange, sweet scent, one that reminded me of Dimresh, but the longer I smelled it, the more offensive it became.

Then he tilted his head, long fangs emerging as he snarled.

In that instant, I knew that this thrall had tasted human

blood before. This was what I would become, what Thomas was so afraid of me turning into.

He tensed, ready to leap at Johann or Thomas.

I had nothing left. But somehow, I reached out and grabbed his leg. The muscles were corded tight, and his skin felt only slightly warmer than mine. He didn't even acknowledge my grab. But it was enough. The leap fell short, dragging me slightly and tilting my head so I could see Johann.

There were four thralls. Too many. One had already jumped on Thomas.

Johann met my eyes. For the moment he was safe in his spot on top of the wagon. He held a bag in his hand. My gaze flicked to it and back to him.

"Trust me," I said. But it came out too quiet, drowned out by the growls of the other thralls as they prepared to leap at him. I was a thrall—I knew what they could do.

Johann threw the bag at me. Part of me hoped the other thralls would go for it as well, giving Johann and Thomas time.

But they didn't. The scent had drawn them, but they wanted human blood, the real treat.

Good. That just meant more for me.

The bag was a tightly woven cloth bag, but it didn't survive the fall onto the leaves and sticks of the forest. Blood spilled onto the leaves and loam. I instinctively rolled over and lapped it into my mouth.

As soon as the metallic taste touched my lips, I was lost in the pleasure of blood for the seconds it took for me to drink. I licked up leaves and dirt along with the spilled blood, but I didn't care. The weakness began to fade, the hole in my leg the stake had left mending along with another shock of pain. It wasn't enough, not nearly, to drive away hunger, but there was enough blood to get me on my feet.

Just like the first time, taking strength from a cat who'd

once comforted and warmed me.

I blinked, my muscles momentarily heavy. But the feeling passed as I took in the scene.

Three thralls, and a fourth currently trying to rip out the stake in its leg that pinned it to the ground. One was biting Thomas, so efficiently the scent of human blood didn't even enter the air to tempt me. A thrall's bite wouldn't turn him, not like a true vampire's, but if he lost too much blood, he would die just as surely. Two more were leaping at Johann, who kept them at bay with a crossbow. But each time he aimed a shot, the other thrall would jump for him, unbalancing the wagon and causing his shots to miss their hearts. One shot hit a thrall's foot. The woman snarled and ignored the pain, leaving flesh behind as she lifted her foot from the ground and sprang again.

If I did nothing, the thralls would obviously overpower them. I could share the blood.

I would be just like them. That dead-eyed, insect-like gaze.

I tensed, the hunger a constant pain in my stomach. Then I leaped for the man who'd stepped over me.

My fangs, my best weapon, sank into his neck, my hunting instinct helping to aim my bite. Along with the foulest blood I'd ever tasted, my teeth found flesh and filth, nothing but decay. The same sickly-sweet scent as before filled my nose, something that reminded me of Dimresh. Maybe their master.

I held on, drinking blood that turned my stomach, letting my fangs rip through tendon and muscle. I'd never killed a thrall before, and wasn't sure I could. But I wasn't going to let them kill Johann. Or even Thomas.

I wasn't going to prove him right. I wasn't. I should have attacked the one draining Thomas, but I didn't know if I could resist being so close to his blood. Even now, as close as I was, the hunger roared. If I scented it, I would be lost.

"Kaiden," Johann called. My name anchored me, letting

me ignore the tantalizing scent for a few moments. A stake whistled past me, thudding into flesh and ripping a cry of pain from one of the thralls that faded quickly. The stake had hit its heart.

I'd given Johann the time he needed. Another shot, and the rustling of leaves from the thrall on the ground trying to free its leg fell silent.

I expected the thrall in my grip to fight me, to turn and take in the threat. But he was too fixated on Johann, on blood, and he never even attacked me, only growled and tried to lunge out of my grasp as Johann raised the crossbow and took him through the heart too.

He went limp, and my fangs detached from his neck as he slumped to the ground. He lay on the leaves, a stake through his heart. In death his eyes looked human again. They were brown.

"Kaiden," Johann said. Thomas lay behind him, the thrall that had been biting him not dead but pinned to the ground by her legs. I supposed he hadn't wanted to risk shooting her in the chest and hitting Thomas.

A gust of wind blew toward him, sparing me from the tempting scent.

Johann covered Thomas's neck with one hand. He didn't cover everything. Thomas had other marks on his neck, too, old, faded scars.

Foolish, to have been bitten twice.

Johann raised his crossbow and pointed it at me, breaking my focus on Thomas's neck. The stake he held was sharp and deadly.

I narrowed my eyes, but I didn't move. Of course. He'd wanted to tie me up first before giving me blood. He didn't trust me. He never would.

"Do something," I said, my mouth filling with saliva. Thomas's skin looked pale. "He's wasting blood."

"Don't attack, Kaiden," Johann said. "And don't run. Please."

"Then stop pointing that thing at me!" I growled.

The metal pieces of the crossbow shone in the moonlight. Johann had aimed perfectly. One flick of his finger, and I would die. I was fast, but not that fast. This was just like before, that night by the river.

But this time fear didn't come. Maybe it was the sound of his heart, something in his breathing, that made me so confident. Maybe it was some other sense, an instinct I didn't know I had. But I wasn't surprised when he lowered the weapon.

"Keep watch, Kaiden," he said.

"I will." I turned, moving farther downwind. My mouth still watered, and my body ached with weakness and hunger. The bit of animal blood I'd gotten was nowhere near enough, and the thrall's blood was filling but foul.

But my master's commands no longer thrummed in my mind. There was no more drive to kill Johann, to return to the castle. I hadn't realized how much of me was simply his orders.

I wasn't sure what was left. Hunger. Fear. A need to survive.

I caught sight of one of the dead thralls on the ground. A wooden stake jutted from her chest, but at least her eyes were closed. She lay next to the one I had attacked, two bodies on the leaves by the wagon.

They were thralls. But they'd been human once, as I had. I wondered who their master was, or if they'd been too driven by bloodlust after biting humans to obey one.

The other thralls Dimresh had turned had died too. I hadn't cared then. They'd never shown anything other than bloodlust and scorn for me.

And I them, I supposed. Thralls had no friends, no companions. I had followed Master's orders. That was all I had.

Now . . . there was only blankness, like the quiet shroud of a night with no moon.

I was a servant, but what did a servant do without a master?

"Kaiden," Johann called. "Get in the wagon. We're going to go back. Thomas needs treatment."

He came around the wagon, meeting my eyes. He wasn't holding his weapon. "I won't tie you again. You can help keep watch. Please, Kaiden. Thomas will die without help."

He smelled of fear and exhaustion. Of humanity and life and blood.

I obeyed.

Chapter Ten

Thomas's heart beat slowly and weakly, every so often fluttering the way a deer's did when it approached death as I drained its blood. I knew the sound well.

Next to me, Johann snapped the reins across the horse's back. The wagon seat jolted as the wheels hit another bump. The jerking distracted me from my focus on the potential prey in the back of the wagon. The moon cast milky light over the forest, but most of the light was blocked by the trees that stretched over the pitted road. I saw and smelled no sign of any recent travelers, or at least no sign I could detect over the foul scent of thrall's blood and that strange, sickly sweet smell that still pervaded my clothes.

"Anything, Kaiden?" Johann asked.

"No." He always asked me when I lifted my head, using my name in that calming way he had. He probably thought I was scenting for blood as well as any potential danger.

"If I hunt, I'll—"

"No," Johann said, and I gritted my teeth. "Stay with me."

The moon had passed its highest point, only hours left in the night. My hunger made my body weaken and my mouth water. I found myself struggling harder and harder to listen to Johann, to focus on the future and my choice and not the scents and sounds of animals around me—and the weak, easy prey in the back of the wagon.

"How far are we from . . ." I trailed off. Johann had told me nothing about the hunter's encampment, including what it was called.

"The barracks. Two hours. It took us three to get to the river."

The river. I shivered when I thought of it. "We won't cross it again?"

"We crossed it twice before when you were tied." He glanced over at me. "To make sure."

I didn't realize I was clenching my teeth until my fangs poked my bottom lip. "To make sure of what?"

He snapped the reins again, the horse snorting in annoyance. "That the connection to your master wouldn't reassert itself once you were back on the other side."

"How would you know?" I'd been unconscious, and when I woke they'd seemed more concerned about me being violent than my still being linked to my master. No, not my master anymore. Dimresh.

Johann turned in his seat, finally paying attention to me. "Do you still feel the connection?"

I paused for a moment, as if listening, but I didn't really need to. It was an absence of weight, a worry or cloud that was no longer there. Like the absence of hunger once I ate, or the absence of exhaustion when I woke. "No. He's gone."

"So are your scars."

It was my turn to stare at him. "What scars?" But a moment after I spoke, I knew. My hand went to my neck.

I hadn't thought of them for longer than a day after I saw them the first time. The only mark on a thrall that didn't heal — the bite from the master who had turned them.

The skin on my neck felt smooth and unblemished.

"How . . . how did you know it would work?" I said.

Johann sighed, his breath fogging in the night air. I hadn't realized it was that cold. "We're hunters. We know a lot about what we hunt."

Something flared again, like hunger but not, the feeling of missing the killing bite or the sight of prey running away. My fangs pricked my lower lip. "Why don't you tell me, then?" I said, my voice coming out a growl.

"What's wrong, Kaiden?" Johann said, but this time his using my name just made things worse.

"You," I said, my fangs snapping on the word. Words boiled out of me, unfettered by the weight of my master's orders on my brain. "You tell me nothing of what to expect. You drag me across a river, tied up, and the crossing hurt. I felt like I had died, again. And when I wake up, it's to you and Thomas" — his name came out a growl — "discussing whether or not to kill me. Why was I out of the wagon, on the ground? Were you going to kill me no matter what? And after I've helped you kill thralls like me, with only a mouthful or two of disgusting thrall blood to go on, you still tell me nothing of why we did this or what the plan is. Will you leave me in the dungeons again, or tied up in the wagon? Will you prevent me from eating until I am as weak as when I woke after the river? Will I get shot again when we get to your encampment? Or maybe Thomas will just kill me when he's healed." My words hung in the air for a few moments. The animals around us had gone quiet, wary of the noise I'd made.

Johann's shoulders tensed. He blinked a few times, his mouth opening and then falling shut. Finally, he broke the silence. "I'm sorry."

I didn't respond, not sure what to add. He spoke again, his breath winding around the words. "If you want to hunt, go. Find a deer. Just . . . please, come back? I promise, after this . . . I'll be more fair to you."

His heart rate picked up. He was still nervous about me going off alone. As if I would go and hunt someone, as those thralls had.

"If I wanted human blood, I would have it by now," I snapped. His heart picked up its pace, but I was gone before he could say anything else.

The leg Thomas had shot buckled as I jumped from the wagon, and my speed faltered faster than I would have liked. Soon I was trudging through the trees, my legs heavy. Even if I hadn't been forced to cross a river tonight, I had eaten very little. I needed to find slower prey than I was used to.

I listened, scenting the air. It was very late, but I did catch the scent of something rotten on the wind. A sick predator.

Disease didn't matter to me. I followed the scent, finding a shambling, sick coyote that had stopped to rest in a thicket. It was small and thin, too many days of illness interrupting its hunting.

In seconds, it no longer felt its illness, and I stood straighter, muscles thrumming with power. Now I could see even more keenly, scent even better. I found and ate blood from a boar after that, finally assuaging the constant hunger.

Overhead, the moon had grown closer to the horizon, the bright moonlight casting long shadows through the trees. Johann would be back at the encampment in another hour, most likely.

I could stay here. I could find a cave or dig a hole, make a place for myself somewhere the sun wouldn't reach. I could live here and eat animals, my new home along this abandoned road in an overgrown forest. That would be my choice, no one else's.

But that was hardly better than before, a life spent in alleys as a slave to drink. No, it was worse. At least in the village there had been people to observe, life going on around me. There had been people I cared about. I couldn't remember them, but I knew that was true.

I didn't know if Johann would show me kindness. I'd thought he might once. And I certainly knew no other hunter would. They would be like Thomas, and I snarled when I thought of him.

But I still found myself tracing the path back to the wagon.

73

Maybe I trusted Johann. Or maybe, without the presence of my master in the back of my mind, I felt alone.

It wasn't difficult to track Johann and the wagon, which still carried the damp scent of the shallow river. I jogged over the broken, unkempt dirt road, careful to avoid crashing into the fallen trees or overhanging branches that every so often blocked the path. The roads near my village were nothing like this—humans routinely had people clear them after large storms, or work to smooth the dirt and fill in mud puddles so wagons wouldn't get stuck. One of the workers had been killed by one of Dimresh's thralls. Without the protection of the river, alone on the road, the temptation had been too great for her.

My stomach was full for now, but I wondered if the temptation would ever prove too much for me. I didn't have my master telling me to kill Johann, but I didn't have his command not to drink human blood either. I hadn't been able to avoid drink in life. It felt foolish to think I could overcome a similar thirst in death.

Horse hooves and the creaking of wood broke through my thoughts. I picked up my pace, not making any effort to hide the sound of my feet on the muddy road. The last thing I wanted was for Johann to shoot me thinking I was another crazed thrall.

"Kaiden?" he called, his voice wary.

"I'm here," I answered before leaping into the wagon seat next to Johann. The horse's ears flicked, and it tossed its head.

"What did you hunt?"

"Coyote. Boar after that." I licked my lips, but the metallic tang of the animals' blood was long gone.

"We'll be returning to the barracks soon," Johann said. He maneuvered the reins in his fingers, the horse pulling us around a fallen, rotted log. After that, we exited the forest, the abandoned road smoothing out into a well-maintained one.

The horse began trotting faster, huffing as it did, sending white clouds from its nostrils. Ahead of us, a black smudge marked what must be the castle. What Johann called the barracks.

"And what will I do?" I asked.

"I . . ." Johann huffed a breath, sounding like a smaller version of the horse. "I can't know for sure. I'm sorry."

I fell silent, staring up at the bright moon. Somewhere, I knew that some people said it gave off its own light, but on full moons like this one, I could almost feel the burning tingle that warned of dangerous sunlight, and it made my eyes water. I looked away, back at the forest we had left, an inky smudge.

"And I'm sorry about more than that," Johann said. "I haven't been fair to you, Kaiden."

I just nodded. "That's true."

"I don't think you realize how unique you are," Johann said. "You said you were recently turned. How long has it been?"

"Two months." So little time, but it felt like longer.

Johann jolted next to me. "You know nothing, then, do you?" When I glared at him, he added, "I mean no offense. But I'd always thought . . ." He shook his head. "I'm sorry. Truly. I've been treating you like . . . like a combination of an animal and as if I had some sort of vampire lord tied up in the dungeons. But really . . . as far as vampires go, you're like a child."

"I'm no child," I growled.

"No, I don't mean it negatively. I just mean you don't know much about what you are."

"Do *you*?" I snapped. "You said you know a lot about what you hunt. Teach me." As I spoke, I pictured the thralls we'd just killed, how black and dead their eyes had looked until they had truly died.

"Do you know what true thralls are like?" Johann asked. "Dimresh had other servants, didn't he?"

Dimresh's other servants, the ones who'd died when we first attacked Johann. They hadn't been like the mindless things we'd seen tonight, but they hadn't been like me, either. I remembered their constant squabbling anger, how each would stay alone and hunt alone unless ordered to work together by Dimresh. When I approached them, I'd gotten only snarls and growls or quick curses. I had never learned their names.

Then again, until Johann had reminded me of mine, I hadn't had one. Maybe thralls never did.

"There were others," I said. "You killed them."

"I'm sorry." He truly sounded sorry, and I didn't understand why. I had felt nothing when they died, focused only on my own fear and will to survive. I had never truly known them.

"Do you . . . *mourn* the thralls you kill?" I asked.

Johann sighed. "You ask hard questions. But . . . not usually. I suppose I mourn the people they were before they were turned. But killing a thrall is merely laying to rest what should already be dead. At least . . . usually." He met my eyes.

"But you think I'm different."

"You *are* different. Were any of the others who served Dimresh like you?"

I shook my head, and when I wasn't sure if he could see my gesture in the moon's dim light, I said, "No."

Johann cleared his throat, looking ahead. "Hunters are taught and trained by killing thralls. Sometimes, after their vampire lord is killed, they must be exterminated as they become even more mindless without their master. They're motivated by blood and have very basic desires—a male thrall will tend to target the blood of pretty young women, for example. But most of what makes them human is gone. They're

as strong as two men and faster than a wildcat, but their behavior's predictable, so they're easy to kill." He sounded like
he was teaching a student, not describing what I was. "They
will, without fail, fall into a trap if they think there's easy
blood to be had. They're only dangerous when their master is
near, if there are a large number of them, or if they take you
by surprise."

"Which is how Thomas got bitten," I said.

"Yes." A measure of annoyance, or maybe disgust, entered
Johann's voice. "Luckily, the bite of a thrall won't turn you."

"You have to be bitten by a vampire to be turned," I said.
"Otherwise you die."

"That's right. A vampire has to drink all but a few drops,
and they will make a thrall. We're not sure how they make a
new vampire, not completely. Most think if they let the victim
drink some of their blood before turning, the victim will become another vampire, not a thrall, but I think there's likely
more involved."

"If I kill Dimresh, do I get his blood?" I asked, and I'm sure
my hunger showed in my face and voice.

"I . . . see no reason why not," Johann said. "I've never
heard of such a thing."

I narrowed my eyes. "But you said killing him would make
me a vampire. And . . . how did you know that crossing the
river would sever my connection with him? You clearly know
more than you're telling me."

"Yes, Kaiden." Johann sounded tired. "Taking his blood
won't make you a vampire, but killing him will. I think. I'll be
honest with you. I suspect more. I theorize more, and so far,
I've been right. But what I think and what hunters are
taught . . . they're not always the same thing."

I blinked. "What do you mean?"

Before he could answer, someone called out of the darkness. "Ho there. Johann?"

Another hunter. I tensed.

"Let me see if I can get you somewhere a little more accommodating than the dungeons," Johann said. "I will tell you everything I know — and suspect. But for now, please, just keep being good."

"Johann? Thomas?" the man called again, and soon enough he rode up out of the shadows on a large white horse. The animal's nostrils flared when it caught my scent. He held a lantern, but the weak light clearly didn't illuminate us. "Back before morning, I see. Your horse looks ready to fall over."

"It's Johann," Johann called out. His heart was racing, and I wondered why. "And . . . Kaiden. Thomas is injured."

There was a pause. "By what?"

I understood then. Everyone would think I had attacked him. My word wouldn't matter, only Johann's would. All I could do was keep silent and let him defend me.

Be good, Johann had said. I gritted my teeth. He had made me promises. Hopefully he would keep them.

"Please, we have to hurry. Go and open the gate," Johann said.

The man nodded, turning without a word and kicking his horse into a gallop. His lantern looked like a firefly as he darted across the dark empty field to the castle.

"Thomas will be fine," I said. "He's weak but he'll live. His heart flutters a bit, but it won't stop."

"How do you know?" Johann asked as he slapped the reins against the horse's side, the wagon moving faster. The animal's breath was labored, but it, too, could keep going.

"I can hear his heart. It beats weakly but steady now." I nodded at him. "I can hear yours too."

"You see?" Johann said. "I will teach you what I know. But it seems you have a lot to teach us too."

CHAPTER ELEVEN

I could only hope Johann was right as we approached the castle a short time later. The man from before had alerted people, it seemed, and I could hear and smell the small group. My mouth watered, too, at the knowledge that there were so many people inside, so much blood to be had.

Be good, I told myself. Let Johann talk.

I told myself this wasn't like the village, full of vulnerable, unsuspecting people. I spotted the woman who'd shot me last time, and I ducked low in the wagon seat. Susana. I had a made a point to remember her name. Five hunters stood outside the wooden gate, and all of them wore leather clothes that would protect them from my fangs. Lesalie, the Master Hunter, wore a metal gorget around her neck. I wondered why they all didn't wear one. Thomas wouldn't have been bitten if he had.

"Johann," she called out, and I lurched forward when the wagon stopped. "Anthony told me Thomas is injured, and I see the thrall in the wagon seat with you. What happened?"

I ducked lower at the click of a crossbow.

"We were set upon by four crazed thralls on the edge of the Gold River. One bit Thomas, and he needs medical attention. Kaiden helped me dispatch them. He doesn't need to be tied up."

Dispatch. That was a strange way to say kill.

"The *thrall* helped kill other thralls?" I could hear disbelief dripping from Susana's voice. "More likely he bit him himself."

I gritted my teeth, a suppressed growl tightening my throat.

"He *didn't*. Believe me, without him we would both be dead. We need to—"

"Believe *you*. The man who reads old legends and fairy tales. The man who's killed fewer vampires than anyone else here."

"A man who'd rather talk to thralls than kill them," someone else added.

I risked raising my head, and when I did three crossbows were trained on me. Only a shot to the heart was deadly, but I'd learned how much getting shot by them hurt. If I was injured at all, I didn't doubt they would finish me off before I could run. They were no thralls, but thralls had been human once too. We were all animals, and their instinct was to kill me just as much as I would kill my own prey.

They stared at Johann the way Dimresh's old thralls used to stare at me, judging and contemptuous.

"Why do they hate you?" I whispered.

Johann held up his hands, letting the reins drop. "We can discuss this after Thomas gets help. But Lesalie, you did agree to let me attempt communication with the thr—with Kaiden here. He helped us fight off thralls, and Thomas will support me once he recovers. Please, let us in and let us both rest."

"This is foolish!" Susana shouted. "I'll just kill it now." I heard Johann's heart pick up. "It's not like you'd stop me." She aimed her crossbow

My muscles tensed, and I instinctively bared my fangs. One question clanged in my mind, kept me from running away into the darkness of the night.

Would Johann defend me?

"Enough!" Lesalie's voice rang out, full of authority. "Johann is right about one thing—we're wasting time. Bring the wagon in. If the thrall so much as bares its teeth at anyone, shoot it."

I shut my mouth and kept my lips tight over my teeth as the wagon rolled past the metal gate. Smells filled my nose — mostly smoke and the acrid scent of churned mud and discarded waste, but also the scents I had learned to hunt — rushing blood and the sometimes foul, sometimes delicious scent of humanity.

"Don't move for now," Johann whispered as the wagon stopped. One of the hunters climbed in the back to check on Thomas. "They're looking for excuses to kill because they're trained hunters, that's all. They don't hate me."

Hunters they might be, but the strongest scent, drowning out the rest, was fear as the hunters approached the wagon. I kept my head down, trying to look as harmless as possible under the gazes of the men and women with weapons designed to kill me.

Not moving became difficult when a sharp point was placed at my back, just behind my heart. A minty scent did little to mask the scent of fear from the man behind me. "Don't move, thrall," the man hissed.

"Peter, that's not helping," Johann said.

"He's weak, but not bleeding," Susana said from the back of the wagon, and I assumed she was talking about Thomas. His heart fluttered as they moved him, but I didn't dare turn around. "As long as we get some meat in him and let him rest, he should recover."

"Keep this thing away from him," Peter said. I kept silent and still.

"Enough, Peter," Johann snapped.

"What do you plan to do with it?" Peter shouted back, my ears ringing.

"That's a valid question," a woman said. My skin prickled with unease. I hadn't noticed the Master Hunter come close. She was the only one who didn't reek of fear and anger. "I thought the plan was to keep him chained and in the dungeons after the link was severed, Johann?"

"We should kill it now," Peter said. "It's a bloodsucker!"

"He's intelligent!" Johann shouted back.

"So are vampires, but we kill them!"

"Enough!" Lesalie shouted. "Johann, answer the question. Why is he not chained?"

Johann took a slow breath. "Does he look like he needs to be?"

I moved my head, so slowly that a human could follow the movement, to look at Lesalie. "I didn't bite anyone," I said. "Only the thralls that attacked us."

"Do you want to feed, though?" Lesalie asked. She wasn't aiming a weapon at me, but part of me didn't doubt she had some plan in place if I was foolish enough to attack. "Do you still crave human blood, even after crossing the river?"

I could lie, but there would be no point. "I still crave blood, yes."

The sharp point of the stake dug farther into my back. "You see?" Peter crowed.

Lesalie's eyes narrowed, the way Johann's had that first night by the village. Calculating.

"Johann, he's your responsibility. He stays with you. Keep him away from others. If he steps out of line, even for an instant . . ."

"What?" Peter demanded, but the crossbow was pulled away from my shoulder blades. "You're letting it *live*, after it admitted to wanting to kill us?"

"That's not what I said." I tried to keep the growl out of my voice.

"Kaiden, enough. Come with me." Johann stood, climbing down from the wagon. He huffed as he jumped the final few feet from the wagon seat. I followed, my skin prickling with vigilance I only used to feel when Dimresh would draw near to order us to do something.

Peter, a man who looked younger than Johann and yet was twice as weathered, glared at me. I felt the weight of his eyes on my back until we left the entranceway and entered the courtyard of what had once been a castle.

But this was no castle built for entertaining, or for a rich noble to show off his wealth. Walls surrounded us on every side, just like Dimresh's castle, but spikes jutted from the top, leaving no space for a walkway. At least none I could see. Past the square of the courtyard three towers loomed, each ringed by another set of walls that formed tunnels between them. Small holes let beams of moonlight shine through near the top of what would be parapets, where archers could pick off invading forces. There was no way to tell from the exterior where to focus an attack or where the leader would reside. The center of the three towers, presumably, but in my estimation that would just be more open space.

"This way," Johann said. As we approached the tower on the left, I picked up more sounds, more smells. People, dozens of them. A small number for a castle this size.

"Who are the others?" I asked.

"Servants, cooks, hunters in training. And not many," Johann said. "We're as self-sufficient as we can be."

"How many vampires know of this place?"

"The wandering ones always find us," Johann said. "But we never let them live for long when they do."

"How do you defend this place if you can't kill someone like Dimresh?" I asked, staring at the structure. As far as castles went, it wasn't large, maybe half the size of Dimresh's, but it was still a castle.

"Vampires like Dimresh aren't concerned with anything outside their territory. The lesser ones without territory of their own are the ones we worry about coming here. But there's nothing to fear, Kaiden. You're safe here."

Something in his voice hitched, some hint of uncertainty, like a deer lifting its head when I'd been sure to make no sound. He wasn't sure. Or he was lying.

But before I could ask, weakness entered my limbs, my eyelids drooping. The moonlight had waned, just slightly, and the pitch-black sky showed the barest hint of purple.

"Sunup, eh?" Johann guessed. Or maybe he knew how sunup affected thralls. He knew so much about us. "Hurry, then. I'll put you somewhere safe."

I was sure it would be safer for everyone else in the castle, not as much for me. As long as it wasn't another dungeon.

Fatigue dragged at me as he led me through a wooden door studded with stakes, and then through long, twisting hallways lined with torches and what looked suspiciously like solar flares, the charged glass and soot waiting to be activated by a single spark.

"This entire place was meant to kill us," I said. "Why did you put me in the dungeon before?"

"Changing your mind?" Johann asked.

"No." I blinked heavily, focusing on not stumbling into a wall that was studded with stakes. They smelled of old blood.

"Through here." Johann swung open a door, and the scent of dust and grain met my nose.

"This is a storage room. There's a basin of water, too, if you need it." I couldn't imagine why. Water wasn't blood. "I'll be one room over, but I don't recommend wandering around. Understand?" He stared right at me, brown eyes boring into mine. I must look just as tired as I felt. "I'll bring you food even before you wake. So don't go anywhere. I don't want to chain you again. Can I trust you, Kaiden?"

His words were heavy in my mind. "You can," I said.

"Good. I promise I will see you tomorrow and have food ready when you wake." He turned his back to me.

"Wait," I said.

"What?"

"I . . . I'm sorry about Thomas," I said. "And about . . . your reputation."

His mouth set in a line. "My reputation was bad before you. It's not your fault. It doesn't matter."

"It *does* matter," I said. Johann raised both eyebrows. "They are your . . . peers." As the other thralls had been mine. "You shouldn't let them treat you badly."

"Why do you care?" Johann asked.

"If they truly believe I'm dangerous, then they're letting you risk your life," I said. "It's not good if your peers don't care if you die. That is what . . . thralls do."

Dimresh's servants had died. The thralls tonight had died. I hadn't known any of their names, and I couldn't get that thought out of my mind. But I did know they hadn't cared for me. Not one of them would even blink if I'd been the one left dead on the ground.

"You truly are different, Kaiden," Johann said. "No matter what the others think, I know that's true."

"I know," I replied. As he left, shutting the door and leaving me in a storage room in the dark, I truly believed it for the first time.

Thralls didn't feel. But I did.

CHAPTER TWELVE

Johann didn't return before I woke like he'd promised. Hunger brought me energy and restlessness, and with it the dark, almost uncontrollable craving. My fangs wetted with saliva. My muscles tensed, aching to run and leap.

I wasn't used to waiting to feed.

Grain crunched beneath my feet as I paced the room. My instincts told me the sun had set just recently, but there were no torches lit in the hallway outside, and no residual light entered the room. Even with my night vision, I was blind without any light at all. My hearing sharpened in the darkness, my nose picking up subtle scents beneath dust and spilled grains.

Rats. There were two in here, eating into one of the bags.

I could strike without seeing, and soon enough one of them filled my mouth, its blood a snack that curdled my stomach even as I drank it. Rodents didn't have good blood.

I threw the carcass away when it was empty, coughing at the taste. Even as I did, I scented for more, but my nose wrinkled at the stench of it — and my own odor. I stank of old blood, the sickly sweet smell of the thralls from the night before, stale grain, and now rat. My stomach turned at the memory of biting the other thrall. That scent was foul and the taste of its blood worse.

Thralls didn't bathe. No life meant no sweat. Before my turning, I'd been dirty too, sleeping in alleys and covered in mud and filth and sometimes spilled alcohol. But my master bathed — I remembered the scents of oils and flowers, his routine before he left to find his latest victim. He knew the importance of appearance. He was beautiful.

Maybe it would be harder for others to hate me if I didn't look like a disgusting thrall. Maybe Johann would like the way I looked.

Focusing on the heat that thought elicited distracted from the hunger just slightly. My body and mind had toyed with this feeling since meeting Johann, memories of pleasure that I still wasn't sure I could feel.

I sat back in the darkness, nose still twitching at the scent of rat, and focused on thoughts of Johann. His clean brown hair, brown eyes, and his warmth. The warmth of his body, of life, and the scent of his blood . . . no, not his blood. Him. His musky maleness, sweat and pine, the sharp, deep scent of another man. He was not just prey to me, not like other humans. He acknowledged me. That made it easier for me to acknowledge him. And I liked what I saw.

I stroked myself once through my thin, frayed pants, hissing at the pleasant sensation. I remembered this. But the sensation was muted, fleeting, as were most things other than bloodlust. The desire burned in me like an ebbing fire, one that sent out small sparks before it died.

I was so hungry. I stopped stroking myself, leaning my head back against the wall. I did want Johann. I wanted to want him even more.

But I was a thrall. Even if I could feel the physical sensations I wanted to feel, he was a human and a hunter. If I did one thing wrong, stepped one hair out of line, he would kill me like he was trained to do, and I couldn't even blame him for it.

Desire burned for a time before bloodlust overtook it, as it always did, and soon I began to weaken from lack of blood. It had been too long. Where was Johann?

He'd told me to stay here, but a new emotion took the place of the pure physical desire. Johann wouldn't just leave me here. Even if he hadn't promised me he would return, a hunter leaving a hungry thrall alone in the castle would be foolish. And Johann, unlike Thomas, didn't seem stupid.

Something must have happened. Johann had even said that lesser vampires sometimes attacked. I didn't quite know what a lesser vampire was—I had known only Dimresh and thralls like me—but the common scent on the thralls came to mind. Their master. It must be.

I paced for what felt like eternity, my feet sending more grain scattering around the floor, but the rats weren't stupid enough to come back with me present. Finally, with a low growl, I went to the door, the lock giving way to my strength when I pushed it open. The metal clanged on the stone floor.

I would be good, I told myself beneath a fog of hunger. But I had to find Johann.

I paused for a moment, but only silence greeted me. The air was stale and still. I retraced the path we had taken in my mind, but my memory was hazy with fatigue from the morning before and the confusing circles of the castle itself.

My mind couldn't tell me where to go, but my body moved on its own, hunger driving me out of the tiny room and down the tight hallway. No torches burned, and I was careful as I passed the wooden spikes set into the wall.

A breeze tickled my skin, the promise of cool night air, and with it came a scream.

My senses sharpened. I lifted my head at the scream, prepared to leap on what would be easy, terrified prey. But the sound came from far away, and something else burned beneath an instinct to hunt.

The scream could be Johann's.

I sprang forward, no longer caring about the potential traps and dangers of the castle hallways. I let the scent of fresh air and the sound of yelling guide me. It got louder as I ran, the screaming mingled with the clang of weapons and the twang of bows and the sounds of running feet on grass.

And there were the growls of thralls. I knew it. My feet slid on stone, and I caught the scent of human sweat and fear on the air. My mouth watered, my run turning into the frenzied lope I used when going in for a kill.

The scent was coming from a tightly shut door down a turn in the hallway. It would lead outside, to battle and panicked humans, easy blood. My stomach was hollow with hunger and it stole the strength from my body, but desperation made me charge through the wooden door anyway, ignoring the stinging pain of the wood cutting my flesh as I went through.

"What the . . ."

"It's that thrall!"

I was suddenly surrounded by prey. No. I clenched my teeth, fighting the hunger, fighting the dark instinct that threatened to overtake me even though I no longer served a master. Not prey. Humans. Johann.

I had to focus on Johann. I was here to . . . what?

"Kill it!" a woman shouted. I blinked, focusing in the dark. Susana, her finger outstretched and pointing right at me. Past her, a bounding thrall with sightless dark eyes was about to sink his teeth into her neck. It would get her long before I did.

Then it crumpled midleap, a stake sticking out of its chest. Another man shouted near me, his voice deafening in my ear. "Two more coming at us!"

"Where's their lord?" someone else shouted. An arrow whizzed past me into the distance, and my focus snapped in two. I ached for the blood of the humans around me, but I couldn't ignore the other thralls.

There were at least two dozen of them, moving like the hunters they were as they stalked and leaped on the humans, and more lay dead on the ground. Stakes jutted from the chests of some, while others sizzled, victims of what must have been a solar flare. There was a fine carriage overturned in the front of the courtyard, just by the gate, and while I couldn't see anyone or pick out individual scents, I could smell the fear of the people huddled inside.

The vampire hunters were trying to help them. Whoever was in the carriage had probably fled this way when they realized they were being stalked, but they hadn't made it far enough. And now the thralls were frenzied with so many humans around. Some massed around the carriage, while others had gone after the hunters who were trying to fight their way through to get to the carriage. There were fewer hunters than I had thought. Only five shared the courtyard with me.

A stake hit the dirt near my feet, and I darted out of the way. As I did, a thrall turned to me, her growl a clear warning. "Get away," she demanded. "This prey is ours."

Prey. Johann. Where was he?

"There!" someone shouted, and a dozen wooden arrows flew at once from the parapets, arcing over my head. More hunters.

"No!" the thrall shrieked, and she dashed off, so fast I could barely follow her movements. She threw herself into the trees, but the branches didn't cover her from the sharp wooden arrows that thudded into her body.

As they did, a strange dark mist emanated from the trees. Fear rooted my feet, a fear somehow different than the fear that greeted me when I saw a weapon designed by hunters to kill me. It was a memory of the fear I once had when I was human, a fear of a creature greater than I was.

The mist solidified into a man with dark hair who wore fine robes, his mouth stained with blood. A thrall would never waste blood.

The scent of the spilled human blood should have driven me to madness, but staring at the vampire kept me motionless. He lifted his head, and as one the thralls gathered around him, some of them dying to another volley of arrows that fell from the parapets like rain. He curled his upper lip, revealing the sharp points of his fangs. The thralls growled all at once, the sound like thunder. They surrounded him like a pack of dogs.

All of the thralls except for me. He turned his head, his gaze boring into mine.

This was a vampire. Not my master, a vampire who had a vested interest in keeping me around. This was a vampire who wouldn't even see me as food. I was an insect to be crushed. A tool to be used, like he'd used the thrall who'd just died for him.

For a moment, I missed my own master. I had no one to protect me. A thrall without a master was truly nothing.

"Kaiden!"

Johann. His voice was faint, and when I turned, surveying the courtyard, I didn't see him. Then one of the thralls lunged toward the carriage, and through a hole in the wood, a stake took it in the heart.

Johann was beneath the carriage, trapped. I scented the air, smelling him and two others, a man and a woman, along with their fear and fancy perfume.

I had no time to wonder how he'd gotten under there or why. He was either very foolish or very brave. Maybe both. But now the vampire was staring at me.

"A thrall with a name?" he asked. "Who is your master?" The chaos in the courtyard faded, or maybe it was just my focus on the vampire in front of me. Another volley fired, but it passed through him, striking only the thralls. He could turn to mist at will, something those in the village had said my master could do. No. He hadn't been my master when they'd said that. And he wasn't my master now.

"*No one* is my master," I said, a growl entering my voice. "I am . . . Kaiden."

"You are a thrall," he replied, his nose crinkling. "You

smell like one. You're no vampire, I'm sure of it."

"I—"

He turned, ignoring me. A hunter flinched when the vampire glared at him, a man with long dark hair who'd dared to run close enough to set off a solar flare. My legs tensed to leap away, the lighter clear in his hand. One spark would incinerate the vampire and any thralls close to him.

The vampire misted and reformed next to the man. The glass of the solar flare shattered when the vampire grabbed his wrist. The sound of bones cracking echoed across the field.

The vampire opened his mouth, sinking his fangs into the hunter's neck. The battle resumed around me like a clock ticking once again. Stakes and arrows flew into the crowd of thralls who once again scattered and leaped at those hunters who were on the ground. Others shielded their master. Tools. Expendable animals that would die for him while he killed.

This vampire used his thralls to hunt. Why had Dimresh made me?

"Kaiden!" Johann's voice again, so faint. "Run!"

An arrow struck my back on the right side. The wood sent a dull ache through me and drove me to my knees. If the arrow had penetrated on the left side, I would be dead.

No one here cared if I died. Not the hunters, not the vampire, and certainly not the thralls. No one but Johann, and I wasn't even sure about that.

I had to be good. And there was one way to prove it.

Even if Johann's story was true, this vampire wasn't my master, and I wouldn't become a vampire if I killed him. But I knew the right thing to do. Vampires had blood too.

Pain tore at the muscles in my back. The vampire fed on the man who'd already gone limp and gray in his arms. The scent of blood overpowered the stink of fear and the rotten, sweet scent of the other thralls, a twisted version of the scent that came off the vampire. His eyes were closed in pleasure as he drank from the man. Next to him, a thrall leaped in the way of another stake, and another thrall pounced on the hunter who'd fired it from their position by the curve of the castle.

My stomach growled with hunger, and I sprang toward the vampire.

I was a good hunter. I rarely missed a killing bite. I hadn't been like this in life — this strong, this fast, my muscles propelling me swifter than a human eye could see.

But the vampire wasn't human. He opened his eyes, blood dripping from his mouth as he pulled away from his meal. He jumped back, throwing the still-bleeding man toward me.

Maybe he meant to slow me down. Or maybe he thought I would feed on the man instead, ignoring him.

I almost did, the scent of blood overwhelming. But I didn't stop. My leg muscles bunched as I jumped again off the ground, my hands outstretched toward the vampire. I was a thrall, a perfect, mindless killer. But I wasn't mindless, and I knew exactly what I wanted to kill. I was faster than an arrow, and much more determined.

I met his eyes midleap. The whites showed, his bloody mouth open in an O of shock.

My claws raked across his face, across his eyes. If I could just grab him, I could bite him. I could have his blood.

He bellowed in pain or anger, and shoved me hard, with more strength than I had ever felt before. My body jolted when I hit the ground, and I rolled, my arms and legs scraped and aching. My head swam. Nearby, the hunter lay, his heart thudding dully in his chest and blood still trickling from his neck.

I could feed from him, like all the other thralls would. But it wasn't him I wanted. I wasn't like them.

I tensed my muscles, fighting to get on my feet, to spring again at the vampire, who was covering his bleeding eyes with one hand. The courtyard swirled around me.

"Now!" a faint voice shouted. Maybe Johann, maybe someone else from the walls above the castle. Maybe the vampire, ordering my death. It was hard to focus through the haze of pain and the ringing still in my ears from my head hitting the stone.

Then something slammed into me, growling loud in my ears, and more weight joined it. I clawed at the other thralls, my nails drawing rivers of blood and furrows in dead flesh. But then there were three of them, four, then more, and they pinned me down, their fangs sinking into my skin and ripping my strength out of me with every bite. I snapped my fangs at empty air, and one of them scored a gash across my face.

I hadn't had enough blood. I was too weak, too slow, to fight so many thralls who'd already had human blood this night. And the vampire was already healing from my attack, blinking the last of his blood out of his eyes.

I had been stupid to attack a vampire. Now his thralls would rip me apart. I stopped fighting when a bite from one of the thralls went through the tendons in my arm, and another snapped the bone in my leg. I didn't feel the usual tingle of immediate healing. I would never get blood to heal it.

No. I didn't want to die.

"Johann," I said. Above me, the stars began to darken. I closed my eyes.

Then the thralls shrieked all at once.

Chapter Thirteen

The sound of the thralls screaming was nearly as painful as their attack.

My head swam with a combination of weakness and the deafening sound all around me. But the bites and scratches stopped. One of the thralls bounded over me, toward the castle. On his neck, the fang marks of his master began to close, the scar fading.

The vampire was dead. The darkness I had seen hadn't been my life fading, but arrows covering the stars. And with his eyes injured, one had finally hit home.

Without him, the thralls were in chaos. They threw themselves at the hunters, all control gone, and were mowed down in droves. Without their master, the tide had turned. They were vicious animals without minds, thralls that had fed on human blood and now could think of only that.

But the hunters adjusted immediately. They baited with blood and then rained arrows and stakes on the thralls. One hunter swung a sword in a flashing arc, taking off a snarling thrall's head in an expert sweep. No amount of blood would give her the healing needed to recover from that.

I rolled onto my side, pain and fear sharpening my senses in a way I hadn't felt since before dying. I called out. I didn't want to die, not again.

"Johann," I said. My voice came out weak and breathy. "Help me."

A shadow fell over me, and I stared into the eyes of a woman wearing a metal gorget and holding a crossbow.

Lesalie, the Master Hunter.

"Please," I said. "Please, don't." The stars spun behind her, and I blinked, my eyelids suddenly too heavy to keep open.

"As if I would, thrall," she said. She turned her head, her crossbow still by her side. "Come get your project, Johann," she called. Her last words grew fainter as I closed my eyes. "He just saved a hunter's life."

I didn't fully lose consciousness, but I also didn't have the energy to open my eyes as someone carried me out of the courtyard and down into the twisting tunnels of the castle. My leg hung loosely, and the dull pain told me it was still broken. Voices came in and out of my awareness, but none of them sounded like Johann. I never heard my name.

I repeated it in my mind. Kaiden. I was Kaiden. I was hurt but not dying. I just needed blood, and I'd be fine.

But not human blood. No matter how good it smelled on the people around me. I couldn't be like those thralls back there, leaping and snarling like animals.

I was Kaiden. A man from the village of Penthorn. I dove into the ghosts of memories, suddenly so important. I had liked cats. Images of the town flashed through my mind, memories of an old woman, and then further back, my mother and her friends, painted ladies of the night who'd come and gone at all hours when I was young. Most of them were dead by the time I'd been old enough to understand what they did. And when I was, the women weren't the ones who interested me.

There hadn't been many men like me, those who favored other men. And the ones who did were merchants, not interested in poor men without a penny to their name. And soon, I had craved drink far more than I craved sex. Alcohol had always made the world less painful, easing the ache of hunger or the pain of illness. Penthorn was a poor town, and I'd been among its poorest. People used those like my mother until they died, and then cursed them for it. I had been beneath even that, a man left to starve and drink himself to death in alleyways with the rats and cats. I had let men use me for drink the way my mother had let them use her for money.

The thoughts hurt, twisting inside me like snakes. I saw again the vampire overlooking me like I was nothing, and then I saw Dimresh, my once master, walking through the castle as though I and the others weren't there.

Why had he made us?

"Kaiden," someone said, and then a scent I couldn't ignore was placed in front of me. Fresh blood.

I bit down hard on flesh, the rush of blood filling me. Bones snapped into place, and stinging pain eased from dozens of bite marks. Strength made me grab at the bloody offering, my fingers curling around fur.

I stopped, drawing my head back when I realized it was a cat. My stomach flipped, but it was too late, the animal a dry husk.

"No more little cats," I said, throwing the dried animal on the ground. I regretted it when I saw it was carpeted.

"Kaiden?" Johann said.

The room I was in was furnished with a writing desk and a large bed. Tapestries hung by the windows, keeping out what must be chill. Steam rose from a large basin by the door. Books filled a shelf by a curtained window.

I sat up, testing the strength of my healed leg, and when I did, chains clanked. I sank back down onto a dusty cot. A collar and chain fastened my neck to a metal peg set into the wall, fresh dust and stone littering the floor around it.

I was chained again. Like an animal, or the thralls, the leaping, snarling things. Worse than a drunk from a small village.

"Kaiden, are you well?" Johann asked. "I can get . . . something else." He nudged the cat with his foot. "Not cat?"

Johann wasn't wearing his hunting gear, instead clad in more simple leathers that hugged his hips. His chest was bare, his short hair wet. His scent, now mixed with soap, was fresh and intoxicating, and my mouth watered even as my body heated. I craved sex as much as blood for a moment, the scent of him frustrating. Hunger and confusion made me restless.

"I can hunt on my own." I put both hands on the chain around my neck but didn't pull. "Let me go. I'll come back."

"It's almost sunup." Johann didn't get close, but his heart beat steadily. He wasn't afraid of me.

"I'll be fast." I tugged on the chain, but it didn't give. "You said you wouldn't chain me again."

"Only until you've eaten."

"Then let me go." A growl entered my voice.

"Relax, please." Johann put up a hand. "I'll get you more blood. Then I'll let you off your chain."

"I'm not an animal!" I snapped. "You said I wasn't like them!" I yanked hard at the metal links, but only strained my neck in the attempt.

"Hunters almost died tonight, and despite what you did, many of them still don't trust you. Lesalie wants you kept here, with me, for your safety as well as everyone else's. Do you understand?"

I met his eyes.

"We were attacked, and everyone is anxious and frightened. I don't want any accidents from anyone. Can you trust me?" His pleading voice chased away some of the frustration.

I gritted my teeth but let go of the chain. "I'm tired of being good and being treated like . . . like them."

Johann nodded. "I'm sorry. I'll get you blood."

His words hurt, even if he didn't mean it. I wasn't like them. But I still needed blood.

I waited, chained to a wall, until he returned. He held a juvenile pig in both arms, the animal not struggling, though its heart still beat.

"It's been sick. I don't think that matters?" Johann asked.

It didn't. I took what he offered, draining another animal dry. "It would have died in a few days anyway," I said when I was done. I'd tasted sickness in animals before, but it didn't matter to me. It wasn't like I, something already dead, could get sick. Hunger still burned in my stomach, but it was bearable for now. Johann's scent still tickled my nostrils, and I didn't know what the craving in me was—bloodlust or lust. Either way, I could do nothing about it, and again I wished I could be alone with my thoughts.

"You won't let me leave the room, will you?" I asked.

"No. But I can unchain you." He moved close, and my nostrils flared. "I trust you, Kaiden."

He trusted me. I could be good.

Johann leaned over me, flooding my senses with his closeness. It was more than the scent of him, more than the sight of his tanned, bare chest. It was hairs on the back of my neck pricking, my skin fizzing with the tension and heat of a warm, living person inches away from me.

He really did trust me. I clenched my jaw so hard my teeth ached.

The chain unhooked with a key, and I relaxed when Johann moved away. He was staring at me, though, his gaze a weight on my shoulders.

"What is it?" I asked.

"You're covered in your own blood. You've healed now, but . . . do you want to bathe? I already have." He swept out an arm at the still-steaming tub. "And frankly, you smell a bit."

If a human could smell me, I must reek. And he wasn't wrong about the blood. The clothes—well, more accurately, rags—I wore were stained with it, along with the mud and dirt of days past. I'd never thought about clothes before.

These weren't the clothes I had died in, at least. Dimresh had given me these . . . about a month after I got to his castle. The clothes I had died in were gone, I supposed, probably still fraying on the castle floor.

"We can get you new clothes too." Johann said. "If you're going to be a vampire lord, you'll need to learn how to dress." His mouth turned up in a faint smile.

I didn't know how to react to this. Last night, as we came back from the river, he'd said he would trust me and treat me well. Now that he was . . . I didn't know what to do. I'd forgotten so much of my life, and what I did remember didn't have smiling, relaxed men in it.

"Should I wear what hunters wear?" I asked. I kept him in my field of vision as I crossed the room, the carpet soft beneath my feet. The warmth of the bath heated my skin as I got close.

"Whatever you'd like. You saved people today, Kaiden."

I liked it when he said my name. Now it held something real when he said it, not just a way for him to get me to relax.

"I didn't do anything." I took off my shirt, the fibers fraying further as I pulled it over my head. Dust plumed when I threw it on the floor. Streaks of dried black blood marked my torso and arms where the thralls had bitten me. What a waste. "Nothing but scratch him and distract his thralls."

"That was what we needed." Johann had averted his eyes, and I took my pants off, knowing as I did I'd never wear them again. I hadn't realized how filthy my clothes were, how filthy I was. I got into the bath without any further delay, the heat drawing a quiet hiss from between my teeth. Cold didn't bother me, but this heat I felt.

"Vampires are hard for hunters to approach." He moved over to his desk, keeping his back turned, and I wished he would look at me. "The one today wasn't particularly strong, but those like Dimresh give off this . . . aura. Fear aura, we call it, something that strikes terror in the living when they get near. Some vampires, like Dimresh, have auras so strong a human can't even get close to their castle. Those are the ones who've been plaguing us for centuries—and with each one that gets to that level of power who we can't kill, the more danger the average person is in." Johann sighed. "Some hunters think the only thing keeping a vampire from declaring himself a king of a territory is disinterest. But no one seems to know what they truly want, besides blood."

I swirled the water with a hand, flakes of dried blood spiraling away. "Why do they make thralls?"

"For the one like today, because it gives them strength. He had exquisite control over his thralls. A weaker vampire like that, with no castle of his own, benefits hugely from a lot of servants who can hunt for him and protect him. Someone like Dimresh . . . well, I imagine he used you and the others to scout."

I nodded, splashing water over my face and hair. More dust and blood tinged the bath. "But . . . why did he choose me?"

Wood creaked, and now Johann did face me. "I can't answer that, Kaiden. I'm sorry. There's just no way to know."

I had been foolish to ask anyway. "Tell me what you do know about vampires, then," I asked instead. "I know what I am. But what are they?"

"I had thought you might be curious about that." Johann leaned back in his chair, the light from the torches dancing over the muscles of his torso. I hoped the water would hide it if I got too distracted by him. I still didn't fully understand why I lusted so strongly at times. Other thralls didn't, not as far as I could tell.

"Many people think they're just like any other creature—wolves and bears and the like. Or humans infected by some disease, hence their passing it with a bite and blood. Like I

said before, many believe it's the sharing of blood that matters. If Dimresh had shared his blood with you upon first
making you, you would have been a vampire on your own,
not just a thrall. I'm guessing he gave you animal blood when
he turned you."

I nodded, swallowing hard. "It was a cat."

Johann blinked. "Oh. I'm . . . I'm sorry."

I shrugged away the awkwardness, using a cloth to scrub
at my face and chest.

"But I don't think it's an infection. Vampires are something
else—something magical." Johann put up a hand. "I know, it
sounds a bit crazy, and not all hunters believe this. A lot will
tell you I read too many old books. But it makes sense to me."

"What is it?"

He smiled, and I got the feeling not many people listened
to his theories. "Old books and scrolls from three centuries
ago talk about divine magic. Protection from an old god—
spells and purified water driving away dark magics and demons."

"Holy Laurel," I said.

"That's right. Some still use her name or ask for her blessings. In the past, it was said that the blessings held real power.
But something happened. The legends don't always agree on
what happened, of course. Some say Laurel lost a divine battle and died. Others say she abandoned us. Regardless, without that divine magic and the protection of people who used
to be able to wield it, dark magic began to thrive. Dark spells
were put in place, either by evil priests or by vampires themselves. And once done, some magic can't be undone. You see
that a lot in the history books that have survived the centuries."

His words sounded strange, but an old memory sparked in
my mind from my time being alive. "Was that what caused
the fall of the Empire?"

"Yes!" Johann's eyes lit up. "Did Dimresh ever mention it?"

"No." Johann gave a small huff of disappointment. "It was just . . . something I knew. Or had heard of."

"I'm impressed," Johann said. "Many people these days barely know the Empire even existed, and those that do say it simply fell to civil war. Of course, now it doesn't really matter." He threw up his hands, letting them fall on the arms of his chair. "We were united and powerful once. Now, ever since, humanity has been fractured, falling into superstition and fear. A once great empire has become collections of city-states and the tiny villages that supply them, tiny kings ruling what used to be cities in an enormous country. And that's when they're not overrun by powerful vampires like Dimresh. No one protects the old roads, everyone too frightened of the night and the vampires. Only merchants bother learning anything, the other people too afraid and desperate to have time to devote to learning." He slumped.

"You do," I said. "The hunters."

"We try," Johann said. "But you saw what happened tonight. Without you, many of us would have died."

"You were the ones who killed the vampire," I said. "I was just . . . a distraction."

"A damned good one," Johann said. "You scratched his eyes out. A thinking thrall. The vampire must have been shocked."

"Maybe." I pictured the vampire in my mind, the way he'd looked at me at first. There had been nothing in his gaze, no recognition of me as an equal. As anything.

And vampires saw humans as food. What did they value? Who were their equals?

If I became a vampire lord, would I be like him? Seeing everything else as beneath me? Twisted by dark magic, like Johann had said?

A pang of heaviness went through me. Dawn was approaching. I stood, the water dripping off me, and Johann raised both eyebrows.

"Kaiden?"

"I'm . . . tired." I met his eyes, which snapped down and then up to my face. "Do I need to be chained to sleep?"

"No. And I've prepared a box for you, to avoid any daylight. But . . ." Johann's face reddened just slightly, his heart picking up as he fixed his gaze on my face. "Do you want clothing?"

I sniffed the air, trying to scent if he was aroused or not. He must have noticed, because he cleared his throat and pointed at the corner, opposite where I had been chained and farthest from the windows. A wooden box resembling a coffin lay concealed behind another tapestry.

My curiosity and excitement at Johann's display of interest faded when I realized with a pang of fear that the spot where I'd been chained was directly across where the morning sun from the windows would have killed me.

Any moment, they expected me to fail, it seemed.

But I wasn't a mindless thrall, and I had *earned* my life. Or what passed as one.

"I will take clothing when I wake. For now . . . I should rest. I do not want to burn." I glanced once more at the chains.

Johann caught my gaze, and his face paled, but I didn't care to talk any longer. I ran a hand through hair still wet from the bath and climbed into the box.

It felt like a coffin.

CHAPTER FOURTEEN

I dreamed of the sun.

I could see in the dark ever since being turned. But true light, true color, popped in my dreams, the greens of overgrown trees and weeds mingling with the deep browns of the dirty paths by the gray cobblestone village roads. The sky itself was deep blue.

In my dream, I flew like a bird over cobblestones that began to turn white. The broken gray roads around the village became paved and well-trodden, marked with dozens of wagon treads and hoofmarks. In the distance, a city gleamed in the sun, one of the cities of the old Empire Johann had talked about, only now the great stone castle that marked it wasn't fallen into ruins.

I turned, the road that led to the great city leading to all others like spokes on a wheel. One led to my village, Penthorn, and Dimresh's castle, which now was whole and overgrown with healthy trees and well-maintained shrubs.

It was all fantasy, I knew, my brain tricking me because of Johann's words about the Empire of the past. But it felt so real.

I knew my life hadn't been like this. The few memories I had were always at night, lying alone in alleys in the dark. But fantasy or not, my life hadn't always been like that. I had talked to people. I had lived.

Then darkness shattered the dream, and I opened my eyes to nothingness. For a moment, I thought I was back at Dimresh's castle, in the tiny stone room I had slept in since being turned.

But if that were true, I wouldn't be this hungry. I licked my lips, my tongue scraping over my fangs, and sat up.

I was met immediately with the sight of Johann clad in his hunting gear. But at least this time it wasn't aimed at me.

"We're going to hunt, Kaiden," he said. "And then we'll talk some more. Does that sound good to you?"

I stood, then paused, my eyes narrowing at something behind Johann. He turned, then moved out of the way, letting me look in the mirror.

Dimresh had never had mirrors in his castle, at least not in the hallways thralls had been allowed to stay in.

I knew who I was, and I certainly knew what I had looked like. But the man in the mirror looked strange to me. Blond hair and skin so pale I almost glowed in the moonlight that came in through the windows. My muscles were strong and well defined. That made sense, I supposed, with how easily and quickly I could move, but it wasn't strength I'd truly earned.

When I bared my teeth, my fangs were obvious, sharp points threatening to slice my bottom lip if I wasn't careful. And my eyes were pure black, like a rat's eyes, like all the other thralls I'd seen.

I looked away, stomach twisting. They'd been blue once. I remembered that.

"I have clothes you can borrow," Johann said.

I nodded.

"Your old clothes were too dirty to salvage."

I wasn't surprised. Hunger and eagerness to leave this room, to hunt, made me hurry to pull the new clothes on. The fabric was plain but soft and smooth on my skin, and soon I was ready.

"It suits you," Johann said with an approving nod. In the mirror, now I looked almost as I had in life. The clothes didn't fit perfectly, hiding how muscular I was, and a stripe of green running down the front of the shirt reminded of my dream of a sunny day.

The clothes did nothing to hide my black, lifeless-looking eyes, though, and I turned away.

"What color were your eyes?" Johann asked. For a moment, my hunger disappeared.

"Blue," I said.

"If you can become a vampire, then maybe they will be again. But you look good. Don't let yourself think you're like the others."

I didn't know how to respond. How obvious had I been in being disturbed by my own reflection?

"Where will we hunt?" I asked.

Johann gave a quiet sigh. "Follow me."

No stars lit the night sky, only pricks of autumn rain that hit my face and dampened my new clothes when we got outside. At least we didn't pass by anyone else. Maybe Johann had picked a route no one else used, or maybe people knew I would be out hunting. Either way, I appreciated the lack of temptation.

"There are many deer in these woods," Johann said. He still smelled like the soap of the bath, and I tried to focus on that and not the promise of the scent of blood beating just under his skin. "Try not to mess up your new clothes too much, would you?" He grinned as he spoke.

"I told you before," I said. "I don't waste blood." I paused for a moment, an urge I didn't like flashing through me as I licked my lips. He was right there. He wasn't even carrying a weapon I could see.

I fled as the urge grew stronger. I could control my hunger. I wasn't like the others.

And he was right about the deer. I didn't have far to run before I came upon a group of them. Two were smart enough to flee in opposite directions, but the buck stood its ground, likely thinking it could fend me off with its newly grown antlers. Of course it was wrong.

As I sank my fangs into its neck, driving it to the ground, I thought of Johann's story of the old Empire. Vampires were twisted by dark magic. That meant I was some sort of creature of dark magic, didn't it?

I knew nothing about magic. I didn't even know if it was real. Dimresh had certainly seemed magical in the way he moved and commanded me, in his beauty and grace and control, but that could have just been his power as a vampire. And of course, the fact that he'd been my master. And the magic of the old god, Holy Laurel . . . I had heard her name enough in life, I knew, even if I couldn't remember where. But if it had ever carried magic to combat vampires, that magic clearly didn't work now.

The question flared once again in my mind. Dimresh hadn't been like the vampire last night, who used his thralls as weapons and protection. Dimresh hadn't demanded much of us, only to avoid human blood and report anything interesting. And finally, to kill the hunter.

Was that all I had been made for? Information and protection?

I dropped the desiccated deer, my hunger sated. But without the hunger to focus on, my mind worked better, and I couldn't erase thoughts that made me tense and upset. Johann had said we would talk, but I wasn't sure what I wanted to know most. Johann confused me and made me feel things I didn't know I still could feel. And worse, I didn't know if he was aware of that or not. He had looked at me last night, and I thought I'd smelled desire, but I wasn't sure.

"Kaiden," Johann said, and I whirled. Johann had followed me. Impressive, to track me this far without me noticing. Then again, he was a hunter. "Are you still hungry?"

"No." I moved away from the kill. "I suppose you want to talk now?"

Johann tilted his head. "Do you not want to?"

"I do," I said, too quickly. I licked my lips, but I'd been efficient — there was no residue from the deer. "I just . . . there's too much I don't know."

"That's fine." Johann began to walk, and I followed, pushing fronds out of my way when he led me through an overgrown part of the forest. "For now, I will tell you a legend, the legend that made me follow you and talk to you that first time back by Penthorn."

"I'd . . . like that."

He smiled, the moonlight illuminating his face when we moved into a clearing. "Good. It's a tale from a century ago, two centuries after the fall of the Empire. It tells of Lucien, an intelligent thrall. He was different from the others, quiet where they were vicious, thoughtful and brooding when the others were slaves to their instincts. Writings from his master reported that he was cunning, as well, and would suck blood from livestock rather than hunt."

I wrinkled my nose. "He sounds lazy."

Johann laughed, and I liked the sound. "Maybe. But he was smart."

"I didn't know vampires wrote records," I said. Each thing Johann taught me just raised more questions. "Dimresh didn't write. At least, not that I saw." He had spent much of his time alone, though, away from us thralls. I had no idea what he kept in the main keep, or in his rooms.

"Fewer people can write now," Johann said. "In the time of the Empire, they say students of Holy Laurel, called priests, learned to write and spread the knowledge. But now there's little need save for merchants. Not all hunters can read and write either." He sighed. "Most think of it as a waste of time, like chasing stories."

I nodded, thinking of Thomas, and curled my upper lip. "I'm not a story."

Johann nodded. "Maybe one day you will be."

That thought made me smile, my fangs pinching my lower lip. It was nice to think I had a future. "What happened to Lucien?"

"The only hint we have is in records from an old hunter, a scholarly man named Artur. He wrote of a Lucien, a vampire lord of the village, once city, of Brusque. The hunter only found out about him when the village reported that a young man sat outside the ancient castle as the sun rose and turned to ash."

My stomach twisted in fear, my throat tight. I'd never before thought of what a sun death must be like. "He was pinned outside?"

"No," Johann said. "He ended his own . . . unlife."

I blinked, the memory of the alley fresh in my mind. My master in front of me, a beautiful man offering death. I had chosen what he had to give.

I didn't want that now. Choosing life was how I'd ended up here, with Johann. The thought of giving up life again made me grit my teeth. If I died, I would lose . . . this. Being with Johann. Talking to him and living a life I'd thought I had lost.

"Kaiden?" Johann asked. I unclenched hands that I had tightened into fists. "Do you want to hear more?"

"Yes," I said, willing myself to relax. "I just . . . want to know why he would do that."

"It's not known." Johann eyed me, his steps slowing. "Does the thought of a vampire dying upset you?"

"No. Only the . . ." I swallowed. "Only the thought of choosing death. No vampire would do that." Only humans, like I had been.

"He wasn't like most thralls, and I suppose he wasn't like

most vampires, either." Johann stopped walking and faced me. "The castle he lived in was searched by the hunter's guild, but they found little of interest, only the writings of Lucien's previous master. That was how they learned he was once a thrall. But Lucien himself kept no records. There were only the reports from the village. Some said people even visited the castle while Lucien ruled there, but no one could find anyone who actually claimed to have gone. They did report that the vampire never killed anyone, though."

"That sounds impossible."

"Is it?" Johann asked. "You drink animal blood."

"I'm a thrall." By command of their masters, thralls drank animal blood only, and now I drank it to avoid becoming a mindless thing like the others. Vampires . . . I didn't know if they could survive on it. Dimresh didn't need as much blood as we'd needed, but he'd killed someone from Penthorn at least once a week. Maybe human blood was simply more filling.

I had been his servant, but I knew so little of what I was.

"You seem uncertain of that." Johann's mouth twisted up in a smile, and he raised an eyebrow. He smelled even better when he was relaxed and happy. He was at ease with me, finally, and I wished I could be the same

"None of that says that Lucien killed his master, though," I said. "How do you know that was how he became a vampire?"

"Another story." Johann huffed when I tilted my head. "I know it sounds like all of this is just old stories, but that's all we have anymore. But a scroll by a merchant from a guild now since bankrupt mentions hurrying away one night from the castle by Brusque. He saw a vampire bury another who'd been beheaded."

A chill went through me. "Was it Lucien burying his master?"

"The scroll didn't say. It was a footnote in a long list of ir-relevant reports — well, irrelevant to us. But who else would it have been?"

"Why would he bury his master if he killed him?" Nothing Johann was telling me about Lucien made sense. Maybe I wasn't like him after all.

"That I don't know. Loyalty, maybe. Would you bury Dim-resh if we killed him?"

A bat flew overhead, and I tracked its movement. "I don't know." Even in the dark, I could tell Johann could see my eyes meet his. "I know killing him will make me a vampire. Or at least, that's what you've said. But . . . why do you want to kill him?" It sounded foolish as I said it. "I mean, you're a hunter. But there are lots of vampires out there. So why pick Dim-resh?"

"Because no one else believes he can be killed," Johann said. "Or any vampire like him."

CHAPTER FIFTEEN

He'd said that before, or something similar. Dimresh was powerful, with his dark magics and auras of fear. "Why?" I asked. "Why is he that strong?"

"Vampires have different levels of strength. Some say the longer they live, the stronger they are. Others say it has something to do with how much blood they were given by the vampire that turned them. There are also people who think it has something to do with how much territory they claim. We've never found a clear answer, though vampires like the one you helped us kill, those who travel without any territory at all, tend to be weak and easy to dispatch. Usually."

"If he was weak, then I don't know if I can kill Dimresh," I said.

Johann broke into a laugh. "I'm sure you can. You've already impressed me far more than I thought you would."

"What do you mean . . . thought I would?"

"Ah, well . . ." Johann adjusted the cloak he wore, and I was distracted when he let it drop from his shoulders. His muscles shifted, revealing the human strength he held. He was well-formed, just like in my fantasies. "I was talking to people in the . . . Kaiden?"

I looked to the stars, hoping he thought I was just craving blood and not . . . him. "I'm listening."

"Sure." He took his cloak off the rest of the way, wrapping it over his arm—but not in a way that would block access to the crossbow at his hip. "I was just going to say, I heard a lot about you from the village. You were . . . well, the town drunk."

I frowned.

"But that wasn't all. I wasn't totally honest when we first met about what people said about you."

Curiosity and nervousness prickled my skin. "Oh?"

"Some reviled you, sure. Many thought nothing of you. But someone like me, who values stories, talks to many people. Many said you were kind, Kaiden. You never judged anyone, never made a nuisance of yourself. You helped those who got sick from drinking at times—I suppose having learned from experience."

Once I would have been ashamed to admit that was true, but it seemed preferable to what I was now.

"And when some people did offer you hospitality on cold or rainy nights, you never wore out your welcome. One of the older ladies even said you were more polite than most men in town, and that one older woman took care of you most nights."

More polite than most, I suppose. Come inside. You'll catch your death. Holy Laurel wouldn't like that.

Again, outside? You'll catch your death in the rain. More snow tonight than in the cities of the Empire of old. You have to stay in, dear.

"Matilda," I said. "That was her name."

"That's right," Johann said. He stared at me, as though trying to see something in my black eyes. "You remember her? I never spoke to her—I think she's taken ill. I'm sorry. Was she important to you?"

"No." That was wrong. "I mean . . . she was kind to me. That's all. I think." The thought of her sliced me open. Johann had heard more about me than I could remember. It wasn't fair.

"What about you?" I asked, making him blink and lean back. "You've heard about me. But I know nothing about you."

"You want to know about me?" He sounded so surprised. "What for?"

What a strange question. "Why wouldn't I? I'm spending time with you. You're" —I almost swallowed the word—"interesting. And if we do kill vampires, we can do it as partners. It's only fair I learn about you."

Speaking like this, banter back and forth with another person . . . I felt more alive than I had in months. No, not even since being turned. Years. I could almost forget the hunger that burned in me, the fact that the night looked as bright as the day had once been.

"I'm . . . flattered, I think," Johann said with a quiet laugh. "But in truth, I'm not so interesting. The son of a family of merchants from . . . Brusque." He spoke the name quietly, and I could hear pain there. "I traveled with my parents six months a year, trading goods and collecting stories. The rest of the time, I lived in Brusque. It was how I heard the story of Lucien. But . . ." He shrugged. "Brusque fell to a vampire lord. One like Dimresh, powerful and fearsome."

"Lasren," I said.

"You've heard the name?" Johann demanded, leaning forward and making me take a step back. "Where?"

I hated to disappoint him. "From you," I said, "and Thomas. In the wagon on the way to the river."

"Oh." The excitement left his eyes, and I missed it. "I had hoped . . . well, it doesn't matter. Lasren is like Dimresh, a vampire lord of frightening power. No hunter can get near his territory. He was the one who . . . let's say, inspired me to become a hunter." He stared into darkness for a moment, and I could guess what had happened to his family.

"I'm sorry," I said. Plenty of people from Penthorn were taken by Dimresh. Mostly prostitutes and drunks like me, or anyone else who didn't have a safe place to spend their nights. But I couldn't remember if I'd lost anyone I knew to the vampire. My life only came back in fits and flashes. If I'd felt the pain of loss for anyone but my mother, who had died of illness in her bed, it was long gone now.

"It's not your fault." Johann sighed. "Most of us hunters have lost someone. But Lasren . . . he took over an entire city, and killed so many while doing it. Anyone who traveled part of the year, like us, was easy prey. I was . . ."

His heart rate had spiked, his skin going pale. "Don't worry about it," I said. "You don't need to talk about it." And I touched him on the shoulder.

He jumped away, his hand going to his crossbow. I froze, my hand still outstretched to where he'd been standing a moment ago. I was impressed by how quickly he could move, and that he'd been so on edge when I hadn't even noticed it before.

Why had I touched him? I was just a thrall. I closed my hand and moved it toward my chest, meeting his eyes.

"Kaiden, you were . . . trying to reassure me?" Johann said. He slowly lowered his weapon, and when he did, I took a careful step back. "Don't run, please," Johann added. "I didn't mean . . . you just startled me. I didn't expect . . ."

"I'm sorry." I hadn't meant to frighten him, but I'd seen myself in the mirror. The clothes I wore did nothing to hide the power I had, or the monstrousness of a thrall. "I won't do it again."

"No." Johann took a step forward, sheathing the weapon once again at his hip. "You're not like others. You're not a normal thrall, and you're certainly not like Lasren. Or Dimresh." He took a deep breath, and his heart slowed. "It's okay. Here. I trust you."

He held out his hand.

I hadn't touched anyone like this since being turned, my only living contact either with chains or ropes or with the animals I killed. Moonlight bathed his pale hand, the lines and grooves of his skin and the bluish purple veins in his wrist.

I reached for it, his hand hot in mine. His was full of blood, but it was more than that. There was life and history. Hard calluses marked where he held weapons, and when he closed his hand around mine in return, his strength impressed me, for a human. His arm was outstretched, a sure sign he was being careful, but I understood. This was likely as close as I'd ever get to him, and I held his hand in mine, relishing it. I ignored the hunger and focused on feeling what I had lost. The buzzing, warm sensation of contact with another person. No violence, no craving for his blood. Just closeness. Warmth and strength and life.

"Kaiden," Johann said. I expected him to pull his hand away any moment, but he didn't. His heart was beating harder, but for once I didn't think it was nervousness that I would turn on him.

"Johann!" A shout broke through the stillness of the trees, and Johann drew his hand away. I ached at the loss, even as I curled my fingers into claws at the sound of the voice. Thomas. "Johann, where are you?"

Johann blew out a breathy sigh, clearing his throat before calling back. "Here, with Kaiden!"

Thomas was clumsy and loud coming through the trees. How had he even become a vampire hunter? When he emerged into our clearing, he was breathing hard, and his heart beat fast and weakly. He should be resting. But I wasn't about to tell him that.

"The thrall." His mouth was set in a thin line. "What are you doing with it now?"

"Him," Johann said. "His name is Kaiden. He's not like the others, Thomas."

"Yeah? Can you prove it?"

"Look at him!" Johann threw his hand out. "Talk to him!"

"You always do experiments on thralls."

Experiments?

"It's not often you talk to them when you do." Thomas, for all his weakness, moved like a predator as he circled around me, like a cat stalking its prey. He wore a long cloak, but I was certain he carried a weapon. "What did you bring him out here for?"

"To hunt and to talk," Johann said. Anger edged his voice. "What are you doing out here, Thomas? Lesalie has already given me leave to work with him."

"Work with him. Right." Thomas finally fixed his gaze on me. "It's a thrall. You've killed and experimented and dissected enough of them to know."

I thought of the thralls I'd killed, pathetic creatures on the forest floor.

"I don't care how different this one is, if I cut you, Johann, he'd be on you in seconds. You can't work with a thrall. Take him to kill a vampire, and the instant you get injured, you'd have two bloodsuckers to deal with."

It used to be true, the scent of human blood too powerful. Was it still true? My body tensed, my instincts screaming danger, even though there was nothing here, yet, that would harm me. I had resisted it once, during the fight with the vampire in the courtyard. I could do it again, I had to.

"Thomas," Johann's voice carried a warning. His heart rate picked up.

"I talked to Lesalie too. That would be the final step, wouldn't it? We can't work with a dog we can't trust." Thomas glared at me, drawing a knife. "What do you think, thrall?"

I growled, shifting my weight to leap. The wind was blowing toward me, bringing me the scent of Johann's sudden fear. Thomas whirled, the knife flashing as he moved to slash at Johann. My muscles tensed, time slowing as I jumped in front of Johann, leaves sliding beneath my feet. I was a thrall, and thralls were fast.

But in the same moment Thomas sliced his own thumb, smirking as the wind brought me the intoxicating scent of his blood. My world became focused on that tiny drop of red and all it promised. Thomas wasn't Johann. I didn't care about him. He was prey.

"Kaiden!" Johann shouted. His voice was far away. "Don't!"

"C'mon," the human in front of me taunted. "You can be baited just like any other thrall." He squeezed his sliced thumb, the blood dripping down his hand and wrist.

His pale wrist, like Johann's in the moonlight. If I took what I wanted, I would never see Johann again. I would be lost. Worse than dead.

I growled, my fangs pricking my lower lip. The urge to bite, to kill, washed through me, my muscles tensing and bunching, my toes digging into the loam. Saliva dripped down my chin. But I didn't move.

I couldn't do it. I could, physically; I knew that. But I wouldn't. I *couldn't* do it. I hadn't wanted to die that first night when I ran from Johann. And I didn't want to die now, and make everything Johann had done to save me pointless.

I wrenched my attention away from Thomas's hand to his face, his sneer and his narrowed eyes. In his other hand, he held a long stake, and I immediately felt stupid. I wouldn't have died from losing myself to human blood. I would have died from a stake through my heart had I moved.

I spat on the ground in front of him. "You'll need to do better than that," I growled.

Thomas frowned, took a few steps back. He shook his hand, a few drops of blood hitting the leaves. I gritted my teeth against another rush of bloodlust. The hunger would go away. I didn't need human blood. I didn't.

"Fine, Johann," Thomas said. "I'm officially impressed.

Enjoy your thrall. I'll tell Lesalie." Thomas put his thumb in his mouth, and I envied him before I realized how stupid that was.

"Good work, Kaiden," Johann said. His voice soothed my tension. But not all of it. "Damn Lesalie. I didn't think she would try that so soon."

It had been an experiment. A test, one I had passed. But it reminded me of Thomas's words. "What did he mean by experiments?" I asked.

Johann's mouth turned down, and his gaze slid from mine. "Have you ever wondered how hunters know so much about thralls?"

"And vampires in general," I said.

"I am a hunter," Johann said. "But I am also . . . an historian. You probably gathered that much from all my . . . stories." He smiled, but it faded quickly. "But I also worked on gathering information about thralls. And a lot of that was by capturing and experimenting on them."

I swallowed, my hunger gone. "What kind of experiments?"

"How to kill them most effectively." He spoke bluntly. "We're hunters, and most of the time our work has us killing thralls, not the vampires like Dimresh. We learned that their strength depends on how much blood they take, and what kind. Human blood makes them stronger, but also makes them mindless. If they take no blood at all, they don't die, but they become weak and eventually unable to move." I remembered what that felt like after crossing the river. "I also learned how to sever a link to its master — the same thing we did to you. But the one we tried that experiment on before went mad with bloodlust."

I wanted to be angry, to feel betrayed. But I couldn't. I was a thrall. Every other thrall I'd seen . . . before Johann . . . I hadn't even cared when they died.

"Why am I different?" I asked. "If you experimented on me . . . could you help the others?"

"Oh, Kaiden." Johann blinked and reached out his hand again. I took it, once again relishing the warmth.

"I don't know why you're different. But I promise you, I'll help you try to figure it out."

"How?" I asked.

"By teaching you how to hunt. Like a vampire hunter," he added when I tilted my head in confusion. "Because I think the answer to why you're different lies with your old master."

I nodded. I wanted to believe him. And I wanted to believe I was more than just another of his experiments.

Chapter Sixteen

I slept another day away in the lightless box in Johann's room and woke the next night as the sun set. But when I sat up, moving the lid of the box to the side, it was to the sound of Johann's steady, deep breathing.

He still slept, and I was unchained and hungry in his room. He really did trust me.

I sat very still. Did I trust myself?

The window was open, but a rushing breeze took the wind across the panes, not into the room. Outside, the moon had risen. Not a full moon any longer, it still cast enough light to give Johann a milky glow. I crept closer, keeping my steps light so the floorboards wouldn't creak beneath my feet. In the corner of the room, a mouse darted away and disappeared into a crack in the stone wall.

Johann slept soundly, his face smooth and unlined in the relaxation of sleep. He wore no shirt, and judging from the way the light blanket shaped his hips, I doubted he wore underclothes either. I licked my lips.

The only touch I would ever feel would be his hand in mine from the night before, I was sure. But I didn't stop myself from etching this sight of him in my mind. Maybe one day, if I truly did become a vampire . . .

No. There were too many unknowns. I had to stay focused on what was in front of me and not risk ruining it. And staring at a man while he slept, giving in to any form of temptation, would ruin it.

I moved away, more mice skittering beneath the stones. I

wondered if the Master Hunter knew they had an infestation.

"Johann," I said. He didn't stir. I cleared my throat, the dusty feel of pending blood-dryness making my voice weak. "Johann!"

He stirred, blinking in the moonlight. Then he sat up all at once, the covers falling and revealing his lightly haired bare chest. Muscles stood in stark definition on his shoulders and arms. "Kaiden?" He looked around the room, right past me, until I stepped into a shaft of moonlight. "Did I . . . did I over-sleep?"

My mouth curled up. "I take it you wanted to wake before me?"

"Of course, I . . ." Johann jumped out of bed, and I was gifted with the sight of his naked body, his muscular abdomen and slim hips. Not to mention his tight butt. I gritted my teeth against a surge of very different hunger, but at least it wasn't bloodlust. If I focused on pleasurable feelings, maybe I could forget my constant craving.

"I wanted to be ready to hunt as soon as you woke. Sorry." He began pulling on clothes. "It's hard to adjust to being to-tally nocturnal, I suppose."

"You don't sleep the entire day, do you?" I asked. Foolish. I slept all day, but twelve hours was a long time for a human to sleep.

"No. I stay up a few hours after you would fall asleep and get up a few hours before. Usually. But in preparing to teach you and talking to the Master Hunter, I suppose I stayed up too late." He pulled on a shirt and then a belt, which looked complicated until he fastened it with no effort. It held a cross-bow and ammunition. "But it's for the best. I have tools to train you with, and more proof that you're safe. No thrall would see a sleeping human and not bite him."

No thrall. It all came back to that. Everything I did was more proof I was safe. I just hoped it would be enough for others to trust me. I also wished that everything I did wasn't being monitored and tested as some experiment in Johann's mind.

"Are you ready?" Johann said. "First thing is for you to hunt. Then meet me by the gate. I'll show you what we work with."

Curiosity buzzed in me as I filled my belly with blood from a deer by the castle. I was quick, and I hurried back to the dark form of the castle, pausing only when I heard the Master Hunter's voice.

" . . . can't believe it," she was saying. "I only do since it's Thomas who reported it."

"We can trust him," Johann said. "He's even shown evidence of emotions. And . . . caring, I think."

"Caring? For who?"

"For . . . me." I huddled in the trees, not risking looking and being seen. I wanted to hear what Johann thought, desperate hope burning in my hollow chest. "I think he craves more than just blood. He wants closeness to another person."

"Is that true, or just your reading too much into things?" Lesalie's voice was harsh. "Don't let your hopes and stories trick you into getting too attached. It's . . . I mean he's certainly different than most. But he's still a bloodsucker."

As much as I hated to admit it, she was right. Even if I could act on the lust I sometimes felt, so close to Johann, to his warmth and neck and blood . . . it wouldn't be safe for either of us. I shouldn't even consider it.

"I know," Johann said, his words and the disappointment in his voice as painful as a stake shot. "I'll be careful. It's just . . . exciting to finally be able to talk to a thrall. Or vampire. Whatever he is. This could change everything."

"Only if it works," Lesalie said. "But I do hope it does."

It was time to show myself. I jogged out from the trees, sticks on the muddy path pricking my bare feet. Lesalie and

Johann stood by the gate, and all around them lay dangerous vampire-killing weapons.

I stopped a few feet away.

"It's safe, Kaiden, don't worry," Johann said. "These are the tools we want to train you to use."

"Come closer, thrall," Lesalie said, her tone that of someone used to being obeyed. Almost like Dimresh. "They won't bite." She chuckled at her own joke.

The weapons lay out on a cloth in an arc around Johann. Some I knew. A crossbow lay next to a series of wooden stakes of increasing size, the last of which were simply wooden spears. A few even had lichen growing on them. Vials of liquid looked harmless, but I knew better, remembering the burning pain of whatever Johann had put on the chains that had bound me. Nets lay on the ground too, also covered in lichen and fresh dirt. More conventional swords and knives and a few throwing axes lay side by side, though most of them were rusty. And there was a flare, just like the one that had incinerated Dimresh's other thralls.

"I can't use that," I said, pointing. "It would kill me too." I hoped it wasn't charged.

"Good eye," Lesalie said.

"First things first," Johann said. "Do you know how to kill a vampire?"

"I know how to kill thralls," I said. "Or more accurately, I know how you kill them." It was meant to be a joke, but Johann frowned instead of smiled. "Stake through the heart," I continued. "Cut off their head. Or sunlight."

"There are other ways," Johann said. "Do you know why wood is used and not metal weapons?"

"I know that wood hurts more," I said. I hadn't been turned long enough to be shot through the heart with anything metal, thankfully.

"Don't quiz him," Lesalie said with a toss of her hair. "Just explain."

"Sorry." Johann picked up one of the long stakes, and I couldn't help but take a step back. "Wood once contained life. Or at least it once was alive, and the more life it holds, the stronger its effect. A freshly cut stake is the most effective. Thralls—and vampires—are hard to kill because as long as they have blood, they can heal from any normal injury. The residual life in wooden weapons slows that healing."

I narrowed my eyes. "Animals are alive, but I heal from their bites and scratches with no problems."

Johann shrugged. "It's theory. But it holds true for many things. Water infused with fresh flowers or newly fallen leaves will burn and weaken a thrall, which is what I treated your ropes with when I first brought you here."

"I remember," I said.

"And of course, bright, heated light from the sun—or a so-lar flare. They are magic from the old Empire, and not some-thing we can make any longer." The solar flare lay on the ground, a glass case supported with brass that wound around the outside. It looked like any other lantern, except instead of flame, a black rock lay inside the glass. "When lit with a spark, that rock you see there heats up, the light reflecting through the glass and sending out rays as bright as the sun."

I nodded. I'd seen the light that had burned Dimresh's thralls. "What is the rock made of?" I asked.

"We're not sure," Lesalie said. "We think the rock itself is a form of coal, though not one we can produce now. It may have been made with magic. But once done, some magic can't be undone, or so they say, so it still works even after all these years."

I remembered the sound of breaking glass from the battle with the vampire in the courtyard. "How many are left?"

"Not enough," Lesalie snapped.

"So," Johann said. "You know what kills thralls. And the

same works on vampires. But they have abilities you don't."
He hefted a wooden stake. "If I threw this at a full vampire,
they could form into mist and be untouched if they saw it
coming."

I nodded. I had seen the vampire in the courtyard do that.

"And there's simply no way a human could sneak up on
one. They have to be distracted or asleep. Solar flares will
work even if they're mist, but aren't always deadly to a full
vampire. And the herbal water will only work if they drink it,
which . . . well, I don't know if that has ever been tried. But
hitting them with it will only slow them down, not stop
them."

Vampires were like me, but better. Suddenly it seemed impossible.

"Typically, a hunter will enter their castle during the day
and kill them. But a castle like Dimresh's is cloaked in . . .
well, it must be magic. The fear aura. No human can get close
unless invited, day or night."

"I can't travel during the day," I said. "I have to sleep."

"So you can get into the castle, but not when he's weak. I
can kill him while he's weak, but I can't get in." Johann
sighed. "We need a plan."

"What if I drag you into the castle?" I asked. "Chain you in
a box and take you in even if you're afraid?"

Lesalie laughed. "You have some odd tastes, thrall."

"That won't work. I'd die of fright." It sounded like he was
just weak until he added, "Hunters have tried such things before, chaining themselves to a boat and sending them along a
moat to enter a castle with a powerful vampire. That was the
vampire Timaeus, who still rules a castle near the city of
Dremasque. We found the hunter in the boat after it had circled the castle once, dead of a heart attack."

I growled, Lesalie tensing when I did. "So it has to be me,
then?"

"Either we find a way for you to stay awake during the day," Johann said, "or we teach you to fight—and kill—vampires who will be fighting back."

I eyed the weapons. "Fine," I said. It felt like agreeing to pick up and use poison. "If a human can do it, I should be able to."

"Then let's begin," Johann said. "I'll teach you to use these." He tapped one of the crossbows on the ground with his foot. "We call them stakeshooters. And if that fails . . . well, you'll learn to fight with a normal stake too."

CHAPTER SEVENTEEN

I was stronger and faster than Johann. I could sense things he couldn't. I could hear his breathing and his heart rate change when he exerted himself, and I knew when he was tired and would begin to slow down.

But for that first night and every night after, he still batted away my stake as though it was a fly every time I so much as thought about hitting him with it. This night the moon was nearly full waned, the forest by the castle pitch dark. Even then, Johann met my wooden weapon with his, batting away my clumsy stabs, the air filled with the now-familiar sound of wood hitting wood. Even if I'd been using a metal weapon, I doubted he had anything to fear. He had talent honed from long practice. I much preferred firing the stakeshooter, a simple matter of aiming the weapon, but ammunition was limited, and I knew I would have to learn to fight in close quarters.

Laughter tittered from the gate to the castle. The audience tonight was the largest by far. Hunters were drawn to watching me get beaten over and over. I'd learned to put up with them. Their whispers were a constant background noise that blossomed into laughter when Johann disarmed me with a flick of his wrist. Pain spiked in my forehead at the strike of the wooden stake.

"Better," he said. "But not good enough."

"Still can't hit you, can it?" someone called out to Johann. I think it was Peter. I was slowly learning their names, though every night the faces changed. The flow of activity in a hunter's encampment at night depended on what mission they were on and whether they were assigned to patrol that night. And many times I'd heard mutterings of how they missed the sun and sleeping at night like they were supposed to.

"Pathetic, for a thrall," Thomas said. He'd recovered some of his strength since that night, but his breathing was still labored at times, and his skin too pale.

"Practice will help," Johann called back. I picked up the long stake, the wood smooth in my hand. A weapon that would kill a vampire and not harm a human in the same way. Well, not unless I thrust it through him as he had told me to.

Leaves shifted. I whirled and lunged at him with the weapon, aiming for his chest.

And once again he batted it out of the way, his wrist angled just enough to cause the weapon to slide along the edge of his. "You fight predictably," he said. "And you keep falling for my feints." The tip of his wooden stake lashed at my forehead again like a snake, leaving another bright spot of pain. "If you fight like this, a vampire will rip you apart."

A vampire. I growled, the sound quieting some of the chatter around us. Johann was training me like a human, but I wasn't one.

I lunged again, the same way. Once again, his stake met mine, his mouth turning down.

This time I let it happen. I let the wooden stake drop, the weapon falling behind Johann. No human could do this. But I wasn't human.

I darted behind Johann, faster than a hunting cat, and picked up the weapon. In one motion, I threw it at his back, though not nearly as hard I could have.

It struck, Johann letting out a gasp of breath. The weapon was blunted and I'd held back, but he still staggered forward. The wooden stake bounced onto the grass.

The whispers around us quieted, and somewhere a stakeshooter clicked. I froze.

"Good," Johann said. He coughed, then drew in a full breath. "That wouldn't have worked on a vampire. But it shows you're thinking."

"Took it long enough," someone said.

Johann frowned. "Kareena," he called. "Weren't you supposed to begin a week's shift patrolling the merchant road tomorrow night?"

"What of it?"

"I suppose Lesalie didn't tell you. I'll take the duty for you," Johann said. He picked up the wooden stake. "And so will Kaiden."

Muttering broke out. "Once you begin learning to use that speed and agility effectively, I won't be a match for you," he said, handing me the weapon. "The next step is to learn to hunt things that will be."

"And you don't think he'll hunt you?" Kareena called out.

I ground my teeth. "Haven't I proved myself to you all yet?" I snapped, my voice ringing out through the darkness. "If I wanted human blood, I'd have taken it by now." I picked out Thomas in the crowd. "Some of you are easy prey."

Johann sighed. It was silent for a beat, and then laughter filled the air from some while voices rang out from others.

"Why don't you try, thrall?"

"It stared right at you, Thomas."

"I've killed so many of your kind!"

Johann put his hand on my shoulder, and I froze again. Voices quieted. "I trust him," Johann said. "Lesalie has given me permission to begin training him to hunt. I know a lot of you think what I'm doing is madness, but Kaiden here may be the answer to finally eliminating vampires like Lasren and Dimresh." He surveyed the crowd. "It's been three centuries since the Empire fell, and we've watched what remains rot while the vampires take over. It's time to take some risks to fight back."

Silence greeted his statement, along with faces full of different emotions. Fear. Anger. And in some, acceptance.

"C'mon, Kaiden," he said. "Let's take a break tonight."

I didn't need a break, but Johann, of course, was human. He turned, and I turned, too, guided by his arm as we walked away from the group. He was so warm, and for a human, strong. The scent of his clean sweat and the residue of the soap from his bath filled my nose. I swallowed hard, letting the urge for blood and the urge to feel more of his body against mine surge through me. I could never fulfill either desire.

Focusing on that fact helped, but not as much as before. The bloodlust for Johann was always there, always a horrible, dreadful certainty that if I let my guard down, I would ruin everything. But the other sensation, my desire for his body, grew stronger every night. And him touching me right now wasn't helping.

I pulled away as we neared the barracks, missing his closeness as soon as it was gone. I focused instead on the scent of hay and horses that emanated from the stables.

"Kaiden?" Johann asked. "I didn't realize the other hunters spectating was getting to you."

"They weren't," I snapped. "Aren't, I mean." I narrowed my eyes. Was that true?

"For what it's worth, if they truly thought you were a threat, they wouldn't treat you like that," Johann said. "I know it's hard to accept, but they see you as something different too now. Most of them don't like what they see, it's true, but they don't fear you in the same way."

I nodded. I still didn't like hearing their laughter and scorn. It felt too much like . . .

Like how I'd been in life. A drunk. Easily ignored, cursed at. The son of a whore, as though I'd done something wrong when in reality I'd just been unlucky to be born to someone desperate.

But my being bitten wasn't the same. I had chosen it, hadn't I, that secret that burned in my chest and filled me with shame. This was my fault. I had no right to be angry if I was disrespected. And that thought hurt the most. But if I could hunt thralls, hunt vampires, maybe I could make up for that mistake.

"Kaiden?" Johann said. "You seem distant."

"I'm . . . thinking," I said. "Tell me about what we're going to do. Hunt on the merchant road?"

Johann smiled. "Indeed. I talked to Lesalie about it before you woke. I know you may not feel like you are, but you're making good progress. I've had to work a lot more every night."

"Thank you."

"Awfully polite for a thrall." He laughed, his voice dull among the stones of the barracks as we entered. "That mostly just means I'm tired. I hope you don't mind if I rest up for a bit, especially since I'll need to prepare for our trip tomorrow during the day while you get to sleep. I'm assuming you agree to go?"

"That's fine."

The path to his room was safer than the one he'd shown me that first night, with spikes only every few feet and normal torches hung on the walls, not solar flares. The steps of the tower wound up in a tight curl, his room opening up on what must be the second floor. I had no sense of what other rooms might be above me—I was always with Johann, and he never took me anywhere else. Safety, I supposed, mine and theirs. The angry faces of the hunters were fresh in my mind.

I'd learned to like Johann's room. My box was still small and uncomfortable, too much like a coffin, but the rest of it was strangely comforting. While Johann took his boots off and sat at his chair by the desk, I looked at his bookcase, where small carved wooden figures sat on either side of each shelf. I picked up one that was carved like a cat, the details of the whiskers and fur artfully done.

See, he likes you. A voice in my mind flickered from memory. Matilda. She had . . . taken care of me. Johann had mentioned her. I chased the memory of an old woman and a cat, but it was like clawing at cobwebs.

"Kaiden?" Johann said. "Is something wrong?"

I hadn't realized I'd growled in frustration. "Where did you get these?" I asked.

"Oh." Johann stood, moving close enough for me to be surrounded by his tempting scent and the fizzing sound of his blood. I swallowed, trying to focus. "These are just trinkets I kept. We had others—we'd mostly trade them for other minor things—beads from Timet, near the lake, or finely woven silks from people in the city of Leoren. Although I guess the true old capital is destroyed, but the city that calls itself that." He held out a hand, and I gave him the carving. He gave it a fond smile, his eyes distant.

There were only eight of them, two on each side of the shelves. Little decorations—such a human thing, and they made my mind work, something I wanted to remember on the tip of my tongue. "Why do you keep them?" I asked.

Johann sighed. "My father carved these for me when I was young." His voice was soft. "I kept them with me all the time and had them when my parents died."

I swallowed. "I'm sorry."

"No, I'm glad you like them." He handed me the cat. "You seem to like cats. Or hate them. I can't quite tell." He raised his eyebrows.

"I . . . I like them. Matilda had one." I curled my fingers around the small wooden carving and placed it back where it belonged.

"Matilda. Second time you've mentioned her. What do you remember?" Johann asked.

Kindness. A warm couch on cold nights. Dolls and old books. Prayers that didn't work. Some sort of sickness. I gritted my teeth, my fangs showing. "She was kind," I said. "And . . . took care of me when I was ill. Or prayed for me. Something."

"To Holy Laurel, I imagine," Johann said. "My parents used to do the same thing, even though it didn't work. Some people hold on to old traditions even harder when they don't do anything. Maybe that's why I like to read old stories." He chuckled.

"How old were you when they died?" I asked. Johann's smile faded, and I wished I hadn't asked.

"Fifteen," he said. "Ten years ago now." I wanted to apologize, but he kept talking. "Merchants live dangerous lives. We need them—they trade goods, keep civilization going. They trade stories. But any journey that can't be done in a day is a risk. They knew that. And they got lucky for a long time, until it ran out." He shrugged, but I could read the tension in his shoulders, hear the tightness in his throat. "At least I learned that night that vampires don't need that much blood. He drained them and left me."

I remembered the vision of Dimresh in the alley, a powerful vampire. To see something like that and live, while others died . . . I couldn't imagine. A faint horror went through me, a cresting sadness, but it faded too soon. The emotion was so negative, but I wanted to feel it, to understand, and then it was gone. Thralls didn't feel.

So instead I reached for Johann, placing my hand on his arm. He smiled and took my hand in his.

"Thank you," he said. "It's all right. I'm a hunter now. I can protect others from fates like that—and I hope you can help me."

I nodded. "I will."

But even as he smiled and let go of my hand, I wondered what that would mean for me. I wasn't a true hunter, even if I had successfully won one bout with Johann tonight. I was still a thrall.

CHAPTER EIGHTEEN

"I prepared a wagon for us," Johann said the next night after I'd hunted. I met him back at the entrance to the barracks, and we walked toward the stables. "The storage is lightproof, just like before, but it's more comfortable. You can sleep there during the day. The Maleras helped me construct it."

"Maleras?"

"Ah." Johann stopped before entering the stables. "The merchants you helped save when the vampire attacked."

The overturned carriage and the scent of fear. "They're still here?"

"Indeed. They were grateful, to me and to you." He swung the stable door open, the scent of horses growing stronger. An oil lamp inside was lit, and light spilled out onto the path.

"But not enough to meet me." Not that I could blame them.

"Well . . . no." Johann huffed a breath and turned to face me. "But they understand, Kaiden. And I know it's hard to believe, but a lot of other hunters are starting to also. People know you're not like the rest."

"I . . . believe you." The first night I'd come here, they'd all wanted to kill me. They probably still did, but now they at least recognized I was something other than a mindless thrall.

But it still didn't mean others wanted to meet me. Even if I helped Johann, like I'd said I would last night . . . I was still a thrall. A bloodsucker. A dangerous tool.

"You don't seem happy."

I met his eyes. What a strange thing to say. "Are you?"

Johann made a strange humming noise. "I . . . about what?

You? Yes. I suppose I am."

"Because I can help you kill vampires?" I said.

Johann took a few steps toward me, silhouetted in the flickering light from the stable. "No, Kaiden. I mean, yes, that does make me happy. But . . . I'm happy to have met you. You're unique, yes, and that's fascinating. You're also a kind man who's lost a lot, and I want to help you. When I look at you, I don't see a thrall. I see a sad, lonely man who wishes for more out of his life. Am I wrong?"

Something clawed at my chest, pain that wasn't true pain, and I finally figured it out. Lonely. A creature that could only exist at night, cut off from the true life and light of day. That's what I was. The laughter and talk of the other hunters, Johann's mentioning how he talked to and got help from people who were too afraid to meet me, memories from last night of Matilda and a house I'd once stayed in and now could never enter . . . They all hurt because of that word.

I was unique. But because of it I was alone.

It hurt, but it felt good to recognize what I'd been feeling. "You're not wrong," I said. It took strength to admit it.

"You know, if you can successfully kill Dimresh . . . you don't need to be a traditional vampire lord and live in isolation. You could stay with other hunters."

"Right." I somehow doubted others would accept me. Staying with Johann, though . . . that thought was tempting.

I waited outside while Johann prepared the wagon and hitched up the horses. The night air was damp, the sky starless. Hunting had been even easier than usual.

"What are you going to bring?" I asked Johann as he led the horses out of the stable. One of them huffed at me, and I wondered if I still smelled like a thrall even beneath the soap I'd been using each night before sleep. "What sort of things do we expect to see on the merchant road?"

Johann climbed into the driver seat, picking up the reins. I followed with a leap, landing lightly beside him. "Have you ever been on the merchant road?"

"No."

"Perhaps that was a silly question." Johann flicked the reins, and the horses began to walk at a steady pace. Johann bumped against me, and I tensed for a moment against another surge of mingled bloodlust and desire.

"Not many people travel if they don't have to—not anymore. But like I said last night, merchants who make their living selling goods between cities typically take this road. It leads in a circular path through three major cities and past seven villages. And, of course, it's a favorite hunting spot for thralls and any vampires who don't have a castle of their own."

"So hunters patrol it," I said.

"That's right. It's easier to patrol portions of the road than to assign a hunter to escort every single merchant wagon or caravan. There just aren't enough of us."

"How many vampires are there?" I asked.

"That is a good question." Johann clicked his tongue, and the horses picked up their pace. As they did, rain began to fall, tiny spots of dampness on my head and face. "We keep logs of the most powerful ones. In our region, that's Lasren, Dimresh, and Amira. They've caused the city-states near them to fall, and they prey on the remaining villages. Lasren sometimes comes out of his castle to feed." He frowned, and I knew he was thinking of his parents. "As for wandering vampires, or thralls . . . there's no way to know. But we kill them often."

I nodded. "Too many," I said. The wagon bumped along a dirt path. A stone archway covered the side of the road, enclosing a worn stone statue that looked dark gray in the damp of the rain. The lantern swinging from the wagon illuminated dead grass and carvings along the side.

"A shrine to Holy Laurel," Johann said when he followed

my gaze. "People used to leave offerings at shrines like that, but no one has done it for likely two centuries now."

"Did the magic ever truly work?" I asked.

"I believe it did," Johann said. "Old books that survived the fall of the Empire are filled with incantations and prayers to Laurel for protection. That was what she was god of — protection."

The shrine was so small, and the statue was nothing more than a formless gray lump, whatever it had depicted lost to time. "Do you know any incantations?"

"Do you want to try it?" Johann said with a chuckle. "You're not afraid of invoking holy magic? You're a thrall, you know."

"You've said it doesn't work. I suppose I was just . . . curious."

"Let's try it, then," Johann said. "C'mon." He pulled back on the reins, one of the horses snorting. The other began to crop the grass.

I followed Johann to the edge of the shrine. The stone archway reached just over my head, and when I got close it shielded me from the sound of the rushing wind through the trees and the falling rain. It smelled like wet grass and stone, no different than any other building in a forest.

"Holy Laurel, guide us as a tree is guided to the sun," Johann said. A memory flashed in my mind. Matilda had invoked Holy Laurel when letting me sleep in her house. A ward against rain and cold, I suppose, or maybe she'd thought it would reassure me.

"Bind us with your protection, once, twice, thrice, in the vines of humility," Johann finished the prayer. Then he clapped his hands once.

I paused for a moment, waiting. But nothing happened. One of the horses snorted again, shaking water from its mane.

"What did the book say it was supposed to do?" I asked.

Johann shrugged. "It never said. That's part of the problem. The old books gave you instructions on how to pray, said that some prayers carried power that couldn't be undone, but never actually said what was expected. I guess it was common knowledge back then. But now . . ." He leaned down, staring at the carvings. "It's just lost, I suppose."

Cracks ran through the statue, and moss grew along the edges of the cracks, as though some sort of tree were trying to break through the stone. Perhaps when the Empire existed, people had taken care of it, but now it looked as though it would be mostly destroyed in a few more decades.

Laurel can't keep you warm anymore out there. Matilda's words echoed. *But she wouldn't appreciate me letting you freeze.*

At least it had helped me remember something. I touched the statue, the stone smooth and cold. When I took my hand back it smelled like wet earth, probably the moss that grew along it. Life seeking a place where people had placed dead stone. If Laurel was ever here, or if she was ever real, she wasn't here now.

"How far until we get to the merchant's road?" I asked.

Johann pulled his cloak tighter around himself. "We'll arrive just before dawn. We'll patrol each night for a week, or until you feel ready to challenge Dimresh. Does that sound good?"

"Yes. I . . . I want to kill him. And help you."

"I like to hear that." The ground squished beneath his boots, the rain picking up. The horses stamped the damp ground as we got back on the wagon. Johann covered his head with his jacket, exposing his well-muscled torso as he adjusted his clothes. He looked and smelled so good.

No. I had to be good. I could resist it.

The abandoned shrine faded into darkness behind us as we rolled away.

Chapter Nineteen

Dawn began to break before we arrived, the wagon slow on the wet ground. I closed my eyes to the scent of rain and the lingering scent of Johann, his clothes stored in the dark space where I slept.

Rain drummed in my dreams, clouds darkening the night even further. A flash of lightning illuminated a broken statue by the side of the road.

A hand touched my shoulder, and warmth spread through my body, the sensation even better than easing my hunger with fresh blood. "Come out of the cold, Kaiden." Johann's voice was deep in my dream . . .

I turned at the touch of Johann's hand. His brown eyes shone in another flash of lightning. He wore nothing, just as he had that night as he slept. Rain dripped down his muscular chest and flat stomach, sliding down to nestle in the curls of hair just above a sight that made me lick my lips.

His hands moved from my shoulder to my chest, and then around my hips. The warmth grew, turning into a burning heat.

I knew this feeling. I wanted it, wanted him.

He pressed himself against me. His scent and closeness mingled, maleness and pine mixed with electric heat like the lightning, more alive than anything I'd ever experienced. I grabbed him, my fingers digging into his muscular arms. The heat became fire. He was mine.

His muscles were taut beneath my fingers, but he couldn't resist as I pinned his arms in place. Lightning flashed again, his brown eyes flickering. His pulse beat in his neck.

Hunger mixed with lust, and he leaned his head back, his hips jutting forward. My body jolted with pleasure even as the familiar taste of blood entered my mouth.

My eyes snapped open to the darkness of the wagon, and I bit my lip hard against a surge of disgust that mixed with the usual hunger of waking. My own blood filled my mouth, and I spat it out, my stomach flipping as though I'd eaten something solid I couldn't digest.

It was a dream. Just a dream. Johann was fine. I hadn't bitten him.

I didn't want to bite him. I didn't.

"Kaiden?"

I swiped my hand over my mouth, and when the stars of a clear sky met my vision, I leaped out of the wagon, landing lightly on my feet next to one of the horses. It whinnied, its ears pinned back.

"Whoa." Johann grabbed the horse's reins. "Calm down, girl. Kaiden . . . are you doing well?"

I blinked, focusing on Johann. The real Johann, not the bitten one in my dream. His large shoulders and muscular chest strained against the tight coat he wore. But on top of that, he wore a long sash filled with stakes for the stakeshooter he held in his right hand, and two more long stakes were tucked into his belt, along with bottles of what I knew would be more of that burning, herb-treated water.

He was a hunter. He would be fine. What had happened in my dream . . . that would never happen in reality.

He would kill me first.

"Kaiden?" Johann said. "You're looking a little . . . Did you cut yourself?"

"I just need to hunt," I said.

"Are you well?" Johann's eyes narrowed.

"Do you not trust me?" I snapped.

Johann frowned. "No, it's just . . ."

"You've tested my bloodlust over and over. Then Lesalie did, with Thomas. Then you had me fight you, with the risk of me drawing blood." I swallowed hard. "And you're wearing more hunting gear than I've ever seen you wear and carrying a stakeshooter. Can't you trust me?"

"I suppose it's my own fault you're this jumpy." Johann gave me a wry smile. "And you should know by now that I trust you. Fair?"

I gritted my teeth. It wasn't even him I was frustrated with. "Fair."

"Go and hunt. But remember, this is the merchant road, and the sun has just gone down. Think. You'll be hunting, but so will other thralls. And they won't be hunting animals, will they?"

"Are there really so many?" I asked.

"Go hunt," Johann said. "You look hungry. Then come back and we'll talk."

I was too hungry and sick at myself to argue.

The dream haunted me as I entered the forest, and I ran fast, putting as much distance between myself and Johann as possible. I was a thrall. I needed blood. And I could never be close to him the way I wanted. Be his partner and equal, when there was the constant risk of me losing control. I'd been foolish to ever touch him that night in the forest, and then again in his room. I couldn't have him. I couldn't experience his life in my hand and not be tempted. Johann had learned to trust me, but my own dreams betrayed me.

Even if he trusted me, I couldn't trust myself.

I bit so hard into a doe that my fangs scraped against its vertebrae, and I growled after I finished drinking. I needed to focus. If I was going to live my life the way I wanted, the first thing I had to do was kill my former master. And that meant learning to kill things like me.

Dreams meant nothing to most humans, and they should

mean even less to a thrall.

The hunger gone, I traced my path back to Johann. "Come on out, Kaiden," Johann said.

Water dripped down my neck from overhanging branches, even though now the sky was clear. The moon was just beginning to grow in the night sky, and even the stars gave more light. A good night for thralls to hunt. "How did you know I was there?" I asked.

"You may think you do, but you don't move silently," Johann said. "Most thralls can move more quietly than a human, but humans don't move all that quietly compared to true beasts."

I frowned. "I wasn't hunting you," I said. "Or really trying to be silent."

"Next time, try to move quietly and see," Johann said. "Tonight, you're not hunting blood. You're hunting thralls."

"Right." For a moment, I let the night air and sky overwhelm me, scenting and listening. Bats flew overhead, and an owl's talons clutched against dry bark. Mice and insects crawled over leaves and twigs on tiny legs. A light breeze brought the scent of more deer and a tinge of woodsmoke.

"If they're hunting," I said, "they'll be that way." I pointed.

"And why do you think that?" Johann said.

"Because I smell smoke. And even an animal knows that where there's smoke, there are humans." I gave Johann a thin-lipped smile. I didn't want to show my fangs.

He smiled back, and I was more pleased than I should have been. "Good," he said. "I trust you. Go on ahead. Guard them until I get there. See if you can be silent. Take this with you, and don't hesitate to use it if you need it."

I swallowed as I took the wooden stake. He trusted me. I was going to approach a group of people, not hunters, people who would have no protection. They would be easy prey, like all the people in my old village. And I had no master's command to tell me not to drain them.

But I had Johann's trust. I had to believe that he was right about me. I would be good.

I moved into a silent, distance-eating lope, scenting the air as I did. The rank odor of smoke was faint, but soon it was joined by the unmistakable aroma of cooked meat and the pungent reek of overworked, flatulent horses.

I froze at the sound of human voices — I'd found them. A group of . . . three. Maybe four.

I crept closer in the darkness, placing each step with care and avoiding brittle, dry twigs and leaves.

Their scents came to me first, a man and three women. No, one woman. Two girls. One had an edge of rot about her that was old, recovering from some childhood illness.

I blinked. I remembered this scent. Another child had it when I was young, a sweet, sickly smell that accompanied her bursting blisters. I'd had it once too. My mother and all the ladies in the Stuck Pig had taken care of me.

The other child had died. What had her name been? I gritted my teeth. What was her name?

"Do you hear that?" I lifted my head at the words. They couldn't have heard me. I hadn't moved.

I crept closer, taking even more care, my feet silent on the forest floor. Their fire was out, but in the dim light of the stars, I made out their forms in the trees. The woman held her daughter, a mound of cloth holding another. A larger form, the man, stood and drew a sword from a scabbard at his hip, facing away from me into the forest. A horse snorted, and a wagon wheel gave a creaking groan.

Maybe it was Johann. But that hoped died at the growl that came from the other side of the trees.

"Who's there?" the man yelled. He held his sword differently than Johann held his stake, lightly out in front of him at an angle while he balanced on the balls of his feet. That would be fine technique for fending off a human.

But it did nothing against the lunging thrall that leaped out of the trees.

The man shouted as the thrall impaled itself through its stomach on the sword. The smell of foul blood and sickly sweet rot filled the clearing, along with the living man's fear. The thrall's teeth snapped on air. It clung to the sword as it stumbled back, the man letting go. One of the girls screamed, the sound ear-piercing.

I'd never been impaled, but it clearly didn't matter if it was metal. The thrall took one or two steps back, tugging at the metal. Then blood and filth spattered the ground as it ripped the weapon out of its body. It would heal and kill the man and his family. Easy blood. I licked my lips.

No. The man and his family weren't my prey. The thrall was. And impaled on a sword, it was the easier prey.

I dashed out of the forest, lowering the sharpened stake Johann had given me. Left side, in the chest. The thrall's black eyes met mine, and he snarled, but then the wood struck home. The stake sank in more easily than I expected.

The black eyes turned gray, and then the thrall fell. The stake pulled free from his chest as it did. Now it was just a man, his innards strewn around him as the healing stopped. The sword, too, fell to the ground.

"Thank you," the man said behind me. "Thank you so much."

"Are you a hunter?" the woman asked.

The thrall lay dead on the ground, stinking and rotten. The deer's blood turned in my stomach, and I blinked hard. I had done it. It had been easy. The thrall hadn't expected it.

A thrall that killed thralls. I didn't feel any different. But I certainly didn't feel like a hunter.

"Come, hunter, share some of our food. It's not much, but we owe you." The man put a heavy hand on my shoulder.

I growled, and the man sucked in a breath, the air tinged with fear once again. "No," I said. "I . . . I have work to do."

I darted back into the safety of the trees. The man stared after me, unseeing, peering into the darkness I had disappeared into.

"Was he a hunter?" the woman said. Her voice had risen in pitch, and she bounced the child in her lap. "Or . . ."

"Hunters can be strange, that's all," the man said. "We'll be safe here if there are hunters about. I told you."

"He moved like the vampire," one of the little girls said. "Didn't he?"

"Don't be silly, Samantha," her father said. "Vampires wouldn't kill other vampires."

Would they?

Johann had told me Lucien, a thrall, had killed a vampire. But thralls were different—servants, and mostly mindless. But would a vampire like Lasren kill a vampire like Dimresh? Could they? Humans killed each other. But I'd never heard of a vampire killing another—for territory or for anything else.

Just another mystery. Maybe Johann would know. I would guard the area, as he'd said, until he returned. I didn't have to think about the thrall I'd killed, a thrall like me.

Twigs snapped and leaves rattled. I turned back. The man must still be trying to look for me.

But this wasn't the man. I curled my upper lip. More thralls.

I hoisted the stake in my hand, the wood still wet from the other thrall's blood. I could sense them more than truly see or hear them, four shapes moving in a tightening circle around the family. The man hadn't even picked up his sword yet.

How humans survived the night, I had no idea. There was no sign of Johann yet.

"Be careful!" I shouted, my voice rough in the night air. "More thralls coming!"

One of the girls shrieked again in response. Growls came from all around me. I turned toward the small encampment, readying my stake. I prepared to stab the first one that made a move toward the family.

A dark shape bounded through the encampment, ripping a scream from the mother's throat and an angry bellow from the man. And then it darted right past him.

At me.

My muscles tensed in a few moments of crucial shock and indecision, and when I hoisted the stake, it was too late. The thrall slammed into me with a blow twice as powerful than any practice strike from Johann. The stake flew from my hand, and the stakeshooter in my belt cracked beneath me.

Johann had given me that.

I snarled, rage darkening my vision. I wasn't going to fail now. I wouldn't let Johann down and let this family be killed.

I grabbed at the stakes in my belt that would have fit into my stakeshooter, hoisting the wood and stabbing down at the thrall that now pinned me. Instead I received another set of fangs in my wrist, another thrall grabbing my arm.

I strained, but another grabbed my legs, and another my arms. Four on one. Anger died away as realization set in.

They weren't hunting the family at all.

These thralls were hunting me.

CHAPTER TWENTY

"Johann!" I shouted. I got a hard punch across the face for my trouble. Bone in my jaw cracked, pain spiking into my head. Another thrall bit into my arm, fangs scoring bone the way mine had crunched against the vertebrae of the deer I'd eaten. My ankle snapped, and I cried out. Hunger met the pain, an immediate need for blood to heal the damage.

I spat my own useless blood onto the leaves and tried to ask what they wanted, but then slammed my broken jaw shut at the pain.

The thralls carried me like a sack of grain, one pinning both my wrists together and the other holding my legs. They moved fast, as fast as I would, but didn't speak. There was no planning, no discussion. One grabbed a fawn as they jogged, and when the others noticed, they growled for it. A brief, fang-snapping fight resulted in the original thrall keeping her kill.

These were not thralls like me. But it was clear they had orders.

I needed to fight back. I had proved it tonight — thralls were easy to kill. But first I needed blood. To do that I would need to overpower four thralls.

I blinked heavy eyes. I *needed* blood. Pain flared again in my ankle as one of the thralls carrying me twisted it again.

Focus. I had to focus. Where was I going? Where was Johann?

"He's going to sleep," one said. They sounded far away. "Do we wake him?"

"Master didn't say," the other growled back. "Keep going. Gotta bring him back."

Bring him back.

Bring me back. Master.

Dimresh.

I writhed in their grasp, summoning the last bit of energy I had to try to bite the one holding my hands. The thrall twisted my wrist, snapping it, and I moaned in pain and hunger. I needed to heal.

I needed blood.

"Hurry," voices said. "Bring him back."

Hunger woke me, somewhere in darkness where the smells that surrounded me were nothing but wet dirt and mold.

Underground. No food. I growled, my stomach hollow and my fangs sharp. Answering growls met mine. Shapes around me moved, leaving me alone.

I needed to hunt. I needed to get away. I pulled myself up on all fours, my wrist sending shooting pain when I put weight on it. My ankle dragged.

So hungry. I needed blood. Anything alive.

Mice squeaked, but crawling was too slow. The rodents scrambled away from my clumsy, grabbing fingers. I stumbled after the sounds of mice and crawling insects, toward the mouth of a cave where starlight illuminated moss and twisted, dead trees.

I grabbed at a squirrel that got too close, but it darted away, and I fell onto stone.

A statue stared back at me. Or half of one, hewn from the base, the other half a few feet away. A shrine to Laurel, at the mouth of a cave.

Johann. Dimresh. A day had gone by. I had slept a day, underground, with the thralls who had taken me. They must be hunting. If I could hunt and heal, I could get away, back to Johann.

I needed blood so badly.

I pushed myself up, ignoring the weakness and pain in my wrist. It wouldn't kill me. Nothing would. I was a thrall. But not like the others. I had to get away, to get back and learn how to hunt properly. If I couldn't even kill four thralls, I had no hope against Dimresh.

A bird landed on the shorn head of the statue, and I grabbed at it with my good hand.

But I got only stone as it flitted away. Off-balance, I fell, growling, next to the statue again.

A god of protection. Holy Laurel.

I fought to speak the words Johann had, and they sounded wrong and distorted coming from my broken jaw. "Holy Laurel, guide us . . . me . . . as a tree is guided to the sun. Bind me with your protection, once, twice, thrice, in the vines of humility."

I didn't know what I expected. But nothing happened.

Of course not. Even if she still had power, she wouldn't protect a thing like me.

My eyes fall shut again. I existed in a black void of hunger and exhaustion for a few moments.

You're going to die one of these days, you know.

A man spoke in my memory.

He slumped next to me against a stone wall, the scent of alcohol surrounding us both. "I, at least, have a wife to get home to. She takes care of me. You what, sleep in the street?" He chuckled. "I get to tell her I'm at least better than that drunk whoreson." He tipped his bottle back then clinked it against mine. "Really, though. If the drink doesn't get you one day, the bloodsuckers will. Ain't no protection from them these days. Not many merchants come here anymore, and this stuff's getting harder and harder to make. If you could just stay sober for a day, I would help you —"

The memory faded when I fought to open my eyes. I remembered that hunger for the burn of drink. But the hunger for blood was so much worse.

A squirrel sniffed the ground near me. It froze when I tensed. I could catch it. Even a little blood would help. Once my wounds were healed, I could fight.

"He moved," a voice growled. I lunged for the squirrel, but it had already started to run when the other thrall spoke. I was too late.

"Break his other leg, then," another thrall growled. I snarled, growling as they descended on me. But there was no hope.

A thrall leaned over me, growling. The name snapped into my mind, the man from my memory.

"James," I said. His name. He had a wife, a son, even though he drank nearly as much as I had. He'd worked in the distillery. No, he had owned the distillery. "James," I said again. Speaking sent shooting pain through my jaw. "James, remember that?"

Black eyes showed no recognition. He grabbed my leg and snapped the bone in two, and his black eyes swallowed me up into a void of pain.

Dimresh's servants. All from Penthorn, like me. But I was still alone.

The statue of Holy Laurel looked on, useless. Other memories crowded my mind as the pain drove me back into a heavy weakness. Advice from the man who was now a mindless servant of my once master.

"You want help, you gotta help yourself first. You gotta want it, Kaiden."

The stars above me began to fade as clouds overtook the night sky. Or maybe it was just that I couldn't keep my eyes open.

Hunger made me fight when the scent of deer or boar would drift by on the breeze, but the thralls that carried me were well-fed and strong. My struggles were nothing, and soon I stopped trying. Even when the tantalizing scent of blood made my mouth fill with saliva.

"James, where are you taking me?" I asked once through the pain of my broken jaw, the words coming out over long seconds. No answer. They never spoke. They seemed even more mindless than the other thralls Dimresh once had, the ones Johann had killed. I wondered if those thralls had been from Penthorn, too, men and women I hadn't known. Johann could hunt these thralls too. There was nothing of them left.

Johann. Where was he? He could help me. He could feed me.

No. I couldn't have his blood. I would be lost.

But without it, I was losing myself now. To hunger, and to the thralls that were carrying me back to my old master.

Johann was beautiful in my memories, and the pain and weakness softened. If I was going to die, to be lost, then I would fantasize and lose myself in that first. It was all I had left.

Johann stood with me in the clearing by the hunters' castle. He reached out to me, and I took his hand in mine, his skin soft and warm. He let me hold him, never flinching, never moving away. Moonlight bathed his naked body, and the trees cast dappled shadows over the planes of his chest and stomach.

"Kaiden," he said. I pulled him close, and he allowed it. His hot breath rushed over my face and chest. My skin prickled. He smelled like woodsmoke and pine, a sharp scent of life that I missed.

He pulled me into a hug, wrapping warm arms around me. Everything was so warm. His heart beat against my chest, a steady, soothing drumbeat I hadn't realized I missed. He rested his chin on my shoulder and twisted one leg around mine, every point of contact a reassurance. "I trust you, Kaiden," he whispered in my ear.

I sat on the forest floor, the carpet of leaves soft beneath me. Grass, too, and flowers. They didn't bloom at night, but in my dreams they did, small, many-leaved things that glowed in the moonlight. Johann sat next to me, still embracing me, his body soft. His muscles were taut and strong for a human. But not to me.

I hugged him back, his breath coming short as I squeezed him tight, and he moved closer, his naked body pressed against mine. Warmth became heat. He gasped, breath rushing over my neck. He kissed me once, his lips soft and wet. He tasted like mint.

"I trust you, Kaiden," he said. "Please, take me."

I knew what I wanted, and this Johann wanted it too.

He tilted his head, and I sank fangs into his neck. This was Johann. He trusted me. I could take just what I needed, and there would always be more. Blood ran down from the bite, filling my mouth and also hitting the leaves beneath us. As blood filled me, pleasure grew, and Johann moaned.

"Kaiden," he said, and his arms gripped me tighter. "Kaiden!"

"Thrall," a deep voice said, and my eyes snapped open, the moonlit clearing vanishing into dust.

The other thrall carrying me dumped me onto a familiar stone floor. I barely had the strength to lift my head to stare into the smoldering blue eyes of my old master.

CHAPTER TWENTY-ONE

Dimresh was beautiful. Johann was handsome, and even handsomer in my fantasy, but Dimresh was something otherworldly. Long blond hair framed the alabaster skin of his face and cascaded down over silk-clad shoulders. Long, manicured nails caught the faint sliver of emerging moonlight and shone like steel.

"I told you to kill the hunter, drink his blood, and return," Dimresh said. His voice was deep and winding, but it no longer boomed in my head like before. "You disobeyed me." Fangs flashed as he said the last.

"I . . ." Pain made it hard to speak. "I didn't mean . . ."

Blue eyes narrowed. "And now you lie?" He tilted his head and took one step forward, nudging my head with his foot to expose my neck. "You've gotten rid of my mark."

I didn't answer. Speaking hurt too much, and there was nothing I could say.

"Do you consider yourself my equal, thrall?"

I just lay there. I had nothing left. Two nights of travel and one day asleep. At a thrall's pace . . . Johann would be nowhere near, even with his horse. And that was assuming he even cared to come after me. Maybe he thought I'd run . . . or killed someone.

That thought hurt the most.

"Answer me," Dimresh demanded. "Did the hunter capture you? Or did you leave on your own?"

Something in his voice made me think.

Johann had valued me because I was different. And now it

seemed as though Dimresh may have figured that out too. But he wasn't sure. For a hunter, a thrall like me was a weapon. Maybe for Dimresh, I was a threat.

But then why did he go to the trouble of having his thralls bring me back if he could just have had them kill me?

It all came down to the question that had been in my mind since the beginning. I struggled through the pain in my face and jaw to say it aloud.

"Why did you make me a thrall?"

Dimresh blinked once. Then he laughed, a sound I'd never heard before in my two months of being his servile thrall.

"It was your choice, wasn't it?" he said, gritting his teeth at the last and showing his long, sharp fangs. "You wanted me to bite you. You were one who wouldn't be missed, weren't you?"

The cold, dark alley. The reek of vomit and alcohol, and then the slow draining of pain and strength as he'd taken my blood. Then darkness.

"No," I said, my voice breathy and weak. Hunger sat like lead throughout my body. "I—"

Useless drunk. Drunk whoreson.

There were plenty of people who wouldn't be missed. Dimresh killed them, just as he'd killed me. But I had chosen it.

"I hate to disappoint you, thrall," Dimresh said. "But I didn't fully drain you to death because I wasn't hungry enough, and I didn't mind another servant. That was all."

"Oh." The word barely left my lips, more an exhausted exhalation. There was no reason. I wasn't special.

At least not in life.

"But then you disobeyed me," he said, and I expected a killing blow at any moment. My muscles tensed, my instincts screaming at me to flee, but I had nothing left. His thralls had seen to that. "You disappeared, ignoring my summons. The hunter disappeared as well, and I supposed you may have fed from him and been killed. But I didn't feel you die. You just . . . vanished. So I bring you back. And now you're here." He made no sound as he stepped closer, looming over me. "So tell me, thrall. Where did you go? What were you planning to do, as a thrall with no master?"

Blackness threatened the edges of my vision. I opened my mouth, and a spike of pain made me shut it again.

In the corner, a mouse moved. No, a rat. It snuffled along the floor, tantalizingly close.

"It seems my thralls mistreated you," Dimresh said. His voice was warm suddenly, sonorous. Almost arousing. When he knelt next to me, his proximity was different than the closeness I'd felt from Johann. Johann I could sense—the beat of his heart, the scent of his body, the warmth of his life. Dimresh had nothing but presence—like the sight of a mountain I couldn't climb, or the moon overhead. The scent of the rat, a mere few feet away, was more alive than he was.

"You're hungry, aren't you?" Dimresh said.

I managed to nod. I opened my mouth again, tolerating the pain, letting my fangs show. I was so hungry.

"I'll let you make a choice," Dimresh said. "The same choice you made before. Would you like to die? No more pain, no more suffering. No more craving. Just emptiness." He wrapped a hand around my throat, and my body chilled. "You want that, don't you?" His voice took on a strange tone, and something thudded in me, an instinct to run that my weakness didn't let me obey.

"No," I said. "I don't want to die."

"Surprising, considering your choice the last time." He moved his hand away. "Then let me offer you something else. Something you'll like very much." He stood, graceful and silent. "Wait here, thrall."

In a blink he was gone. I was alone.

I wanted to get away. I *needed* to get away. But I couldn't.

This castle had never been a home. It was simply a place I had been, the place I rested during the day. This was my master's, not mine. Mice and rats scurried through the walls, their squeaks a constant background noise, and the scent of rat mingled with the scent of mold. My master's quarters were nicer, I think, with ragged carpets in the hallways just outside what would be the main keep, but I'd never seen them. I was just a servant.

But I wasn't. Now more than ever, that felt true. My master had said more to me tonight than he ever had before. He'd sent thralls after me to bring me back.

Why?

No one knows what vampires want. Johann's words echoed in my mind. I had no idea what my master wanted from me now. If he was angry with me, or threatened by me, he should just kill me. Why go to all the trouble to bring me back here and . . .

I still didn't know what he was going to do.

I should get blood and fight back. All I needed was blood. A mouse wouldn't be enough, but just one rat . . . It wouldn't taste good, but I didn't care. I gnashed my teeth with hunger. I struggled onto all fours, only to fall back to the stone when weakness made my arms shake at my own weight.

I needed blood so badly.

"There," my master said. "I know how hungry you must be, thrall. You see? I brought you something very special."

I looked up, but my master wasn't in front of me. His voice wound around me, and a claw traced a line of pain down my back. Words burned through my skin.

"By my blood, guide him as a blighted tree falls to the earth. Bind him like vines, once twice thrice, by his blood to mine."

I gasped, and the pain multiplied, a line of fire as bad as the burn of the sun must be. I screwed my eyes shut, more pain flaring in my broken jaw as I screamed.

That prayer. It was just like Johann's. Different in some ways, but the most obvious difference, as pain wracked my body, was that it actually worked. Pain screamed inside my body, and the castle walls began to fade into gray.

I lay on the ground, the stars spinning in circles above my head. Pain pounded in my temples, but also in my side, and each breath hurt. The wooden walls of the Stuck Pig formed an alley with the side of James's distillery. The scent of yeast filled the air, the only thing I could smell through the thickness that filled my mouth and throat.

Alcohol hadn't helped. It never really did, but this was the first time, so I'd thought it would. The burning should have helped the sickness in my chest, and the numbness should have chased away the memory of the mother I had lost.

But it didn't.

"Hey."

They wouldn't be calling for me. No one would. My mother was gone, and I'd been sick for days. Everyone knew to stay away from those who caught the black cough. If I was lucky, the vampire would end my suffering before I suffered like she had.

The light of the stars vanished, silhouetted in a woman's shape.

"You're Theresa's boy, aren't you?" Theresa. My mother's name.

"She's dead," I said. Cold seeped into me, worse than pain.

"You will be, too, if you keep lying there. Come on, then. Drink won't help you. Soup will. Soup and warmth."

Pain bloomed in my chest, and I coughed when I tried to stand. She supported me as we walked. I wasn't quite as tall then.

I writhed. The magic — if that's what it was — twisting in my body and finally burning out in a flash of pain in my neck like a blister popping. My fangs jutted into my lower lip.

Dimresh's presence bloomed in my mind like a flower. No. Not Dimresh.

"Look there," my master's voice said. He stood next to me, but he was even more present in my mind, crowding out everything else. Part of me scrabbled at something important, something I'd just lost. "Go, thrall. Drink your fill. I command it."

I snarled, my fangs dripping. When I opened my eyes, I saw an old woman, blood leaking from her neck. She lay on the ground, eyes glazed. Dying.

Easy prey.

"I knew your mother. We were old friends." A familiar voice spoke in my mind as I dragged myself toward the blood. It whispered beneath my master's command. *"Remind me of your name?"*

The woman lay on her side, her neck a mass of blood that made her gray hair look sticky and black. Pain faded in anticipation of sinking my fangs into her neck and drinking in what remained.

Her eyes flicked to mine, and I froze.

Kaiden, I said in my mind to the memory. *You knew my mother?*

"Matilda," I said aloud.

CHAPTER TWENTY-TWO

The woman who'd helped raise me lay dying on the stone floor in front of me.

Matilda. The cats. How had I forgotten?

I had forgotten so much.

"Bite her," Dimresh said. My hunger roared in me even louder than his voice. I was desperately hungry, the craving for blood stronger than any mere thirst I'd ever felt for alcohol in life. The one Matilda had tried, over and over, to save me from.

She would likely die from the wound in her neck whether I bit her or not. Her heart beat as quickly and as weakly as a mouse's would. It would be a waste not to bite her. It was what I wanted. What my master commanded.

The words burned in my brain, the command mixing with what my master had spoken. *Bind him with your vines, once twice thrice, by his blood to mine.* The memory drove pain into my back, spiking my hunger even more.

Magic worked. Johann had said . . . What had Johann said?

"Bite her!" Dimresh snapped.

Johann. Matilda. How had the prayer gone?

"Laurel," I said, and gritted my teeth against the surging hunger. My fangs pricked my lips as I spoke, my own rotted blood running onto my chin. "Protect me . . . as . . . a tree . . ."

Pain flared in my mind, and I growled. *Bite her!* the command thrummed. My hunger turned my stomach. I opened my mouth, my fangs aching from a need to bite, to drink.

"Laurel," I said, saliva dripping from my mouth and

mingling with the blood on my chin. I blinked hard, focusing on Matilda's face.

"Come now, Kaiden," she said. She held my shoulders, keeping me from falling as I retched a stomachful of ale into a basin on the floor. "Ask Laurel to save you from temptation. I do it every night for you."

It had seemed so foolish then. Laurel had no power.

I bit down, drawing more blood. "Laurel, save me . . . from temptation," I said.

"Fine, then," Dimresh said. "If you won't obey, you die."

Why did he want me to obey?

My master swung a clawed hand at me. As I turned, something in me flared — maybe magic or maybe instinct. My fangs met his wrist.

I bit down, and for a moment his eyes looked just like the vampire I'd lunged at in the courtyard, the whites showing. His blood filled my mouth, sickly sweet and intensely filling.

I sucked in a mouthful, my leg and jaw snapping into place with a wrenching crack, before he turned to mist and vanished.

Kill the blond one. The command boomed in my mind, a command to all Dimresh's thralls. *Kill him immediately.*

I growled a challenge to anyone who could hear, then picked up Matilda. She was light as a feather in my arms. Dimresh's blood still worked to heal me, one mouthful more powerful than an entire deer. My wrist snapped into place, and strength filled me as I leaped down dark halls, down the left wing of the castle that stretched around the main keep and would lead out.

I knew the way out. But so did they.

Four forms darted toward me, mindless things drawn to the scent of Matilda's blood. I didn't have time for them. I weaved past, their speed and strength my equal. Less than, since I could predict their every move.

I was different. Dimresh knew it. But why?

The scent of damp earth met my nose. I crashed through a rotted wooden door that led outside the keep, wincing and skidding to a stop at the spiking pain of splinters. The sky was a deep purple, autumn leaves littering the forest floor outside the stone walls.

Growls followed me. I had only seconds.

I laid Matilda down on soft leaves and grabbed a rotted piece of wood from the door. I turned just in time to jam it into the first thrall's shoulder as she tried to go through the door after me.

Johann had told me to practice hunting thralls, and now I would. I didn't know how long Dimresh's blood would give me strength, or if I had enough training to fight four of them. Even if I did, Dimresh would kill me.

But I wouldn't let them have Matilda. She'd saved me and kept trying, even as I fell further and further. I could save her too.

I grabbed at the door, my fingers digging through the soft, rotting wood. Moss crumbled to the ground as I pulled it away, and my improvised stake split in two, one half useless and soft.

The thrall I'd stabbed leaped at me again, Dimresh's orders stronger than her hunger for Matilda's blood. Matilda still lay on the leaves where I had left her, her heart beating as weakly as a bird's wing. At least if the thralls were focused on killing me, she would be safe.

I stepped to the side, just as Johann had done to me a hundred times, and let the mindless thrall impale herself on the wood. Shock drove up my arm as she jammed the weapon deeper into her body.

When the blackness left her eyes, they were brown. I didn't know her.

I wrenched the stake out of her chest just in time, but not fast enough to catch the next thrall who came at me, claws and fangs scoring into my flesh.

"James," I said, and twisted my head to avoid a bite to my neck. "James, please, enough. It's me, James. Kaiden."

He snapped at me, his black eyes unseeing. Dimresh's command still burned in both our minds, but I of course couldn't kill myself. Not again.

I slammed the wood toward James's chest, more snarls coming from the darkness as I did. Weight dragged at my back, and another thrall pulled at the arm not holding the wood. My muscles strained, and I gritted my teeth. James shrieked in pain. Blood dripped from the center of his chest. Sharp claws raked at my face.

I shouted and stabbed again. James didn't even have the mind to dodge it, too focused on slashing at me.

When he went down, I moved forward over his body, almost stumbling at the weight of the thrall on my back. The momentum and the other thrall's grip on my arm pulled me to face him. Another man I didn't recognize. One of the many in Penthorn who'd likely passed me by on the street and never thought anything of it.

He wouldn't let go of my arm, but I didn't need two arms to stab him with the stake. Dimresh's thralls were easier to fight when they were so focused on just killing. His orders made them less effective, not more.

Or maybe it was something else. I felt strong when I reached up and grabbed the arms of the thrall trying to strangle me, snapping her wrists as I threw her onto the ground. One of the girls from the Stuck Pig. Memories flashed like lightning at night, pretty painted faces and long lashes.

Now she snarled and blinked black eyes at me, her painted nails long and twisted. She sprang at my neck, the killing bite all thralls instinctively knew.

She too met the stake, and her body fell to the forest floor with a thump.

Blood dripped from scratch and bite wounds on my arms and neck for a few moments before they healed. Dimresh's blood was powerful. I licked my lips, my stomach hollow. I wanted more.

A soft moan came from the leaves. Matilda. The scent of her blood overpowered anything else.

Saliva filled my mouth, and I spat it onto the ground. No. I wasn't going to lose myself. Not to Matilda.

I took a step toward her. My stomach growled with hunger, my fangs sharp and digging into my lower lip. Her heart beat too fast, too weak.

She was dying anyway.

But she would die in Penthorn, where she belonged. Not here. Not to me.

I lifted her again and began to run.

Come back, thrall. The command boomed in my brain, even as the first hint of exhaustion began to sneak up on me, the first sign of the sun. *Come back!*

I had no intention of doing that. I had too much to do. I knew too much. I had to help Matilda, help Johann, tell him that magic worked. At least when vampires used it.

Burn, then, the command intoned, and pain flared in my neck. I tripped, dropping Matilda. I screamed as agony like fire overcame me, centered on my neck.

No. I had to keep going. I knew what would work.

I lifted her again, her form so light. I kept running. I ran as fast as I could, ignoring the pain in my neck and the heavy feeling in my body as the sun grew closer to breaking over the horizon. My whole body hurt, centered on my neck. I was disobeying my master, and he was angry.

This must be what dying to a solar flare felt like. But I couldn't stop. If I stopped, that meant giving up, and giving up meant death.

I didn't want to die.

The river burbled ahead of me, the old barrier keeping me from my village as a thrall. Johann had shown me what it could do.

Leaping across meant weakness and possible death to the sun if I couldn't find shelter in time. But staying here meant pain and certain death at the hands of my master.

I picked up my speed, heading toward the part of the river where I had used to watch the village. Matilda's house lay in a clearing just across. Across running water.

I jumped, and the pain struck me all at once, so much worse than the burning in my neck. Blackness slammed into me like a stake as it claimed me, and the last thing I felt was falling.

"Oh, Kaiden." Matilda wiped my forehead with a cloth, water dripping down my temples, making me itch. "That was a close one."

My hand weighed a thousand pounds, and shook as I reached to wipe the water off my face. "Am I going to die?"

"Not this time," Matilda said. "It was close. The black cough took you for a few days. But I think you're through the worst of it."

She wavered in my vision. Next to me, a small black cat purred. Its feet were white, as though it had walked through paint. "Why didn't my mother survive?"

Matilda blinked, and water ran down her cheek too. "Death comes for us all eventually, Kaiden. But you have to keep trying as long as you can. Laurel commanded it once."

My mother had believed in Laurel. "Laurel has no power," I said.

"No, that's true." Matilda wiped my forehead again. "But we do."

I opened my eyes to a dangerous dawn. The sky was pink, not purple. Any moment and the sun would clear the horizon.

I had to move. But the weakness, the heaviness in my body, was just as bad as the first time I'd crossed a river. I had nothing. The strength I'd gotten from biting Dimresh was gone.

Thankfully, so was he.

I didn't want to die. I was free again. I had survived this long. I had brought Matilda to safety.

I couldn't hear her heart anymore.

Another heartbeat came closer, a fast, weak one. No, not weak. Just small.

A tiny mew came from somewhere to my right.

My head felt as though it would snap from my neck with the effort it took to turn it. Matilda lay next to me, the blood on her neck black in the dim light. A small cat with a patch of white fur on its nose sniffed at her face and gave another tiny mew.

I didn't have the energy to spare for an apology. The kitten was too trusting, too slow to escape, as I used one last burst of desperation to grab it. But it gave me the strength I needed.

My limbs were still heavy when I sat up, and the threatening light of day made my eyes burn. Matilda's home sat a mere hundred feet away.

There was no sound of any heartbeat from her, no sound of breathing.

Tomorrow night, I was sure, Dimresh would come after me. I would have to leave the village. I had to find Johann.

But for now, I just needed to bring Matilda home.

My arms ached when I lifted her. So light before, now she weighed me down, and my legs shook with each step. Exhaustion from the threatening sun over the horizon slowed me even further. My stomach growled with hunger, and my fangs ground against my other teeth so hard I wondered if they could break.

My steps slowed, my eyes threatening to close. Matilda was so heavy. I felt as though the stone I walked on was clinging to my feet with each step, each time I lifted a leg harder than the one before.

The door was so close. Somewhere a goose honked, and a rooster began to crow. Then someone screamed from somewhere indoors, the sound muffled through the wood.

My legs buckled, and my knees hit cobblestones. Another scream echoed from somewhere farther down the street. "Vampire! Bloodsucker!"

I needed to move, but I couldn't. My muscles tensed, my instinct screaming at me to move, to make it to safety, but there was nothing I could do.

Heartbeats picked up all around me, and shapes flitted in the window of the house next door.

A familiar click. I turned, my growl tired and so quiet I doubted anyone could hear it.

Johann, his hair damp with sweat and his face streaked with grime, held a stakeshooter pointed at my chest. His gaze flicked to Matilda, limp in my arms and her neck caked with blood, and then back to me.

"Kaiden," he said, and the name sent a jolt through me. "What have you done?"

I blinked but couldn't open my eyes again. It couldn't really be Johann, but this didn't feel like another memory. "Nothing," I said. "I just need to get her home. I just . . . I didn't . . ."

"Kill it!" someone screamed. Johann's heart beat faster.

Pain slammed into my chest, and then darkness finally took me.

CHAPTER TWENTY-THREE

Johann's voice filtered through the haze of weakness and hunger that woke me.

"Kaiden. Kaiden, can you hear me? Say something."

Then, quieter, "Please, don't be like the others."

Johann sat on a chair, a long wooden stake across his lap. My chest ached, and heavy weight dragged at my neck, wrists, and ankles. They reeked of herbs, and any exposed skin chafed and burned where it touched the metal.

He didn't trust me after all.

"Kaiden." Johann met my eyes and held up the weapon, the point of the stake at my chest. His arm never wavered, even as his heart beat hard. "Did you bite that woman?"

I would be answering a variant of that question for the rest of my unlife, I was sure. I could only hope the answer would always be the same. "No."

Johann didn't move. Behind him, a familiar clock ticked the time, the numbers on the face worn. I lay on a couch, the chain around my neck hammered into the wooden floor.

I had slept on this couch before, a cat on my chest. This was Matilda's house.

He let out a breath. "Tell me what happened," Johann said. "Where did you go?"

I winced when movement brought more pain deep into my core. The stakeshooter ammunition was still in my chest, sticking out on the right side. My vision blurred, and I fought not to growl. I felt like I had lost everything, again. And I was so hungry.

"How did you get here?" I asked instead. "Why didn't you . . ." Of course I knew why. Johann couldn't fight Dimresh. No hunter could fight a vampire that powerful.

Fear made me tense up, ignoring the burning pain from the chains. I couldn't fight him either. And he had wanted me dead. My once master had wanted to kill me.

"What?" Johann lowered the stake a tiny bit. "Kaiden, what is it?"

"Dimresh killed her," I said through gritted teeth. "And James. And three others from Penthorn. He tried to . . ." I didn't even know the word for it. "He made me his servant again. So I crossed the river. He wanted me his slave, or dead."

Johann let the stake drop to his side. "Kaiden, you're really still you?"

"Yes!" Pain flared from the wood in my chest when I shouted. "I just . . . I wanted to bring her home."

"The woman?" Johann asked. Then understanding dawned. "Matilda. You mentioned her before."

"Where is she?" I asked.

"Buried," Johann said. A pang went through me. I wished I had more memories of her, ones that had survived Dimresh's turning.

The tension went out of him, his shoulders slumping. He rubbed a hand over his face, but it only streaked more grime. "That merchant family you saved told me they'd heard growls from the forest after you helped them. That was all I had to go on. I rode two nights and a day to get here, following a trail I found. My horse died. And when I saw you had gone to the castle with four other thralls, I thought . . ." He threw up his hands. "I didn't know what to think. And then . . ." He eyed me again. "There was blood on her neck."

"Dimresh." I hated myself when my mouth watered at the thought of blood. "He brought her to me. He wanted me to bite her. He commanded me to do it."

Johann blinked. "And you didn't?"

I met his eyes. "You were the one who said I was different. I didn't. Please, believe me."

Johann sighed. Pulling a knife from his pocket, he nicked his finger, holding it up to the light of the lantern in the corner.

I didn't need the light. The smell made my mouth water, made me gnash my teeth. I was so hungry it hurt. The fantasy I had conjured, the only relief I had those horrible nights of being carried, taunted me now.

"Please," I said. "Don't do that. I don't . . . I don't want to want it."

Laurel, save me from temptation.

Had it worked, then? Or had it been instinct that made me bite Dimresh's fist as it swung at me instead of Matilda?

I split my lip with my fangs and wished I didn't see the look of disgust on Johann's face. "Laurel, save me from temptation," I said, my own blood flecking my face as I spoke.

"What?" Johann asked.

Weakness and pain still dragged at me. "Laurel, save me from temptation," I said again. "I . . . I don't want to want it. I don't want your blood."

It wasn't true. I did still want it. But the desire wasn't overpowering anymore.

Had it truly worked?

"If I find you some animal blood and let you go, you won't hurt anyone else here?" Johann said.

"I promise." I wished I wasn't so wretched, so hideous. I would have to start all over again with Johann. My fantasy frayed and vanished. "Please, I promise."

Johann let out another gusty sigh. "I'll find you something." He made no move to unchain me or remove the stake that still sent dull pain into my right side. "Then I want you to tell me what happened. Tell me everything."

I had almost forgotten what a filling blood meal felt like. The pig squealed for a few seconds when I bit into it, but soon the thrashing stopped. Its heart slowed and fluttered.

I stopped for a moment, blood dripping from my fangs. The pig's heart sounded like Matilda's heart before she died.

"Kaiden?" Johann asked.

I sank my fangs back into the artery. I couldn't waste blood. Soon it was a husk, and Johann took the carcass from me. He'd unchained my arms but left my legs and neck chained down.

The healing from the blood worked once I took out the stake. I plucked it from my chest, letting it drop and roll into a sticky puddle on the floor.

"So," Johann said. "What happened? Start from the beginning. Vampire hunters give reports, sparing no detail. So tell me."

I told him everything. Even that Matilda had raised me for some time after my mother's death, even though I didn't remember everything about it. I didn't know how long I'd stayed here. I didn't know why she'd helped me. I just couldn't remember so much of my life.

But I told him everything I did know. Everything except the fantasy that had kept me sane that last night of starvation before being brought to Dimresh. I knew that wasn't relevant. It would never happen.

When I told him about the magic being used, his eyes lit up. I had known they would.

"So he invoked some sort of spell to . . . to bind you again?" Johann said. "Do you remember exactly what he said?"

"Bind him with . . . his blood to mine? My blood to his? One of the two." I shrugged, then winced at the burning of the chains. "I would tell you more if I could."

"No, I understand. You couldn't be expected to remember it, not with all that happened to you."

The last few nights had been torturous. I hoped now with Johann the torture would be over. "Can you take these chains off me?" Johann's eyes widened. "Or do you truly not trust me anymore?"

"No . . . Sorry. No, it's not that." Johann reached over and the chains loosened. I suppressed a growl when one of them slithered down my leg as it fell, drawing a line of pain like a snake. "I'm sorry, Kaiden. It sounds like you went through a lot." He leaned back, rubbing his eyes again. "When you vanished, I thought . . ."

I sat up on the couch, the wood of the armrest creaking when I put weight on it. "Tell me what you did," I said. "How you got here, what people here . . . what's happened here. I want to know. What happened to . . . to Matilda."

"You worked hard to get her here." Johann glanced at the couch but stayed in his chair, slumping farther. His heart rate slowed. "She was well known here. One of the oldest women in the village. She wasn't a practicing herbalist any longer, but people went to her for reminders of old remedies. And she helped raise Kaiden, the town drunk, after his mother died." Johann met my eyes. "You never mentioned that before."

"I . . . didn't remember it."

"Don't feel bad. The fact you remember anything of your life is amazing."

"Did anyone recognize me?" The clock behind Johann chimed eight times before he answered. Eight o' clock. I hadn't kept time since being turned.

"No. Only two people saw you, and I came over because of their screaming."

I thought I'd heard more than two screams.

"I half expected you to return here blood-crazed, and half expected you to . . . well, to have been killed. I was going to rest here after following the trail, and then to my surprise, you showed up, still yourself. Lucky me."

He smiled, but I didn't see the humor. "You gave up on me?"

"Would I have followed your trail as far as I did if I had?"

Good point. "Sorry."

"Don't be. I followed you here, but in the end I didn't help you. I couldn't." His hand clenched the armrest of the chair. "I'm tired of being helpless. I'm supposed to be a hunter, but when it comes to the most dangerous vampires, we're useless. You escaped because of your own strength and maybe some sort of vampire magic. The hunters . . ." He shook his head. "It's like we still think Laurel will come and save us one day, even though it's obvious that magic is gone."

"You have to help yourself," I said. Johann raised an eyebrow. "Just something someone told me once."

"Matilda?"

"Maybe her. Maybe a man named James. He's gone, too, now. Turned. One of the thralls I killed."

"I'm sorry. If it makes you feel any better, it's Dimresh's fault, not yours."

"I know." It still hurt. "They truly were mindless during the fight. Less effective even than the thralls in the courtyard."

"Dimresh is powerful. He may not typically rely on his thralls, and thus when he needed to use them correctly, he didn't have the experience." Johann crossed his arms. "That's good information to have, I suppose."

"I'm mostly surprised he ordered them to kill me rather than go after me himself," I said. "If he had . . ." The thought was chilling.

Johann grinned at me. "You haven't realized it yet?"

"What?"

"You're an intelligent thrall. He was curious enough about you to turn four others to bring you back to command you. You bit him and sucked his blood. He used his magic on you and failed." I didn't understand until he said it. "He was afraid of you."

"But . . ."

"I don't know much about what vampires want. But vampires were people once, and people generally want power. You were a threat to his power. Why risk leaving his castle and hunting you down himself, when you might be able to fight back, when his disposable thralls and the sun could do the job?"

A chill went through me. Johann was grinning, but I couldn't erase the memories of the past few days. "What if he knows I'm still alive?"

"That's why you don't have to worry," Johann said. "He won't come after you if he's afraid of you. You're not the one who has to be afraid."

My jaw tensed. There was so much I didn't know. I was a danger to vampires. But I was a danger to humans too. I didn't belong anywhere. "I'm not afraid for myself." That wasn't entirely true. "I'm just . . . lost."

"Lost?"

"I kill Dimresh. Then what?"

Johann tilted his head.

"I become a vampire lord. Will that mean . . . Will I get my memories back? Will I be able to control my hunger all the time, or will it finally be gone? Will I be able to . . ." I snapped my jaw shut. I had wanted to say *be close to anyone*, but that was too risky to even voice.

"I don't know the answer to any of that," Johann said. "But that's what life is. It's uncertainty. It's learning new things. You can't let that uncertainty prevent you from trying. And everything we've seen so far suggests that this will work. Dimresh is on the defensive. You're discovering magic you can use, and we can learn more about it." His voice rose, and I was happy to see his fervor. "I was so afraid I'd lost you, but you're still you. You're special. You can do this, Kaiden."

I wanted it to be true.
Then screams came from outside.

CHAPTER TWENTY-FOUR

I jumped to my feet and then froze when Johann put a hand on my chest. The contact made my skin fizz with tension, and my body pulsed with his for a moment. I hadn't realized how much I'd missed it.

"Let *me* help," Johann said. "*You* will cause panic."

I curled my upper lip. "I'll be safe. I can hide."

"What do you want to do?" Johann asked.

"I'm learning to be a hunter, aren't I?" I shot back. "This is my town. I can help protect it."

Johann took his hand away. "Fine. But stop baring your fangs." He turned, grabbing a long stake from by the door and a stakeshooter he'd hung on the wall. There had once been decorative plates there, and bits of ceramic dotted the floor.

Maybe they'd been broken when Dimresh took Matilda.

"Stay focused." Johann tossed the wooden stake to me. I caught it smoothly, my reflexes still sound despite my distraction. "And stay out of sight. Don't act unless I call you to." He put his hand on the doorknob. "Prove I can trust you."

I clenched my teeth behind a thin-lipped grimace. "I will."

As another scream rang in my ears, he exited into the night, and I followed.

Penthorn was small. It had been larger once. For every house with a person or family inside, there were two that were abandoned on the outskirts. For every inn or brewery, there was another large warehouse that had fallen to ruin. Most people stayed in the center of town, save for the farmers who worked the outlying fields.

Johann jogged down the street at a steady clip. The night was young, and light spilled from lanterns still lit in some windows. I kept to the alleys and dark corners, darting past the occupied houses and pausing next to the abandoned ones, keeping Johann in sight.

Memories threatened to come to the fore, like a word I knew that wouldn't form on my tongue. I didn't remember who lived here, faces or names, but I knew which houses to avoid and which had lain without people for years. I knew we were nearing the town square, and sometimes visions of lying in these alleys would flash through my mind.

As we got closer, I made out more sounds, not just the heartbeats of mice and the scritches of insects.

"He was here!" someone shouted. "He took him right out of the alley!"

A woman screamed, and this time I heard the name. "Alistair! No!"

Johann picked up his pace, nearing the cheery lights of the torches that burned next to the Jameson Brewery. No, not anymore. Part of the sign had been taken down, and now it just read Brewery.

I paused in the shadows by a large building that lay quiet now but smelled of straw and unwashed bodies. The scent was somewhat familiar. A steady heartbeat came from inside behind a window with iron bars. Whoever it was, they were sleeping, and this was a good vantage point.

"Hunter!" a man called out. The man threw his hands out, his gestures close to nearly hitting Johann in the face. "Where were you?"

Johann's voice was harder to hear. "Tell me what happened."

"Alistair . . . a man here. He came out to piss and never came back. The vampire got him. He must have."

"Did you see it happen?"

"No, but where else would he be?"

Good, Dimresh had said. *Blood gives you energy. Now come with me. Hurry.* His voice had been my entire world. I left the alley—and life—behind without a second thought. My last memory of the alley was the cat, dead and drained.

That wasn't the alley this Alistair had been taken from. But if he was a thrall now, then . . .

"Where are you going?" the man shouted after Johann.

"To check the alley," Johann said. "If the vampire turned him here, there may be clues. Look for drained animals. A thrall needs to feed before anything else."

"You check the alley!" the man shouted, not moving after Johann. I couldn't blame him. "You hunters don't do anything!" he kept shouting, his voice thick with drink. "Every year we lose more. We lost four in the past week!" He threw his hands up, shouting to the sky once it was clear Johann wasn't responding. "A man can't even drink out late anymore!"

There had been four thralls, and I'd killed them all. Dimresh was making more. He had been here, in my village, targeting people I'd once lived among.

My fangs cut into my lower lip. I had lived here as a human. Vampires hunted everywhere, taking whatever they liked, whoever they liked. He had killed Matilda. He had killed me.

My palms stung, and I stopped digging my nails into them. I breathed in the scent of my village, the mixed scents of straw and sweat and horse and the tinge of alcohol on the air from the brewery. Perfume came from the direction of the Stuck Pig, the brothel where my mother had worked.

Memories came in flashes, but nothing concrete. Dark alleys. The taste of alcohol. James laughing at something I said. Matilda's cat purring on my chest.

I thought I'd wasted my life, but no life was ever wasted.

Living was its own reward. I wished I could do it again, live free of a thirst for blood and having to hide in the shadows.

From the jail cell I crouched behind, the man snorted. "Wha—?"

"Be silent."

Once that voice would have a sent a chill down my spine. Just the previous night, it would have made me curl up in terror. But Dimresh didn't have any power over me now. And I had tasted his blood.

I could get Johann. But I was so much faster.

The night air whipped my face. I threw open the door of the guardhouse attached to the prison, the wood banging against the frame, and wrenched the doorknob free along with a good portion of sharpened wood. A man at a desk jumped as I entered. Keys jangled at his belt. I'd moved past him before he could summon the air to scream.

The cells where drunk and disorderly people were kept were in the back, and I reared back to kick in the door. The wood was weak, but the metal lock wasn't. My foot created a hole that wasn't big enough for me to pass through. I clenched my jaw.

Behind me, the guard moaned. A wave of fear assaulted my nose along with the stench of loosed urine. His heart beat in a frenzied, disorganized staccato.

I paused, my hand clenched around the wood. Dimresh was beyond the door. I could kill him. I could feast on his blood.

But the man behind me would die.

But if I didn't move, so would the man in the cell.

I was a thrall. I shouldn't even care.

The door exploded outward. Dimresh stood in front of me, blood ringing his lips. Behind him, the man in the cell lay drained and gray. And next to him stood a thrall.

No. The man's eyes weren't black, but brown. Another

vampire.

"That's the one. Kill him," Dimresh said. Then he turned to mist.

I brought up my weapon, but I was too slow. Thralls were fast, but this vampire was faster. He punched me so hard bones in my chest cracked, the pain agonizing. I flew backward through the wooden door, out into the street. The cobblestones scraped my back, and I lay on the ground. The stars twinkled above me.

Someone screamed, the same woman as before. "Alistair!"

The vampire blocked the light from the torches as he leaped, and that was the only sign I had to move. The wood he held shattered on the ground where I'd lain. When I moved, the taste of my own blood entered my mouth, and I coughed. That was the first time I'd done anything similar to breathing in months.

"Alistair!" the woman screamed again. I don't know if she distracted him or not. But I had enough time to scramble away on all fours like an animal, weakness dragging at my body. I grabbed a few splinters of the wood, but they were all too small.

I had fought and killed thralls. But this was a vampire. I had attacked the vampire in the courtyard, had drawn his blood, but had never killed one.

He moved so fast wind whistled past my ears. Strong fingers with fingernails so long they might as well be claws grabbed my head. I had to fight with everything I had to keep him from twisting my head hard enough to break my neck.

"Stupid thrall," he hissed. "Why does my sire want you dead?"

"Why . . . are you obeying him if . . ." One of his fingers pressed against my jaw and I shut it against the pain. Muscles straining, I growled and clenched my teeth. The vampire was so strong. I had never faced something stronger than I was. I couldn't do this.

The woman screamed again, and so did Johann.

"Kaiden!"

I would never kill Dimresh If I just gave up.

He was stronger than me, but that didn't mean I was weak. I drove my fist into his gut. Unlike the vampire in the court-yard, this one didn't turn into mist. My fist sliced through skin. Blood and viscera slicked my arm. The vampire bel-lowed his pain, and his grip on my head weakened.

I turned and drove my fangs into him, aiming for his neck and instead hitting his shoulder.

His blood didn't taste like Dimresh's, but it was still ten times sweeter and more filling than any animal's. Strength filled me, and I bit down harder.

Fingers dug into my arms, lifting me and throwing me across the courtyard. Stars whirled overhead, and I twisted in midair. I still landed on all fours, the ground scraping my hands and knees. The wounds healed almost immediately, the vampire's blood fresh on my tongue.

I lifted my head and growled at him.

"What kind of thrall are you?" he shouted. His gut was torn open, and blood dripped from his neck.

I didn't know. No thralls bit vampires. No thralls turned on their masters. No thralls resisted the scent of human blood.

But I wasn't a normal thrall.

I tensed to leap at him. But he was faster.

Except he went for the woman who'd screamed. The fool had gotten closer instead of running away. She had a moment to widen her eyes, to whisper "Alistair, no," before he sank his fangs into her neck. Blood hit the ground, a wasteful vam-pire bite, and her skin began to pale. His back was to me.

Easy prey.

"Kaiden," Johann said, and I stayed still. Then the stakeshooter bolt sprouted from the vampire's back and he fell to the ground. The woman wavered on her feet, then sank to her knees.

When thralls died, their bodies simply lay still, their eyes returning to a normal color. The vampire did the same. In death, bloodsuckers like me just looked like a dead human.

"Freshly bitten," Johann said, jogging closer. He raised his stakeshooter, aiming for the woman.

"No!" I shouted. As I did, she met my eyes. Then they turned black, and she fell to the ground, her lips forming a sibilant hissing sound. The vampire had taken enough blood to kill her, but not all of her blood, and that meant turn her. She needed her first blood meal, but her master wasn't there to give it to her.

Dimresh had done this. I gritted my teeth, turning to bound toward the prison where I'd seen him last and then froze.

Men and woman poked their heads out of windows and doorways, bathed in the light of the torches from inside. Some had crept out of the houses that were nearest to the square, peering through the darkness.

All of them were staring at me.

"So much for lying low," Johann said.

The scent of fear floated on the breeze. The torches near me guttered in the wind.

The people who came out at night in Penthorn were the fools and the drunks, the prostitutes and the entertainers. Night was dangerous. Anyone who went out risked being bitten. I had never cared, too focused on finding a drink to worry about my own safety. I wondered how many of the half-dozen people who were walking closer to me, trying to see the man who had fought a vampire, had similar issues.

"Don't be afraid," Johann called out. He put his hand on my shoulder, my muscles knotting and then relaxing beneath his touch. I resisted the urge to lean into it. "For now, it's safe."

A woman was the first to get close, her lips painted bright red. The lantern she held illuminated her colorful, frayed skirts.

She jerked it backward, the light sending dancing shadows around the square. "It's a bloodsucker!" she called out. The men and women behind her skittered away.

"It's safe!" Johann called again. His hand was firm on my shoulder. "There's nothing to fear." He faced me, his eyes dark in the flickering firelight. "Do you want me to tell them who you are?" he whispered.

I opened my mouth then closed it. They might know me. But I wouldn't know them. My life came to me in flickers, not enough to go on. I had died. I couldn't just start again.

And even if I wanted to, if Dimresh truly wanted me dead, telling them my name might only put them in more danger than they already were. And if they thought their turned friends could come back . . .

The woman on the ground was all the evidence I needed to know why that was dangerous.

"No," I said. "Don't tell them anything. Please. Keep them away."

Johann sighed then nodded. "This thrall is my prisoner," he called out. "He obeys me and answers to me." I wondered if he'd planned to say something like that in case someone discovered me. Or from the beginning, when he'd first picked me out as a weapon. "It's for the best if you stay away from him. I'll keep him contained."

Whispers and low conversation came over the wind. The woman with the lantern crept closer, the light burning my eyes. Perfume tinged the air. "How do you keep it controlled?"

Johann's words buzzed in my mind, but I paid no attention. Her question only made me think of the vampire again. Alistair. The woman he'd killed had loved him. But as a vampire, he had fed from her immediately.

Vampires weren't mindless. That hadn't been hunger.

How had Dimresh kept him controlled?

It had to be magic. I needed to understand.

And if Dimresh was seeking to kill me, I had very little time.

"Who was he?" I asked, and the woman jumped when I pointed to the ground where the vampire lay. "Alistair, right?"

She held the lantern up, peering at me instead of the man on the ground. "Yes, that . . . was him. He and Eliza were gonna be married. He was celebrating her agreeing to it tonight. But that ended as soon as the vampire got him, I suspect." She shook her head. "Guess we'll be burying them both tonight, if it's safe."

"They're harmless now. A piece of wood through the heart will end them." Johann kept his hand on my shoulder, and the warmth of it seeped through my clothes. "But it's clear the vampire is increasing his attacks. I urge you to keep indoors, and to tell others to do the same."

"My business will fail if everyone stays indoors all the time. Of course, I lost my husband only a few days ago. You gonna kill the thing, hunter?"

Her husband. James, which made her . . . The light flickered over her face, and I took a step closer, memory beckoning. Johann's grip firmed, and the woman held out the lantern, stepping backward.

"I hope to," Johann said. "Keep me informed. I'll be staying at . . . Matilda's old home. I intend to stay here until the job is done."

"Still extending her hospitality, even after her death." The woman nodded, still staring at me. I knew her; I was sure of it. If she'd been James's wife, she must work in the brewery. But no memories came to me.

"Yes. I'm sorry for your loss. But I swear to you, I will kill him."

"Maybe. Of course, some other bloodsucker will just come by." She sighed. "There's no way to get them all."

"We'll do our best," Johann said. He tapped my shoulder. "Come on, thrall. Let's patrol."

CHAPTER TWENTY-FIVE

Rain began to fall as the moon traveled higher overhead, a soft pattering on cracked cobblestones and the wooden and thatch roofs of a decrepit house. One person snored inside.

"Villages like these are harder to patrol," Johann said with a sigh. His footsteps clacked, rhythmic but uneven, on the stones. "This would have been a city once. But now with more houses than people . . ." He sighed again, his breath fogging. "Someone could get bitten without anyone noticing for days."

I cocked my head. His heart beat faster than it should, yet each breath was slow and deep. "You're exhausted," I said. "It's not healthy."

"That's true," he said. "But I can't rest until daybreak."

"Did you mean what you said?" I asked. "About killing Dimresh?"

"I did." Johann stopped walking. "But you'll most likely be the one to do it."

I nodded. "I haven't killed one yet. I've fought. But both times, you were the one to kill them." A bat swooped overhead. I tracked it as it nabbed an insect out of the air and flew on. "I don't know if I can."

"Neither do I. But all we can do is try." Johann swept an arm out. "I can't let this village get any more depleted than it already is. They'll end up like Brusque."

"Where Lasren is?"

Johann nodded, then let out another heavy sigh. "I know you may not remember your life. But people here still have . . ."

hope, I suppose. They go out at night, try to run businesses and stay functional. Merchants travel through here at times. But if Dimresh decides he needs to kill faster, turn more thralls . . . The people who remain in places like this are essentially bred for their blood, and they know it. They're kept like cattle, but with no guidance at all, just the knowledge that every night someone else will die."

"Why don't they leave?"

"Think, Kaiden. Even if they could get far enough away from a vampire like Lasren in one day, what would happen to an entire town of defenseless people the first night exposed in a land full of bloodsuckers?"

"Easy prey," I said.

Johann grimaced, and I wished I hadn't said it like that.

"I hope you see the purpose of this, too, the importance of protecting people. I know you want to kill Dimresh for his blood, to become powerful. But for humans, for me, there's so much more to it than that."

"I know."

Johann paused, then shook his head. "I'll be honest with you. I worry about you as a vampire. There's no guarantee you'd end up like Lucien, if the tale is even accurate. That Alistair, killing a woman he loved as soon as he was turned . . ."

A man who'd become a vampire had killed his fiancée without a second thought. It was clear Johann didn't know why either. "I worry too."

"Since you told me about that spell Dimresh used . . . I wonder if it's magic. Some old twisted holy magic that robs new vampires of their morals. But the information about that would be in the old temples, which are in Brusque, although Lasren is said to have destroyed most of the old information. And Lasren is more powerful than Dimresh. And if we went there, Dimresh would continue to hunt here." He rubbed his forehead.

I hated to hear Johann sound so hopeless. I stepped closer, making sure he saw me, and put my hand on his shoulder.

He tensed but let me touch him.

"Don't . . . don't worry," I said. "We'll help them." I swallowed. "I'll protect them. There won't be more like Matilda."

Johann's eyes widened, and he smiled for a moment. He put his hand on mine, and his heart picked up slightly. I relished the touch.

"Kaiden . . ." His hand tightened around mine, a reassuring squeeze. "Would you want to visit her grave? It's not far."

I paused for a moment, something twisting in my stomach and chest. Then I nodded. "I think I should."

Johann led me through the twisting streets of the inhabited parts of Penthorn. Farther on, the houses were less close together, forgotten fields that once held crops or livestock taking their place. The moon was still a sliver, the blades of grass silhouetted in faint, silvery light beyond the reach of Johann's lantern. Stars twinkled overhead.

As the field rolled on, small headstones marked graves, and Johann slowed. The scent of fresh earth met my nose.

"There," he said. The lantern light illuminated a freshly carved stone.

Matilda. She cared for many.

Next to it sat two smaller stones, and my throat tightened. I knew them.

"They buried her at noon, next to her sons," Johann said. "A lot of people came to pay respects. She was known for her kindness and her constant hospitality, wasn't she?"

"You remind me of my sons, Kaiden. Twin boys, with blond hair like yours." She helped me sit up, my chest still tight with sickness. *"They died long ago to the pox."* Her gaze went distant. *"I had to burn their things. But there was one thing I didn't burn, a gift I was going to give them on their tenth birthday."* She pointed to a doll,

carved of wood and decorated with dried leaves. *"A little doll of Laurel, for protection."*

"It doesn't do anything," I'd said, my voice raspy.

"I know. But they used to love hearing about her. And I've always believed the comfort it gives is more important than any lost magic." Her eyes glimmered, but she didn't blink the tears away. "What matters is intent, Kaiden. Being a good person is all the protection you need."

"She was a good person, and she still died," I said. My voice came out thick, and my eyes felt hot. "She always believed in others, believed in . . . the protection of being a good person. But no one was there to protect her."

Johann put his hand on my shoulder again, and I put my hand on top of his. Warmth flowed from his touch. "Dimresh brought her to you for you to bite her, right?" he said. "But you didn't. Maybe her protection worked in the end."

Maybe. "But she still died." I'd worked so hard to bring her home.

"Did she want to protect herself, though? Or did she always want to protect others?"

I had no answer, but the words felt heavy in my mind.

"Some people believe that after death we move on to a better place," Johann added. "Maybe now she's somewhere with her sons, safe and sound."

"Do you believe that?" I asked.

Johann nodded. "I do."

"Why?"

"Because when I kill thralls and vampires, they look human again. They died once, but ending their unlife is truly putting them to a peaceful rest. Being what they are . . ." He trailed off. "Are you happy, Kaiden?"

"No." I didn't know if I ever was.

"I'm sorry."

"I want to live, though," I said. "I don't remember much of

my life. I remember her." I jutted my chin toward Matilda's grave. "I remember a few people. But that's all. And before you . . . I remembered nothing. Not even my name."

"None do, except you." A cricket somewhere began to chirp. "Thralls, and even newly made vampires, remember nothing of their life before. I've always believed they already died, and are simply . . . walking undead. They have no morals, just a need for blood in the case of thralls and security in the case of vampires. Intelligent, but there's nothing there. Animated by the blood they drink."

"Or by dark magic," I said, thinking of the words Dimresh had spoken and the line of pain he'd drawn down my back.

"What do you mean?"

"You said there were priests, ages ago." He nodded. "And that the Empire fell when the priests' protection faded and vampires began to rise in power. But . . . what if it wasn't that Laurel's protection faded? What if the magic just changed?"

"So Laurel is now . . . a goddess of vampires?" Johann's brow furrowed. "What kind of goddess would allow that?" His hand left mine as he swung out an arm to indicate the graveyard.

"Maybe Laurel isn't real," I said. "But the magic is. And . . . what matters is intent."

That wasn't the full answer, I was sure. And it felt blasphemous to say it, especially here in front of Matilda. But it also felt more right than believing the magic was simply gone.

"I want to argue with you. But I'd be arguing with something — someone — that has already upended most of what I thought I knew." Johann smiled at me. "I knew the story of Lucien, but I never truly thought I'd meet a thrall like you."

"So . . . guide me, please," I said. "We need to protect Penthorn. I need to kill Dimresh."

"Right." Johann nodded, standing up straighter. "Let's go back to Matilda's. Before sunup, let's focus on what we do know and what you can do. I'm sure Dimresh will attack again tomorrow. And he's clearly after you. I don't want to lose you again."

I smiled, and it was hard to tell, but Johann's face may have flushed in the dark. We turned away from the graves, and I paid one last silent goodbye to Matilda.

I was different, unique, a thrall who could fight vampires. Johann's words echoed. *"Did she always want to protect others?"*

I hadn't saved her in the end, but maybe I'd lived the way I had, as an intelligent thrall, because of her protection. That didn't feel quite accurate. But it was a nice thought.

CHAPTER TWENTY-SIX

"How much of this do you remember?" Johann asked.

Being in Matilda's house was strange. I didn't remember the details from my life except in flashes. The ticking clock, the doll. Other things were new, at least to me — knitted fabrics on most of the tables and chairs, candles that had melted onto the wooden windowsills. The entire place smelled of rosemary. But all of it combined made me feel nice. Safe, in a way, even though I knew I never truly was.

"Some things." I motioned to the doll up above, and the couch where I'd slept some nights. I wanted to explore, to see if more memories of my life would resurface, but there were more important things to be done.

"So, Kaiden. You drank a mouthful or two of a vampire's blood tonight," Johann said. "Does mine still tempt you?"

I blinked in surprise. I sniffed the air, catching Johann's scent, a scent I was growing fond of. It was mingled with soap, and I wondered where he'd gotten it.

"You smell nice," I said. His face reddened in the torchlight from the sconce by the door. "But . . . I'm not hungry enough to be tempted yet."

"Do you think it was the vampire blood? You didn't get very much."

"It . . . it must be."

"Or it could be Laurel's magic. That spell you used. Protecting you from temptation. Could that be it?"

"I . . . I don't know."

"Can we try something?" Johann asked. "When Dimresh

used the magic on you, he used blood. I've never heard of anyone doing that before. If there are some lost rituals to make the magic work, perhaps blood's a part of them. I want to try one, but I'll need to cut myself."

I swallowed hard. "Should I . . . wait outside?"

"Do you want to? I trust you, Kaiden. If I can't work the magic, maybe a thrall can. There are many things we should try before we decide something definitely does or doesn't work. I'd rather have you here, if you think you can resist."

I *had* to. I wouldn't be a monster. And I had to kill Dimresh. "I can," I said. I swallowed hard. "I will."

"Good." Johann led the way into the kitchen and sat at a wooden table. The stained tablecloth depicted flowers. "There are very basic magics priests of Laurel used to perform, at least according to the old books. Let's see if we can do them if we change a few things."

Johann blew out the lamp he held in his hand, the room dark save for the flickering candlelight in the hallway from the sconce by the door. He placed it in the center of the table then folded his hands.

"Laurel, grant us your light to protect us from night."

I tensed. I'd never heard of such powerful magic.

Nothing happened.

"Laurel made light?" I asked.

"Priests of Laurel could light candles. At least, the old histories say so. Any novice priest could light a candle and purify water." Johann tapped the lamp.

"Maybe you're just not a priest," I said.

"Any believer could be a priest," Johann said.

"Maybe you don't believe, then."

Johann frowned.

"Why would you, after years of seeing it not work?" I added.

"Right. But you're missing the point, Kaiden." Johann

195

shook his head. "I don't think it's that. I think it has something to do with vampires. And blood. So maybe . . ."

He met my eyes, then took out a small knife from his heavy hunter's jacket. I swallowed then gave him a nod.

He pricked his finger. The coppery tang of blood immediately filled the room. Johann's blood was mixed with his scent, a spicy bouquet of iron and pine and life that made my mouth water.

"Laurel, grant us your light to protect us from the night," Johann said.

The words burbled in my ears, quiet among the rush of bloodlust that was making me clench my teeth.

The room was still dark, the lamp unlit. Johann sat alone and bleeding, easy prey.

No. I had to focus.

"Hmm . . ." Johann's eyes were dark. "Are you managing, Kaiden?"

"Y-yes." My words came out thick, and I swallowed down bloodlust. I wasn't even hungry, not since the vampire blood, but Johann was so tempting. I wanted him. My muscles twitched, a compulsion to leap, to bite.

"Can you think of anything else your master did to make the magic work?"

"He . . ." I took a step closer, and then immediately away. The scent of him, his body and sweat and maleness, mixed with the blood. "He put it on me. As part of the spell."

"To link the magic to the blood, perhaps?" Johann muttered to himself. He squeezed his thumb, then pressed a bloody thumbprint onto the lamp. My fangs drew my own blood from my lower lip.

"Laurel, grant us your light to protect us from the night," Johann repeated.

Nothing. The bloody thumbprint sat there, taunting me.

"I . . . I kind of thought that would work," Johann said. He looked up, his pulse beating steady in his neck. "Why don't you try?"

"What?"

"Kaiden." Johann spoke louder, his voice commanding, and put his other hand around his bleeding thumb. "Focus. Remember what we're here for."

"Right. I know." I hated my hunger. No, this wasn't even hunger. It was twisted lust, and I hated having it. "What . . . what do I say?"

"Laurel, grant us your light to protect us from the night."

"Laurel, grant us your light to protect us from the night."

Nothing. Johann sighed.

No. The prayer was right, but they weren't supposed to be right. Dimresh hadn't asked for protection when he'd bound me. I remembered it had been strange, different than the one Johann had used on the road. He hadn't said anything about Laurel, after all.

"Maybe try your blood, then," Johann was saying. "Just a bit—"

"Laurel, grant me . . . your light to protect us from the night," I said, driving my fingernail into my thumb.

Pain spiked, but there was nothing. I growled in frustration. What had Dimresh said? How had he phrased things?

It was all about him. It was about intent, what he wanted.

Right. "By my blood," I said, and it felt right, even as the words twisted. "Grant me darkness to protect me from the burning light."

"What was that?" Johann snapped.

Then the light flickering from the sconce in the hallway went out.

Wood crashed against wood, Johann's shape silhouetted in the dim moonlight from outside as he jumped to his feet. "Kaiden!" he shouted, and his stakeshooter clicked when he drew the bolt back.

I blinked in the darkness, the only light the sliver of the moon outside. "I'm right here," I said. Something twisted in my stomach, disappointment at myself, or at Johann for not trusting. Or at the fact that the only magic that worked was wrong. "Was that . . . was that dark magic?"

"Kaiden," Johann said, his voice breathy. His heart beat fast, like a rabbit's, but began to slow. "Yes, that was dark magic. And now that I know you can do that, promise me you won't ever do it again. I thought . . . I trust you, but dark magic is something wholly different. Or maybe it's the same, but . . . that would be worse, in a way. Some magic can't be undone. The old books were very clear about that."

"I . . . I don't want to." My body felt heavy, my stomach turning. My fangs felt long and strange in my mouth, and I relaxed my jaw with effort. "I don't want to be like Dimresh."

Johann moved in the darkness, and I got out of his way, the scent of his fear mixing with his usual alluring scent. He relit the candle in the hallway, and the new light glimmered on the sheen of sweat on his skin.

"What . . . what did I do?" I asked.

Johann sighed and sat down on the couch I used to sleep on. At least he'd put the stakeshooter back in his belt. "A spell of darkness, I suppose," he said. "For a moment I was blind, and I thought Dimresh had found us. And then I realized . . . it was you."

I didn't like the way he looked at me. "I'm sorry."

Johann let out a breath. "Don't be. I've learned more from you than hunters have learned about vampires since the Empire's fall." He rolled his shoulders, his breathing slowing. "And yet I still don't know what kind of bloodsucker you are. That magic . . . if you could cast a fear spell and did it by accident, I would be dead now."

I could have killed Johann. "I'm . . ." I was a thrall. But thralls didn't think. They didn't feel. And they certainly didn't use vampire magic. They didn't lure a vampire lord into coming after them and endanger an entire town. "I . . ."

Johann tilted his head. "Kaiden?"

Laurel truly was gone. Only dark magic remained, dark magic that had erased all the lights in Matilda's home. The doll on its perch above the couch was just that — a doll, with no power at all. No, less than no power. It was a mockery of belief that blurred in my vision. Laurel had turned on us all, and intent didn't matter. I wanted to do good. But all I could do was snuff out light.

"I don't want to be like this," I said, my words thick. "I want to be . . . I want to be alive again."

Why had I given it up? Why had I wasted my life with drink and lying in alleys, throwing away the second chance Matilda had given me? And now I was using dark magic that was anathema to everything Matilda had believed in.

She wasn't here to save me anymore. And Johann . . .

Johann stood, his scent enveloping me as he brought his arms around my body. I froze, my muscles tense.

"Don't cry, Kaiden. I know you would never hurt me."

I was crying? I blinked, my eyes hot and sticky. But right now all I could focus on was Johann. His strong arms around me, the warmth of his body, the scent of his sweat and maleness and blood, his warm breath washing over my shoulders.

Yes. This was what I wanted.

"We can figure this out together, Kaiden," Johann said, his voice loud and sonorous this close. "I know you don't want to hurt anyone."

"Is there a way to go back?" I asked. I wanted to grab him, to pull him close, but instead I stood motionless, my fingernails digging into my palms. "Can I use magic to be human again?"

"I would once have said no," Johann said. "But if the magic works . . . in the way you use it, maybe there's a way to use it correctly. Seeing you and what you can do has given me hope that things can change. So maybe. We can find out together."

"Once I kill Dimresh," I said.

"Yes." Johann rubbed my back. "I'm sure you can do it."

I let him hug me, his touch warm and soft. My confusion faded, replaced with instinct I hadn't known I still had. I liked to be touched. I liked to be held.

But of course I wanted more. My nostrils flared at Johann's scent, his closeness so tempting. Warmth built into heat and kindled hunger.

I licked my lips, closing my eyes, but I couldn't ignore it. My body began to respond, throbbing with that dull promise of pleasure I knew I couldn't fully have. His closeness taunted me, and it only made me want to bite him more. I ground my teeth in frustration. I had to focus.

But I couldn't stop myself as I ran my fingers over his arms, the muscles taut and strong. He pulled back from the embrace. As I ran my hand down his arm he caught it in his, holding my hand again. His eyes smoldered in the firelight from the lamp.

I swallowed, but it didn't do much to get rid of the saliva filling my mouth, the hunger in my stomach, and the very different kind of desire suffusing my body, making me feel as warm as Johann felt.

I couldn't have this. But I wanted it so badly.

"Hungry, Kaiden?" Johann asked.

"Yes." I needed to let him go, to stop. I needed to tell him to stop touching me. But I couldn't. I took a step forward, my body pulsing with need in time to the pulse in his neck.

His hand met my chest. I stopped, my fangs clicking shut. His scent filled my nostrils, a spice of fear mixed with the unmistakable scent of arousal. "What do you want, Kaiden?"

My fantasy filled my mind, along with the memory of my dream. I drove my fangs into my lower lip, hissing out a growl of frustration. Johann didn't move, his hand never leaving my chest.

"I want you," I admitted. But saying it didn't make it any easier to bear.

"I know you don't want to bite me, Kaiden," he said in response. "You don't really want that, do you?"

"No," I managed, frustration putting an edge in my voice. But it wasn't true. I did want to bite him, to enjoy his blood and his body. I couldn't have one without the other. I was a thrall. Life was sex, but blood was life. If I let myself be tempted . . .

He reached for my face, his fingers hot against my jaw. He guided my head forward. The scent of his arousal filled my nose. He was going to kiss me. His lips would feel so good.

Stupid. Easy prey.

His lips met mine, soft and warm and wet. Lust blazed in my body, and I opened my mouth, my fangs long and sharp. His heart beat in my ears, his blood rushing in his neck, his lips.

"No," I growled, and shoved him hard. His arms flailed, and he stumbled back onto the couch. He reeked of sex and maleness and blood, everything I wanted.

"Kaiden, are you . . ."

"I can't." I knew he could see how aroused I was. "I don't want your blood, but . . . I do." The words came out as a growl of frustration. "You can't trust me."

"I do trust you, Kaiden," Johann said, standing up again. He put his hands up as though he would reach out, and I darted away. Johann's face fell. "I know you wouldn't hurt me."

"Don't," I snapped, lacing it with another low, dangerous growl. "Don't tempt me."

"Kaiden—"

"*Don't.*" I gnashed my teeth at his blood and scent. "You

being so close, your touch . . . it's torture."

Silence filled the house. Finally Johann let his hands drop. "I'm sorry. I . . . I didn't think. Do you . . . do you want me to get you blood?" I swallowed. "Or I could let you hunt before the sun comes up. I could lower the drawbridge to the woods. Or there are plenty of pigs and goats roaming around the village."

He talked as though nothing had happened, as though he wasn't standing there burning with the embers of doused desire.

He wanted me too. That made things so much worse.

"I'll hunt," I said. "I'll come back."

"Kaiden, wai—" But I was gone into the night before he finished saying my name.

CHAPTER TWENTY-SEVEN

The moon had sunk low, dawn threatening. I ran through the dark streets of the village where I'd once lived, my speed carrying me past the inhabited houses to where the streets were pitted and worn. Here the abandoned houses had fallen into the streets in places, and in others were overgrown with weeds and roots that jutted from broken stones in the ground.

My body surged with frustration, instincts to kill warring with instincts that had once brought me pleasure. I stopped next to a broken house. One wall had collapsed, the scent of mold strong. Something snuffled in the broken wood and stone, and the scent of fur and blood met my nose along with the musky, sharp scent of dog.

Easy prey. But it wouldn't taste very good. Not like Johann.

My mouth watered at the thought, and I spat on the ground. I couldn't want his blood. I couldn't want him.

He was a vampire hunter. He killed thralls like me. Why was he so stupid to tempt me like this? What kind of fool tried to kiss a thrall?

I should drink the blood of the dog. The mutt smelled like it was going to die anyway. Blood might help.

Rotted wood creaked, and I found the dog staring at me. Its tail — parts of it matted and other parts bald and bleeding — wagged slowly. The animal was missing an ear, and held its head cocked to one side.

I growled. It whimpered and ran on shaky legs, hiding behind another piece of fallen stone. Its heart raced, weak and sputtering with illness and rot.

I sank to the ground, my body tense. Running wouldn't help. Feeding wouldn't help. Pleasure I couldn't have, urges I couldn't fulfill, overpowered other sensations.

I reached down, my mouth falling open and my fangs pricking my lower lip. My eyes fluttered closed, something kindling each time I stroked myself and then dying just as quickly no matter what I did. I imagined Johann doing the same. For him it would be red-hot desire that would crescendo in mere minutes. I groaned, the thought making me hungry again and making my body ache further.

But nothing happened, my touches growing frantic and the pleasure never peaking. My teeth gritted together. Johann would have come by now, spilling onto the ground. I imagined how hot and slick his seed would feel—I wished I could taste that too.

I wanted it so badly. But the pleasure was faint and all too soon I softened beneath my own touch. I hung my head, alone in the dark. I couldn't have pleasure, not like Johann, not even when I was thinking of him. He was alive. I wasn't. I needed to take his life, his blood, to truly have it.

I wanted him so badly. He wanted me. But if I bit him, it would end for both of us.

I had asked Laurel to protect me from temptation, but of course that hadn't worked. Laurel wasn't real, if she ever had been. Now there was only dark magic.

Incantations probably didn't even need her name.

I met the dull glow of the dog's eyes as it peered out from behind the stone. Its heart still beat fast, faster than a dog's should. It would die soon anyway.

"By my blood, bind . . . your will to mine," I said. It wasn't quite the same as what Dimresh had done to me, but something about the words felt both right and very, very wrong. "Bind your will to mine, like vines, and come to me."

I didn't want it to work. But the dog's heart slowing told me it had.

My stomach turned as the dog left its hiding place and trotted toward me. Its eyes still glowed in the faint light from the moon, but its tail no longer wagged. The scent of its illness met my nose, the reek of rot and infection in its fur. It held its head steady, not panting, its breathing slow and deep.

Prey could be controlled. Dimresh had done this to the people he hunted.

I hated it.

"Go away." The dog began to trot away, its legs no longer shaking and its pace even and steady. "Go!" It didn't move any faster.

No. There had to be something I could do. "Run," I tried, and it did, but it showed no sign of the pain it had before. Fur fell in clumps from its body, but it didn't react.

No. What had I done?

I leaped and sank my fangs into it, putting it out of its misery. I should have done that first.

My stomach turned as it died, and for a moment I paused, wondering if I would reject the blood and waste it on the ground. Instead strength filled me, even as I spat out the taste of it, disgust chasing away any remaining pleasant thoughts of Johann.

The further I got from being a thrall, the closer I would come to being like Dimresh. No matter what happened to me, even if I killed Dimresh, I was trapped.

Maybe that was why Lucien had given himself up to the sun.

The thought sent a jolt of fear through me, and that more than anything else chased away the sickness and frustration.

Fear I understood. Fear was what had driven me away from Johann's killing blows that first night, what kept me alive even when in every other way I wasn't.

I wanted to live. And more than that—I wanted Johann to live. I wanted the people in the village to live.

Focusing on that made it easier. Fear was a sign of life, too, one I still had. As long as I could control it, it wasn't so bad. Humans felt fear. I wasn't completely lost.

And clearly, Dimresh could feel it, too, or he wouldn't have sent his thralls and a vampire after me.

Fear aura. That was what made Dimresh so powerful. It would kill humans. I could feel fear, but I could also enter the castle without feeling it.

I was close to figuring something out. Not anything about what I was, but something that would help me kill Dimresh. And more importantly, help Johann and hunters like him.

But the sky was beginning to lighten, and fatigue began to drain my strength, my mind growing fuzzy. I had to get back.

Tension entered my muscles as I neared Matilda's, fear of what Johann would say or think. But that, too, was reassuring. I felt fear. I wasn't completely gone. It was the one thing that linked me to humans, and to Johann.

He waited for me outside the front door, his long hunter's coat rustling when he turned. "There you are."

I skidded to a stop by the front door. "Johann."

"I'm sorry, Kaiden." Johann waved a hand. "Let's talk before it gets light out."

I was afraid I would smell more of his scent, more evidence of his arousal, but the smoky scent of the candles lit inside hid most things. The clock ticked the seconds. It was nearly five in the morning, though I didn't need time to know the sun would come up soon.

"Did you eat?" Johann asked.

"I did. A dog." I licked my lips, though no trace of the blood remained. It hadn't even struggled.

"Let's be honest with each other, Kaiden," Johann said. "But please, let me know if anything gets to be . . . too much for you. I know a lot about thralls, but I know nothing about you." He moved to the couch, the wood creaking when he sat. The way he looked at me was inviting, or maybe it was just my imagination. I stayed by the door.

"I don't want to talk about myself," I said, and Johann's eyes widened. "I don't know anything about myself either," I continued, my jaw tight. "I was alive, and what I remember was pathetic. A useless drunk, like you said once." Johann frowned. "Now, I'm some sort of thrall that can use magic, maybe a vampire or maybe not. I'm a danger." I met his eyes. "And I can guess what you want to know. I want you. I want you badly." My fangs pricked my lower lip. "But I can't have you, in any way, because to have you would mean having your blood. I can't . . ." I swallowed, licking my lips again. "I can't feel pleasure without it."

"I was afraid of that, after seeing you . . ." Johann sighed, the sound reminding me of just how alive he was. "I'm so sorry. I didn't mean to tempt you . . . that way."

"But you want me," I said. The scent from before was unmistakable, the memory of the almost-kiss fresh in my mind. "Why?"

"Why?" Johann laughed. "Kaiden, you're gorgeous. A thrall, yes, but gorgeous. Powerful, a bit dangerous . . . I suppose it's my own weakness. The thrill of hunting is one thing, but the thrill of being with you? An intelligent thrall, one who cares for humans?" Johann threw up his hands. "It clouded my judgment. But don't worry. It won't happen again."

"So . . . you like me because I'm dangerous?"

"You don't become a hunter because you like to avoid taking risks," Johann said. "When I thought you were enjoying yourself, too, the idea was enticing. But if I'm only making you suffer, then it's best not to think about it. Right?"

I took a step farther inside, the heat from the candles warming my skin. "You can just . . . ignore it so easily?"

"Kaiden . . ." Johann leaned back against the couch. "I don't know what to say. Yes, I can resist my urges. I feel desire for you. But the last thing I want is to risk losing you."

"Because you care for me, or because I'm valuable to kill vampires like Lasren or Dimresh?"

Johann leaned forward, his eyes sparking in the flickering candlelight. "Both."

My mouth watered, my body flaring with lust, and I curled my upper lip.

"What's wrong, Kaiden?" Johann leaned back. "Like I said, if it's better not to think about it . . ."

"I don't know," I growled. "You're a fool for admitting that and making me think I have a chance."

"I'm a fool for caring for you?"

"Yes!" I whirled, but he didn't flinch. "I could kill you! I could control you with magic, like I did the dog I fed on. I *want* to." His heart picked up, but again he didn't move, staring at me with those smoldering brown eyes. "I want to drink your blood while I fuck you the way I let men fuck me for drink when I was alive." My fangs dripped saliva onto my chin. "The hunger, the craving . . . it hurts, Johann. It hurts more every day, and everything makes it worse!"

"But you're getting better at controlling it, not worse," Johann said, his voice low. "The reason it hurts is that you care more."

"What?"

Johann stood, and I shrank back against the door. He reached out his hand. "You lost a mother figure. You saw people in the village you used to live in get killed and turned. I haven't been as open and kind to you as I should have. The memories you've told me you have are all bad. And you're worried, not only for yourself but for your village. You may be a thrall, a bloodsucker, but there's real emotion in you, a caring for others beyond what I see in most people, hunters

included. I can't imagine what you're going through. But I can
help you, if you want it. No sex, no desire, until you're ready
to deal with feelings that strong, if you ever are. But I do care
for you, and I want to help you beyond just as a thrall to kill
vampires."

"But why?" I didn't take his hand. "Not like before, why
you want me. Why do you care?"

"You're a man who's lost everything, Kaiden, and yet you
never give up." Johann drew his hand back. "I admire that."

"But I *did* give up." The memory of Dimresh standing over
me in the alley throbbed in my mind like a wound.

"What do you mean?" Johann asked.

"I mean I chose to be bitten," I said. "In the end, when I
was lying in the alley and Dimresh appeared, I chose to die."
The clock ticked on the mantle.

"So he hypnotized you," Johann said. "It's what vampires
do."

"No. It wasn't that, it was . . . I had nothing!"

Johann's eyes widened.

"Or at least . . . I thought I had nothing. Now I've truly lost
everything." I could still taste the dog's blood on my tongue,
and the hunger for Johann still flared in my mind.

"No." Johann held his hand out again, "You made a mistake. It cost you. But you don't have nothing. You have me."

His hand almost glowed in the moonlight, ruddy and pulsing with life. "What if I lose you too?"

"You won't," Johann said. "You have magic, Kaiden.
You're more than just a thrall, and we'll figure out why. And
if you need me to tell you that, then I will, and I'll do it as
many times as you need. I believe in you. I care for you. I'll
help you kill Dimresh, not just for me or the people of
Penthorn, but for you too. To fight for what you've lost. Fair?"

I reached for his hand, the warmth flowing up my arm.
"Fair." I swallowed hard against a mixture of lust and

bloodlust. "But we need to do it soon. The town is running out of time."

"Don't worry," Johann said. "We have the rest of tonight and I have all day. He has to come here to make thralls or vampires, after all. We'll be ready for him."

Chapter Twenty-Eight

M y dreams tormented me that day.

Johann's soft lips, his warmth and closeness, surrounded me in every one of them. And each one of them ended with me sinking my fangs into his neck and ending the dream with a blissful climax that I could never have otherwise. Dreams during the day were worse because I could never truly wake, never find true release, so it only repeated in an endless cycle of longing and searing hunger.

"Kaiden," Johann said, his weak arms pushing me away. I spoke the words I had spoken to the dog, and then he was meek, complacent, baring his pale neck for me as well as his lean, muscular body. Black clouds filled the whiteness of my mind when I took him then, the taste of blood bursting and fading on my tongue.

I woke ravenous, my body aching with an entire day's worth of thwarted desire. I blinked in pitch darkness, surrounded by the scent of earth and the pinprick noises of scuttling insects on the dirt floor of Matilda's basement.

A mouse darted away as I moved, but not quickly enough. Its heart beat so fast I could barely feel it against my thumb. By the time I'd drained it, the rest had fled into the crannies and nooks that led below ground.

Wood creaked, and the voice from my dreams called down. "Kaiden?"

"I'm here." My voice came out throaty with hunger. Something was tossed down, and I tasted it before even looking — pig again, blood rich and thick. Their hearts beat similar to humans, at least.

"We don't have much time," Johann called. "Come up. There are some things I'd have you do."

If I was awake, that meant Dimresh was too. And a vampire could travel from his castle very quickly.

Candles were lit all over the room, and three books lay spread open on the table. Johann was dressed in plain clothes, his hunter's jacket gone. A tight wool shirt hugged broad shoulders, and leather riding pants drew my gaze to his thighs. "Kaiden?" Johann asked.

"I'm listening." I shifted my gaze to the books instead.

"Your caretaker Matilda had a lot of old prayer books," Johann said.

The pages frayed beneath my touch when I ran a finger over them, and I drew my hand back.

"Gently," Johann said. "They're very old."

Spidery script that I couldn't read decorated every page. "Is this our language?"

Johann laughed. "Yes, but written in an archaic form that scribes and priests used to use. I can teach you one day."

"What does it say?"

"Prayers, Kaiden. Old ones, some of which probably worked and some of which were likely just soothing words. But some, I think, are real, and match the ones we have in the barracks."

"That's great, but . . ." I licked my lips and tore my gaze away from his neck. Focus. I had to focus. Why wasn't he wearing his jacket? He didn't even have his weapons, in case I . . . No, I couldn't lose control. I wouldn't. "The prayers don't work now. The words have to change."

"I know. But at least we have something to start with. The other thing is that Dimresh won't have any easy prey tonight. I told everyone in town to stay inside and stay safe."

I doubted everyone would listen. "So . . ."

"So I'll be the bait," Johann said. "Crossing over the bridge, with you, toward the castle, just like that first night. He ordered his thralls to kill me all those weeks ago, after all. It's strange, isn't it? That a vampire as powerful as he is would bother killing a hunter who doesn't even think he can beat him?"

"And he tried to kill me, a useless thrall," I said. That was odd. I'd never thought of it from Johann's perspective before. He'd talked so much about being powerless against Dimresh. So why had Dimresh bothered sending his thralls against him?

"There are risks," Johann said. "Vampires aren't thralls, and not so easily baited. He may not come after us. But I've hunted lesser vampires before. And you're no slouch in combat, you know. Dimresh is clearly afraid of you."

I swallowed. "I don't know if that will be enough."

"You'll have my weapons," Johann said. "I plan to throw everything I have at him, which should do some damage. And you'll have your magic. Look."

More sheaves of paper lay where he pointed to the small writing table by the couch, and the writing on these was in a blocky, easy-to-read hand. Most began with pleas to Laurel.

I swallowed, the thought of the dog fresh in my mind, its flat stare and lifeless obedience. "Did you write these down yesterday? Where did you find the words?"

"Matilda's bookshelves." Johann picked up one of the papers and then motioned toward a stack of books that had been piled next to the kitchen table. "She had quite a few old prayer books she kept near her bed. A lot of people no longer keep them, or they were lost when the Empire fell. This collection is impressive. She must have been a very kind woman, and still devoted."

"She was. She knew the magic didn't work, but she always thought that the intention mattered more."

"I know you don't necessarily trust your magic. But it

could be useful to look over these. Some of the spells vampires use, the one you used for darkness and the one you told me Dimresh used, sound like altered versions of old prayers. The more you know of how magic used to work, the more you may be able to learn what you can do now." Johann held up the stack of papers, a small smile on his face.

He had said altered. He meant twisted. *Dark.* But he wasn't wrong. I took the papers, the smell of ink still fresh.

Laurel, guide us with your searching vines.

Laurel, give us the sun's light.

"Some of them are ones I haven't seen before. Hunters tend to be more concerned with killing vampires than researching magic. I always thought that should change, but survival's more important."

"We're failing, aren't we?" I asked. "Humanity, I mean. We're losing to the vampires, losing more ground."

"I wouldn't say that. The Empire did fall. Vampires have seen to it that no government larger than a village exists. But there's still trade. People still travel, despite the danger. And they can't kill us all. We'll recover. I have faith in that, if not Laurel. Maybe it's just time for humans to move beyond power granted to us by a god. We need to rely on ourselves."

"And kill the vampires," I said. "That's the first step, isn't it?"

"That's right." Johann moved to the door, throwing on his coat. The leather creaked, and bottles of what must be burning herbal water clinked. "Bring those with you and study what you can. You'll be riding in a wagon while I take you across the bridge. By then I hope we can attract Dimresh's attention. The first thing I'll do is set off a flare—don't leave the wagon until I say it's safe."

"And then what?" Fear tightened my throat, even as I predicted his response.

"Then we kill him," Johann said. "It's that or he keeps killing people in the village, and I'm tired of allowing that. Aren't you?"

I nodded.

"You asked me yesterday why I care for you," he said, turning to face me. "What I said before was true. But there's more to it. Seeing you . . . Because hunters like me are too afraid, too . . ." He made a fist. "We gave up. I keep telling you vampires like Dimresh are too powerful to kill, but after a while, it became an excuse. We stopped even trying. And people like you . . . you gave up, too, because of course you would. The world you live in is dying to bloodsuckers."

I clenched my back teeth.

"The hunter's guild was founded two centuries ago to save humanity from the vampires, but even we have gotten too complacent. You saw those like Patrick and Thomas. Afraid of a little thrall." He gave me a wry smile. "But now, with you . . . I never explained this well enough to you. But you give me hope. You resist your bloodlust. You mourn for others." He motioned to the interior of the house, where Matilda had once lived. "And you even care for a poorly skilled hunter like me. You're like an inspiration, a living piece of evidence that things can change."

I didn't know how to respond, his words heavy in my mind. "You're not a bad hunter," I said finally.

He laughed. "We'll see tonight, won't we? I just wanted to tell you all that, Kaiden, before we face what could very well be our death. Seeing you gives me hope. It makes me want to fight even harder. Other people may think I'm crazy, chasing stories and dreams, but at this point, it's all we've got. I'm tired of being afraid and overly cautious, just waiting to see what the vampires will do."

His words warmed me just as his touch would. "Let's go, then," I said, and my fangs probably showed when I smiled. But Johann smiled back anyway.

The wagon wasn't the same one I'd seen that first night. It was smaller, and the place where I lay, reeking of spoiled grain, was a tight fit. But it wouldn't let in the light of the flares Johann planned to set off.

I read the spells he'd written out for me by the light of a tiny oil lamp, the flame giving just enough illumination for my excellent night vision. The words still seemed to flicker and jump as the wagon bumped along the dirt road that led to the bridge. As long as there was wood between me and the running water, I would be safe, but I still tensed as the sound of rushing water came closer.

Johann wouldn't do that to me, not now. He needed me. More than that — he cared for me.

The words in front of me faded in my vision as I thought of Johann's words and shuffled the papers in my hands. I was hope. I was an inspiration.

All I remembered of myself was as a drunk in an alley, someone who'd thrown his life away. I lived now only because of fear of losing what little I had. Johann had given me everything I had now. He needed to give himself more credit. If we survived this, and I really did become a vampire lord, I wanted to learn more about him.

Laurel, bind us to you, once twice thrice, for protection from harm. The familiar-sounding words jumped out at me as I shuffled the papers. That was Dimresh's binding spell, or what it had used to be. A spell of protection, twisted into a spell of control.

Every spell — or prayer, I supposed — that Johann had written down was for things that would benefit people, selfless incantations calling for protection or light or guidance for love. Reading them like this made me feel strange, something inside me both intrigued and disgusted, like viewing a dying insect. I mouthed the words to one prayer, a call for guidance to find someone to love, and as I did I changed the words, an incantation for *let the one I want burn with . . .*

I stopped talking before I could finish the spell, knowledge of what it would do making me dig my nails into the wooden seat of the wagon. If I wanted, I could make Johann want me. I wanted to, selfishly, but not like that.

My twisting of the magic would work, I knew, but only for my own base desires. Intention was what mattered, but the intention for magic now was only for my most selfish thoughts.

Bind his will to mine. Make him burn with lust for me. It was all about control.

What had happened to the magic? Why did it work this way, and only for vampires and thralls like me?

Why was I like this, and why could I use it at all?

A bang from outside interrupted my thoughts, and dread made me drop the papers. Most of them hit me in the face as they fell in the tight space. Another bang from above the wagon, and then the click of a stakeshooter being set.

"Come and get me, vampire," Johann said. The scent of his blood filled my nose, and my mouth watered. He had warned me he would do this. I froze, willing myself not to move. I doubted Dimresh would take the bait.

Then glass broke, and I screwed my eyes shut even though I knew I was safe. Johann had set off the flare.

CHAPTER TWENTY-NINE

I remembered the searing light that solar flare had created, and the aborted shrieks of the other thralls that first night as it had killed them. This time, there was only silence.

Another shatter of glass, and the soft rush like raindrops as the shards hit the wooden bridge. He'd brought three flares, and that was number two.

"Fool hunter." Dimresh's voice wound even through the wooden wagon. "You *will* serve me."

My fingernails scored my palms, my jaw tight. I would *never* let that happen.

Johann clearly wouldn't either. A stakeshooter twanged, and more water hit the ground, along with glass. The last flare, as well as what must have been herb-treated water.

All he had to do was give the word, and I could leave my safe haven.

When Dimresh snarled, the sound shot fear through me. Johann shouted back, unintelligible words full of anger. The wagon jolted. My head banged against the wood, stars flickered in my vision, and the world tilted for a moment. The horse squealed. The scent of fresh dirt from churning hooves filled the space before it was replaced with the scent of fresh animal blood.

"What other surprises do you have in there, hunter?" Dimresh said, his voice smooth and close and no longer edged with a growl. "You stand no chance."

"Laurel curse you!" Johann shouted. "Laurel, by the light of the sun in your leaves, purify the darkness!"

Dimresh laughed aloud. But that was the signal.

Another stakeshooter twanged from outside as I grabbed the only other thing Johann had put in the wagon with me — a long wooden stake, the edge I grabbed laced with metal to protect me from stray splinters. I hit a latch on the inside of the wagon and dropped to the dirt ground. Blood from the slain horse trickled past my feet.

As soon as my feet touched the ground, I leaped at my once-master, the stake hefted the way Johann had taught me — supported in one hand and the power driven by my shoulder, the sharp point aimed for Dimresh's heart.

My once-master loomed in my vision, his blond hair tied back with blue ribbon and his eyes pale. A silken piece of clothing around his neck, some sort of fashion I didn't know the name of, jutted from the front of his silk shirt. I had seen it before, spotted with blood.

His eyes narrowed, and in the instant before I struck, he vanished into mist. I didn't even have time to adjust my aim or prepare to land on the ground before he re-formed behind me and grabbed my ankle. He plucked me out of the air and turned my momentum into a headlong crash into the nearest tree.

Shock drove the strength from my limbs. The stake in my hand cracked in two. My ears rang, bone crunching when I opened my mouth. I took a few moments to heal.

"There you are," my master said, and blue eyes met mine. Then he vanished again as another stakeshooter bolt flew past him and into another tree.

"Get up, Kaiden!" Johann said. "Move!" He aimed the weapon at me, the point of the small stake centered in my vision.

I jumped up and away, toward the trees. Dimresh formed behind me, a blink before he vanished again, Johann's stakeshot once again whistling harmlessly through air.

I hid behind the trunk of a tree, leaves tickling my face. It was foolish, hiding in the darkness from a vampire more powerful than myself, but I didn't know what else to do. Dimresh could turn to mist. He needed to be taken by surprise, just as the hunters had taken the vampire in the courtyard by surprise when I'd distracted him, but there were only two of us, and the plan we'd made hadn't worked.

Johann stood, human and slow, his stakeshooter in his right hand and another stake in his left. "Come out, vampire!" he called.

"He thinks highly of himself, doesn't he?" Dimresh said from behind me. I whirled, but too slowly, and strong hands grabbed my shoulders, pinning me in place and squeezing so hard bones cracked.

He leaped, carrying me, and Johann whirled and fired. Dimresh misted into nothingness again and the bolt caught me in the chest, dull pain sending me to the ground.

"Kaiden!" Johann called, his voice full of horror.

"That's one fool down," Dimresh said, and appeared behind Johann. "Thanks for the help, hunter. You made it too easy. I should have just done this first and not bothered making all those useless thralls."

Dimresh raised a hand. Johann would be too slow, too inaccurate. The pain of the bolt in my chest kept me rooted. A heavy weakness in my arms kept me from pushing myself to my feet.

The papers. The magic. It was all I had. The words would be wrong, the incantations swirling together in my mind, but it was the intention that truly mattered, wasn't it?

"By my blood, bind him to the earth!" I shouted, fighting through pain to touch the stakeshooter bolt jutting from my shoulder, drops of blood smearing my fingers. "Bind him in place so he can't escape!"

Dimresh's blue eyes met mine, going wide. Johann turned,

firing the stakeshooter.

This time Dimresh didn't turn to mist. I could see the realization in his eyes when his trick failed, and the indecision as he tried to leap away instead.

The bolt caught him in the ankle. For the first time I heard my master bellow in pain. His leap took him dozens of feet away, into the trees where he meshed with the dark. And then nothing.

"Kaiden!" Johann ran to my side, warm hands on my shoulders. "I'm sorry." He wrenched the wood from my chest. Blood poured onto the leaves, and pain made me curl up on myself and grit my teeth, bloodlust and weakness warring. I wanted to bite him so badly.

"It's funny," I said with a wheeze. "Thomas was so concerned about me attacking you." I coughed. "And then you shoot me in the middle of the fight."

"It's not over," Johann said. His heart beat hard in my ears. His pulse was pounding in his neck, the artery so obvious. "Focus, Kaiden!" Johann shouted. "He's still out there. Hurry and get up or Dimresh will kill us both!"

He was right. I had to focus. I forced myself up, pushing Johann away when he tried to help. I had to fight. I had to help. I couldn't let pain beat me. I would be a hunter, like Johann.

Johann. So handsome and so delicious.

This was bad.

"That was close, Kaiden," Johann said, peering at my wound. "Only a few inches lower and . . ." He swallowed. "Are you in much pain?"

"I . . . I'll be okay." The wound should heal now that was the bolt was out. I blinked slowly. Hunger sharpened my senses and my mouth watered. I just had to deal with the hunger. I'd done it before — every night.

Then something dark shot from the trees and Johann

gasped and doubled over, the wooden stake he'd been holding shattered. There was no scent of blood, thankfully, but I could see the pain in Johann's eyes, sense the careful way he drew a breath.

Dimresh stood in the clearing, his eyes full of fury. His ankle still bore the stakeshooter bolt, but he was just as fast and deadly as any vampire.

"Your hunter friend is going to die, thrall," he said. "May as well finish him off."

Johann whirled and shot at him again. Pride filled my chest at Johann's strength and determination, fierce glee making me smile when Dimresh skittered away again, wincing as he landed on his injured leg. He didn't look so lordly now.

"Fine, then," Dimresh said, and my amusement faded at the expression on his face. "I'll rip him and you apart like we did when we first fell."

First fell. That was important, it had to be. What did it mean?

But I had no time to think as Dimresh leaped for Johann, fangs bared and clawed fingers outstretched.

Johann turned, but he would be too slow. I might be too slow. But I had to try. Not even to kill Dimresh, but to protect Johann. That was what truly mattered.

Dirt bunched under my foot as I moved in front of Johann. Dimresh slammed into me with more force than anything I'd ever felt, either living or undead. My head snapped back and forth from the impact, and blood welled from gouges Dimresh ripped in my chest.

I snarled, baring my fangs, and snapped at Dimresh through the haze of agony and shock. Fine silks tore in my grabbing hands. Scraps littered the forest floor when he jumped away.

"Afraid of a thrall, vampire?" Johann called. "Why don't you come at me again, and feel his fangs next time!"

His words helped calm the whirling confusion in my mind. Dimresh was afraid of me. He didn't want to fight me head-on. Thralls fought with no concern for their well-being, but Dimresh wasn't a thrall. He didn't want to get hurt.

He really was afraid of me. That meant I had a chance.

I growled, the sound low and feral, and even Johann's heart picked up. Darkness filled the spaces between the trunks and branches of the trees, and the milky glow of the half moon was weak. "Come out," I called. "Or I'll . . ." I didn't know what would anger him, what would make him desperate, so I guessed. "By my blood, I . . ."

I didn't know what I would say, but it didn't matter. The threat of magic was enough. Dimresh came at me like a blur of darkness, the reflection of moonlight in his eyes the only thing I saw.

I didn't have a weapon, but I had Johann's training. This time I caught the attack, letting Dimresh whiz past me faster than I could ever hope to move, and I kicked out when he landed. My foot hit his shoulder, and might as well have hit a metal forgestone for all the good it did. My leg shook with weakness.

I turned the moment back and slashed forward with fingernails, hoping to grab him. He couldn't mist again. If I could just get my fangs in his neck, I could win. I could become a vampire lord.

Instead he grabbed my wrists, jolting my body and sending pain and weakness radiating from where the stakeshooter bolt had been in my chest. "Idiot thrall," he snarled.

A stakeshooter twanged behind me, and Dimresh ducked out of the way, impossibly fast. His mouth formed a rictus when he grinned, his fangs digging into his own lip the way mine did when I was close to losing control of my hunger.

But Dimresh was always in control. "By my blood," he said, and then it was my turn to leap at him, to stop whatever spell he would use.

My legs buckled, just enough for my attack to fall short. He jumped, his strength taking him into the trees. "Let all who come close to me be stricken with thorns of fear."

I froze, a rush going through my body and then past me, as if I had jumped forward without moving. Dimresh stood in the tree, his gaze fixed. Not on me. On Johann.

Johann's heart began to pound. The scent of fear-sweat filled the air, a rush of acrid adrenaline. His eyes were wide, the whites paler than the moon, and he fell, his heart going faster and faster. Harsh, wheezy, short rasps were all I heard of his breathing.

Fear aura.

The stories Johann had told me flashed in my mind as fast as his heart now pounded. A man dead in a boat, having gotten too close. The magic that prevented any human from getting close. Terror powerful enough to kill.

Johann's heart beat faster than a bird's, and then began to sputter and jolt, a disorganized chaotic rhythm. His weapon fell from his hand.

"No!" I shouted.

Dimresh laughed.

"Johann, fight it!"

His eyes fell shut, the blood in his body slowing. My mouth watered, and I spat against a mixture of hunger and sickness. He was dying. I couldn't do anything.

"Easy prey, Kaiden," Dimresh said. "Run."

He would kill me when I turned my back . . . and if he followed me, Johann would die. We'd never had a chance, and now Johann would die, and me with him. My fangs scored my lower lip, my weakened legs and arms shaking with frustration. I couldn't beat fear. Any second, Johann's heart would give out. I'd heard the pattern before in animals overcome with fright, deer and rabbits falling victim to their instinct.

Like the dog by the ruined house, its heart weak and sputtering. The one I had controlled.

My stomach turned as I spoke the words. "By my blood, bind your will to mine," I said.

Dimresh's eyes narrowed, the glow becoming two slits.

"Johann, don't be afraid."

His heart slowed, the pattern resuming its normal cadence. And then Dimresh leaped for me.

"Johann, shoot him!" I shouted. Faster than a blink, faster than a human who had seconds ago barely been able to breathe, Johann snatched the weapon he'd dropped and aimed for the vampire.

He fired at the same second Dimresh hit me, his long fingernails digging into my chest. Blood sprayed his fine silk shirt and scarf, both mine and his from the stakeshooter bolt that slammed into his side.

He screamed. His grip on me weakened, and I grabbed his arms in mine, forcing his fingernails from the gouges they'd left in my chest. I snapped my fangs down toward his neck.

He twisted faster and wrenched away, limping, his face pale. Blue eyes met mine, full of hatred and fear.

I tensed, preparing to leap again, my muscles quaking and my fangs bared.

Dimresh, my once master, turned and fled.

Weakness overtook me, and I sank to the ground.

CHAPTER THIRTY

I needed blood so badly.

My head hung, the leaves and dirt I sat on all that filled my vision. The raspy sound of insects in the trees filled the silence now that my master was gone.

"Johann," I said.

"Yes?" His voice was emotionless, alive but somehow dead. His heart beat a steady rhythm.

By my blood, bind your will to mine.

"I did it to save you," I said. "You can . . . stop now."

He didn't move, didn't speak. I had bound him to me, like the dog, and I didn't know how to undo it. He stood straight, motionless, but his eyes were empty.

I couldn't find the will to move. All I had to do was command him, and Johann would give me his blood. Saliva dripped down my chin, mixing with the blood from when my fangs had dug into my lip.

"Johann, stop obeying me," I said. I wanted to hear his voice, to hear him laugh or wince in pain. To tell me the fight wasn't over, that Dimresh was in his castle and weak and I should go and finish him off. But he didn't.

"I am bound to you," he said.

"Stop it!" I shouted. My stomach twisted with hunger, and my legs and arms shook. "By my blood . . . be yourself again! Sever the bindings!"

Magic was about intent. He should be free of it, free of me.

Johann tilted his head as if considering it. "I cannot."

Some magic can't be undone. The books were very clear about that.

No. "Johann, please," I said. "Be yourself! Obey only your-self!"

"I am bound to you."

I wanted to run, or maybe attack. Instinct shrieked at me that something was wrong, my weakened muscles tense.

"I've killed you," I said. I had put the dog out of its misery. The thought made me hungry, and I hated it, hated every bit of myself and what I'd done. "Please, stop."

"Tell me what to stop doing and I will stop it."

"No!" My shout silenced the insects in the trees for a moment. "Johann, please . . . ignore my will."

"I cannot."

Some magic can't be undone.

No. I needed help, needed Johann. "Laurel," I said, turning to prayer, and then shut my mouth. Laurel was long gone. "Johann, tell me what to do!" I shouted. "Tell me how to help you!"

"Command me," Johann said. "My will is yours." His eyes met mine, their spark gone.

Was this what Dimresh did to his victims? Did they go to him willingly, ask to be bitten and killed?

Was it what Dimresh had done to me?

"Johann," I said. "Would running water help you? Would it remove the spell?" I shouted before he answered. "Go walk into the running water of the river!"

He turned without protest, heading toward the bank where the bridge met the water. Hope gave me strength.

I needed blood, but I wouldn't take his. Not like this. I fought to stay upright, dirt and loam soft beneath my knees. I was so hungry. I needed to hunt. I needed to feed.

I needed Johann.

Splashes came from the river, light then heavy. Any moment I expected Johann's voice, his laugh, his call of my name.

More splashing, then less, the rush of the river unchanging.

"Johann?" I called. No answer. "Johann, come back!"

My body grew heavy when he returned, water dripping from his neck and shoulders, his shirt and coast soaked through. The thick, muddy scent of the river clouded the scent of him, and he seemed even less alive than before.

"Johann, please be yourself. Please . . . please."

"I follow your will."

I couldn't do this. I couldn't keep resisting my hunger and fix this all at once. I didn't want Johann like this, the way I had been as a mindless thrall when I was first turned. No, worse. I was different, unique, a thrall with a mind. A thrall with the powers of a vampire.

Maybe I wasn't a thrall at all. I had powers and had misused them, and I didn't know enough to fix it.

Dimresh might.

All of it came back to him. The vampire who had turned me. If Johann was himself, he would finish the job, not lie on a forest floor growing weaker by the minute.

He had admired me because I never gave up. I wouldn't give up again. And I wouldn't give up on Johann.

I was so close to the end of this. Fight Dimresh. Ask him how to fix Johann, or he would kill me. That was all there was to it.

But first, I needed blood. I only had to deal with the hunger for a little bit longer.

I couldn't think of biting Johann or the temptation would become too strong. I staggered toward the fallen horse, the animal still hitched to the wagon. Each step was torture, and it was made worse by Johann walking beside me, matching his steps to mine. Waiting for instruction.

"Wait," I said, and he stopped. I could still feel his eyes on my back as I sank my fangs into the fallen horse. The blood filled me with energy and lessened the pain in my shoulders and chest.

It didn't chase away the heavy despair that had settled in the back of my mind. I had a plan. But I wanted Johann, the man who'd given me a second chance, and I couldn't shake the fear that I might have lost him forever.

I didn't know what I would do if I couldn't save him.

I was sure that none of Johann's, or any hunter's, plans for sneaking into a vampire's castle had ever gone like this.

The sight of the castle was familiar, more familiar than the village I'd spent my life in. The old black stone of the first wall, slimy with mold. The ruined, rusted gate that led through it. And the looming main keep flanked by two long stone wings that were the hallways and small rooms we thralls had lived in. The keep itself listed to the side, old wood that had once supported the stone rotted through. The door that led to the hallway I had once lived in was still broken from my fight with the thrall, but the body was gone. Only broken grass and traces of fur marked where a wolf must have come for an easy meal.

Johann followed, both noisy in his living—his breathing, his heartbeat, his heavy steps—and silent in a way that made me dread what would happen to him even if I succeeded.

But his steps were steady and his heartbeat sure. His will was mine, not Dimresh's, and he wouldn't be afraid of whatever magic Dimresh had put up around the castle. He was my weapon.

Johann had wanted to kill Dimresh, to kill vampires like the one that had killed his family. I could make sure he did it. Or if he couldn't, I could.

I tested the weight of the long wooden stake I held, taken from the wagon, and made sure the stakeshooter in my hand was loaded. I was not as fast at reloading as Johann was, but one shot might make a difference.

"Do you have your weapons?" I asked.

229

"Yes."

I wished his voice carried the tone I was used to, or that he used my name the way he always did. I hadn't realized how soothing it was. "Be prepared," I said. "He may have made more thralls." I doubted it, but Dimresh could accomplish things faster than I thought possible. It had taken two of us to weaken him. Now . . .

I didn't know. I didn't know if I could do this, and I paused outside the gate, staring at the splintered wood. I was alone, just like before.

I shoved down my feelings, swallowing against a surge of heaviness that had nothing to do with lack of blood. I didn't have time to feel. I had to kill Dimresh and understand how magic worked and fix Johann. I could be a vampire lord and do things I hadn't dreamed of. From there I could fix things. I had to believe that.

"It will be dark," I said. "Follow me." I wished he would respond.

The walls of the castle began to surround me. My steps were silent, but Johann's feet created a heavy tread that sent mice and roaches scurrying down the dirty, dusty stone.

I had spent so many nights here, two months of being turned, traveling through these halls either on my way out to hunt or on my way back. The sounds from the main keep often echoed in the halls, mixing with the growls and curses of the other thralls. We passed the stairs that would lead down into the dungeons, the small room where I'd slept likely empty and dusty now.

"Johann." My voice sounded dull against the stone. "What was this castle like before? During the Empire?"

"I don't know," Johann said. I expected him to say more, to offer a story, but he didn't.

I gritted my teeth and hurried onward. I couldn't take this silence, my having failed Johann even if I succeeded. There had to be a way.

Memories of my life as a thrall flickered strongly in my mind as I walked down the corridor, everything forming into one long blur of stone hallways, snarling thralls, and constant hunger.

Ragged carpeting began to decorate the floor as I neared the main keep of Dimresh's castle. I turned down one more hallway and paused by the intact wood and iron enameled doors that would lead to Dimresh's quarters. My memories ended here. I had never been inside.

But now I was no servant. I would kill him and take his quarters for my own. I gripped the wooden stake I held more tightly. I could do this.

"Johann," I said. "Please, don't be my servant."

"I cannot."

"Then help me kill the vampire. Be fast and strong, but above all, *do not die.* Understand?"

"Yes."

I shoved the door open.

Color met my vision. Firelight glowed over red and gold carpets that decorated the floor, and shredded tapestries hung from the rafters, dividing the room. Wooden pillars jutted from four corners, supporting the structure, and stairs wound up to a second level between two of them. Beams crisscrossed the stair, low enough that most men would have to duck going up them. More wooden beams crossed the room, thick ones that likely provided support and also blocked access unless we walked one path. The room smelled mostly of wood, with a hint of rot that spoke of age, and beneath it all was the unmistakable scent of human blood. My mouth watered.

Johann moved ahead of me, pushing past a shredded tapestry. Fibers clung to his shoulders before swinging back into place.

Rusted weapons hung from struts in the wall. Some had

fallen, ax heads and spear tips tarnished and useless. Some blades were so old they looked like rocks. Or maybe they'd just been poorly forged. Johann kept walking, ignoring the weapons, following the only path he could since the beams of the structure blocked every other way. This would lead to the stairs.

Dimresh hadn't built this castle, but whoever did had defense in mind. But I wasn't human, and I didn't have to follow it.

"Johann, stop," I said. He froze in place.

We were walking into something that had been built to be a trap. I was sure of it. "This way," I said. "Climb over the beams and past the fabrics."

Johann obeyed me. I didn't know if he was naturally a good climber or not. He found handholds on the beams, raising his body up with no effort at all. His heart didn't even pick up as he swung himself toward the staircase, bypassing a ten-foot wall between sections of the keep.

I hoped he was still alive in some way. The way he moved . . .

No. I had to focus, I had to believe I could help. I followed him, taking the path he'd climbed through in two jumps.

I was greeted with soft carpeting, pillows strewn over the floor, and dilapidated wooden shelves. Dust filled the empty spaces where books must have rested.

I swallowed down sudden fear. Just because the shelves were empty . . . there had to be some way to save Johann. I didn't need books, especially not some old book written in spidery script I could barely read. This keep hadn't been a place for priests anyway, at least not judging by the weapons racks we'd passed.

Something growled behind us. Johann, wordless and emotionless, whirled and pulled the trigger on his stakeshooter. I crouched and growled an answering warning as the shot struck the thrall in the chest. It hit the ground and didn't get up. Her hair was long and blond, but facedown I couldn't recognize who she'd been. Someone from my town, I was sure.

Under my control, Johann was just as effective at his job. Maybe more. I didn't know whether to be proud or horrified.

"I didn't think that would make a difference," Dimresh said, his voice carrying from above. I whirled, facing the stairs. "Come up, thrall. Kaiden. Let's talk."

CHAPTER THIRTY-ONE

My upper lip curled. How dare Dimresh use my name? Johann started toward the stairs. I grabbed his arm, his warmth and closeness helping me resist the growl that threatened to leave my throat. I had to believe he was there, somewhere, and if I did something stupid, I would lose my chance to help him.

"I have nothing to say to you," I called up to Dimresh, thinking of Matilda as she lay bleeding on the floor, a "gift" from Dimresh. "I'm not your thrall. You can't offer me anything I want."

"I wouldn't be so sure of that." I whirled, Dimresh's voice now behind me. He'd come down another way onto the level where Johann and I were, and stood nestled between two crossing beams, his arms across his chest. There was no sign of the injuries he'd sustained before, his silk clothing and pale skin unblemished.

This time I did growl, my muscles tensing, but I stayed in place. My fingernails dug into the soft wood of the stake I still held.

"I see you're struggling still," Dimresh said, his voice sonorous. "You have a human hypnotized, and you haven't even bitten him. You have magic like a vampire lord, but still crave blood like a thrall. You have no idea what you're doing, do you?"

I ground my back teeth together, my fangs pinching my gums. "What do you want?" I snapped. "You've tried to kill me and failed, so now you want to make a deal?"

"I won't lie. I'd rather have you dead. But unlike thralls, I have no desire to fight and risk myself when I can give you what you want and we can both go our separate ways. How does that sound?"

"How do you know what I want?"

"Do you know how vampires make other vampires?" Dimresh said instead.

I curled my hand into a fist. "They bite them and . . . let the person drink their blood before they become a thrall," I said. That's what Johann had said, wasn't it?

Johann stood motionless, waiting for orders. If he knew, or still remembered, he gave no sign.

I had hypnotized him, Dimresh had said. How did I undo it?

"Not exactly," Dimresh said. He waved a hand as if he held a fan. "It's a bit more complicated. You are right that it involves blood, but not by drinking it. You bit me, after all, when I tried to offer you that woman, and yet you are still . . . whatever you are." His eyes flashed with anger. "Drinking blood is not the same as sharing it. You bite your target, and then you must share your blood."

I narrowed my eyes.

"You bleed into their wound, sharing the gift true vampires have."

The gift true vampires have. "Your blood?"

"Yes." He stared down his nose at me, and I had a flash of another man staring down at me as I lay on the ground. I knew well that look of judgment. "The blood weakens the hunger and bestows you with magic."

"But . . . I have magic. Why are you telling me this?" I could tell he was seeing how I would react, waiting for me to get it, but it wasn't coming together. "Just tell me what you mean!"

He sighed. "I will share my blood with you. That will ease your hunger. You will be a true vampire, not this . . . half thrall that you are." He made a shooing motion at me. "Then you will leave here. You will give me Penthorn and go off and make your own territory, make your own thralls."

I gripped my stake tighter. "You expect me to agree just to that?" My muscles tensed, and I licked my lips, my fangs sharp against my tongue. "What about . . ." I almost said "Johann," but stopped myself. That was a weakness Dimresh could exploit. " . . . learning magic?" I said instead.

The tips of his fangs flashed in a brief smile. "Already want more, do you? You should consider yourself lucky I don't kill you."

"Maybe *you* should consider yourself lucky I don't kill *you*," I growled. "Why should I listen to this? You'd only make this deal if you thought you had something to gain." I took a step forward, but he didn't flinch. "Are you afraid of me? Of Johann?"

"Are you turning me down?" Dimresh said, his voice cold. "Choose wisely, thrall. This is your last chance, and then I'm done being generous."

Generous. As though sending me off with nothing was generous. With Johann still mindless because of my own ignorance. He stood motionless, as lifeless as the weapons he wore.

"Why did you hypnotize him?" Dimresh asked, and I snapped my gaze away. "You clearly haven't fed on him, or you wouldn't be speaking now." He tilted his head, and I saw another flash of fang. "If you agree to my terms, I could teach you one more thing. How to use your will to bind others, or unbind them, the way you wish it. That work is . . . sloppy."

"You would teach me that?" I said. "I could . . . let Johann go?"

"If that is what you wish," Dimresh said. "Would you find that fair? I turn you into a full vampire. I teach you how the hypnosis spells are supposed to work. You leave here, taking your . . . friend with you. I never see you again."

That was what I wanted. Johann would be free. I would be free of hunger, able to enjoy something other than the burst of blood on my tongue. My future shone ahead of me, something I chose, another opportunity. Fantasies of being with Johann swept through my mind in a flash of lust that burned out like ash as soon as it began. But if I made this choice . . .

"I'll . . . I'll do it," I said. "How is it done?"

"Very simple," Dimresh said. "First, drop that stake, please. And that wooden shooting contraption."

I let the stake fall, the wood landing softly on the carpet. The stakeshooter I laid down. Dimresh then leaped, landing on his feet more lightly than a cat. He stepped over the fallen body of the thrall Johann had shot. "You must cut yourself, or I can do it if you're not prepared. Then I will bleed into your wound."

So simple. Almost too simple.

"You will enjoy being a vampire," Dimresh said, his voice deep and inviting. "Oh, you'll still have those weaknesses to wood and to flame, and to the sun. But the hunger will be weaker. Your power will be greater. And minor things like the fangs of animals and metal weapons won't touch you." He drew closer, stepping past Johann. I swallowed down unease when he kicked the stake away. When he kicked the stakeshooter, wood snapped against the stone wall. "You're making the right choice." He stopped in front of me, blocking my view of Johann. "You can take a castle of your own. I can even teach you the fear spell, to keep out anyone you don't want. Something no bastard would ever dream of."

He might be using magic on me. I wasn't sure, and I was likely immune anyway. But it sounded so nice.

He raised his hand, his nails shining like diamonds. I raised my own, and a sharp nail razed a line across the meat of my arm. The pain was slight, the cut thin.

"Hold still." Dimresh raised his hand, beginning to close it so that his nails would drive into his palm. The blood would drip into my wound.

I glanced up at Dimresh, his blond hair and blue eyes, his fine silks. He was beautiful, just like that first night. A vision standing in an alley, just like he stood now in the narrow hallway.

Dimresh drove his nails into his palm. He didn't flinch.

I had wasted my life in Penthorn, and then I'd turned my back on it.

Blood appeared on his palm.

Magic is about intent, Matilda had said. *Laurel may not be real, but she once was, and her kindness lives on, I'm sure.*

The blood ran into the creases on his palms.

I would be a vampire lord. Something no bastard would ever dream of, Dimresh had said. Was I a bastard? I had never known my father. Many people didn't. My mother had died young, I her only child.

Why had he called me that?

The blood began to pool, sticky and black in the low light.

Dimresh stared down at me, just as he had before. I'd made a choice then too.

You never give up, Kaiden, Johann had said. *I admire that.* He still stood motionless behind Dimresh. Brown eyes met mine, and a jolt went through me.

The blood beaded into a drop, ready to fall.

Would he admire this? Would Matilda? Would Johann choose freedom over leaving Penthorn to a vampire? He was a hunter. He would have died fighting.

Dimresh gripped his fist tighter, the blood nearly falling.

I didn't want to die. I didn't want to lose Johann. But I didn't want this either.

The drop fell, and I pulled my arm back, instead leaping for Dimresh's throat.

His lips turned up in a snarl, and long nails raked my face. My fangs snapped on air.

"Mistake, thrall," he said, and any trace of kindness or softness in his voice was gone. So was he, a mist dissipating and floating up the stairs. He had gotten rid of the effects of my spell somehow, probably when he'd fed on the thrall Johann had killed.

"Johann," I said, my face stinging from the pain of Dimresh's nails. "Kill the vampire!"

Johann turned, his face still expressionless but his body as fast and as efficient as a cat closing in for the kill. He gripped his stakeshooter in one hand and pulled a short stake from one of his long coat pockets with the other before turning and running up the stairs.

Watching him, the man I admired more than he could ever admire a thing like me, made my fear fade. No matter what happened, I wouldn't let him die. Not like this. If I died fighting Dimresh, defending Penthorn . . . then at least Johann would be free.

Dimresh didn't want to fight me because he was afraid of losing his status, his rule of Penthorn, his castle and his power. Thralls were vicious and fierce because they had no fear, nothing to lose. What I had to lose . . . I wasn't a mindless thrall. But I would lose far more, become something worse, if I didn't fight with everything I had.

A sound began to hiss against the side of the wooden room, a susurrus of pattering. Rain. The noise hid the creaking of the wood as I darted past Johann, moving on instinct, letting my ever-present hunger drive me onward.

The second floor was plush and inviting, carpets and tapestries lending warmth and softness. Books lined wooden shelves, and the scent of something heady and smoky replaced the familiar scents of dust and rot.

I clawed at tapestries that blocked my way, revealing an entrance to a bedroom where more tapestries surrounded the softest, most lavish mattress I had ever seen lying on the floor, each blanket made of silk and laid one atop the other so that they made a rainbow of luxuriousness. A chimney stood next to it, cold and filled with gray ash that had the same scent as the rest of the room.

Johann caught up to me, his body tense, either searching for Dimresh or waiting for more orders.

"By my blood, bring us light and the choking smoke to kill our enemies," Dimresh's voice intoned.

The fireplace ignited, the strange scent growing stronger. I didn't need to breathe. But Johann did, and almost immediately his breathing brought heavy coughing.

I snarled, growling. "By my blood, bring us darkness to protect us from the burning light!" I snapped. It had worked before.

The light in the fireplace winked out, as did fires that had once burned in sconces by the stairs. I whirled in the direction I'd heard the voice, straining to see through the pitch darkness. I would kill him. I *had* to.

Johann's coughing eased, but not completely. His breath came in wheezing gasps.

Johann had brought me here, and all I'd done was seen him be hurt and abused. He was just human, and the risk was too high. I was tired of seeing him in pain, even in the horrible state I'd put him in.

"Follow me," I snapped at him, trying to keep the edge from my voice. "Keep yourself safe."

This was my fight now.

I couldn't see. But there had plenty of moonless nights where I'd tracked prey just as wily as I was. Cats, cougars, wolves, all had fallen to my fangs.

My eyes narrowed. Dimresh would too. He was no master, no powerful vampire. My hand tightened around the stake in my hand.

He was just prey.

CHAPTER THIRTY-TWO

M y feet made no sound on the carpeted floor. The wooden grains of the stake sent tiny pinpricks of pain into my hand.

My fangs lengthened, my lips wet with saliva borne of anger and hunger and focus. Darkness enveloped me, and the sound of Johann's raspy breathing became the only thing I could hear.

Soft fabric touched my face and brushed over my shoulders and head. I tore at it with my fingernails. What must be a hanging tapestry fell to the floor with a soft thump and the stench of dust. With no light, I had to navigate the way I did in the woods on nights with no moon, using my knowledge of the forest and the scent of trees. Of course, I had no idea of the twists and turns of the room, or where there might be nooks and crannies for Dimresh to hide in. My body felt heavy, caution keeping me from leaping forward.

Dimresh, like me, was dead. The only scent of life in this place was Johann, his piney, pleasant scent still in my nostrils. There was no way for me to track Dimresh, not by scent, light, or sound.

Hunting a hunter meant predicting what it would do. He thought of me as prey, and Johann was prey. Johann was an easier target, but if his breathing changed, I would know immediately where Dimresh was.

He would attack me; I was sure of it. He would wait until I stepped somewhere where I could be taken down easily. I stopped moving, straining to hear anything.

Johann's breathing mingled with the creaking of old wood from a light wind outside and the scritches of what must be mice beneath the floorboards. I'd never find Dimresh this way, and would only fall into a trap in a castle I knew nothing about.

"Johann," I commanded. "Shoot to your left." The string twanged, a bolt hitting wood with a thud.

"To your right." I was likely just wasting ammunition. But it was better than waiting.

"Shoot until you hit him!" I snarled. The string kept twanging, bolts of wood hitting and bouncing off the ceiling and beams. Five, six, then seven times, and still no sign of Dimresh.

I gritted my teeth. "By my blood, let your bolt hit my enemy!" I snapped. The stakeshooter clicked.

A rush of air shot past my face, and Johann gasped.

I leaped in pure darkness onto the form that had grabbed him. I was met with slashing claws, Dimresh's long fingernails, and a blow to the gut that made my stomach turn.

I didn't let go. Not now. Not when I had him.

My own fingernails tore through silk fabric and dug into skin that was somehow tougher than boar hide. A snarl rang in my ears. The form beneath me twisted and lashed out. Pain exploded in my shoulder as fangs as sharp as needles dug into it. Lights flashed in my eyes even as I returned the bite, tearing at a flap of skin that must be an ear.

Dimresh bellowed and turned to mist, my teeth slamming shut on each other.

No. "Johann, throw the herbal water!" I shouted. I had no idea if it would work.

A lid popped, and a splash of water hit my chest, wetting my shirt and sending more burning weakness into my body, worse than any bite from Dimresh.

Something thudded, and a hissing voice chilled me. "I will

kill you both, old blood or not," Dimresh said.

I had no time to think about what his words meant. I struck at the source of the voice.

Dimresh did too, fingernails that were more like claws raking toward me even as I stabbed with my stake. It hit wood, and then snapped in two. I overbalanced, and as I fell, Dimresh's fangs sank into my neck.

Pain and weakness made me cry out. I reversed the stake in my hand and stabbed upward, into Dimresh's back.

His bite stopped, his scream making my head throb with agony.

But then he twisted again. I had missed his heart.

Claws raked at my face. A hand like iron grabbed my wrist, wrenching me first into the air and then onto the floor, threatening to break my arm. Then I was hoisted up again, as though Dimresh was above me.

I scratched and kicked out, but my struggles met only air. Somehow, even in this darkness, Dimresh could see and I couldn't, because he avoided everything I did — every snap and kick and struggle. Another hand grabbed mine. I snapped at where Dimresh must be, *had* to be if he was holding both of my wrists, but my fangs clacked only against my own teeth. I growled, but it faded into a whine as Dimresh squeezed my wrists, the bones grinding together. Pain made my head swim. Maybe he was behind me . . . or maybe he was in front. I couldn't tell. All I could hear was Johann's breathing, and my own skin tearing beneath Dimresh's fingernails. I kicked behind me — my foot hit nothing. In return, Dimresh twisted my wrist, snapping it.

Then Dimresh shrieked again, hissing in agony. Another bottle popped. The sound made the pain clear.

Johann was still throwing the herbal water. And Dimresh's shriek was above me.

His hold on my wrists slackened and I fell, my wrists

sliding out of his grip. All I wanted to do was sink to the ground, take Johann's blood, and recover. Instead, I jumped up toward the sound of the hissing, steaming herbal water on skin, where Dimresh must be hiding in the rafters.

This time, I wouldn't miss. And this time, I used a weapon I was familiar with, one I had honed every night since being turned.

My leap took me up into more darkness, my hands finding purchase on wooden beams. I swiveled my head toward the sound of boiling vampire skin.

I lunged, and this time I sank my fangs through silk and fabric into Dimresh's neck.

The taste of his blood filled my mouth. Copper and richness, tinged with the faint scent of something else, like the sweet whiff of something putrefying nearby.

I drank. I ignored the hissing of the herbal water on Dimresh's skin, his sudden, frantic slashes at my chest and the back of my head. Another bottle of water shattered. More of the burning water hit both me and Dimresh, but Dimresh's blood healed me even as the water singed.

His clawing grew weaker, the pumping of blood into my mouth slowing. "I should have killed you when you first disobeyed me," he whispered.

I bit harder, but I couldn't cut off his voice. "You still don't know what you are," he said. "I could tell you."

The last words of a dying man. No, a vampire. He'd lied to me again and again. I wouldn't be tricked.

Another bottle shattered, and he hissed in pain. I kept drinking. My hunger was gone, but soon, he would be too.

"You're making a mistake," he said. "If you care about humans, doing this . . ." He shivered, and my teeth ripped at dry skin. "Thralls can drink animal blood. Vampires can't." The words came out as a whisper. "You will *need* human blood. You will . . ."

He was lying. He had to be.

"The curse will kill you like the rest," he said. He spoke so faintly no one but a thrall could have heard him. "You're making a mistake. Kill me and you'll never know what you are. What we are. You're making . . . a mistake."

The last bit of blood flecked my lips. I wasn't hungry enough to lick it off.

I waited for one last gasp from him, one last word. More lies.

But there was nothing.

I blinked and saw him, faint in darkness that suddenly wasn't as pitch dark as I had thought. Dimresh lay still, as desiccated and dead as any deer or boar or wolf I'd ever fed from.

I leaned back on the rafters, staring. The faintest bit of moonlight streamed in from a tiny crack in the molded wood and stone of the castle. I hadn't been able to see it before.

I curled my hand around the wood of another beam, and it shattered, dangerous splinters raining to the floor. I winced at the noise.

I was stronger. I could see better. And I wasn't hungry.

But I didn't remember anything more than I had before. I had become a vampire. But somehow, I still didn't know what I was.

A steady background sound began to grow faster, and it took me a moment to realize it was Johann's heart. I whirled, leaping down from the rafters faster than a blink.

Johann stared straight ahead, unseeing in the dark, his eyes wide and sad. "Kaiden?" he said. His voice was back—full of feeling and confusion and life.

"Johann!"

He whirled and stumbled. His heart beat erratically, and bones I hadn't known were damaged creaked. His breathing came in gasps.

245

"Kaiden," he said. "You did it. You . . ."

Then he fell, his eyes falling shut.

"Johann?" His heart beat, slow and weak. But that was all.

I reached out to touch him, to shake him, and stopped. My nails were long, sharp, and jagged, as Dimresh's had been, the fingernails grown out to become weapons. I shrank back, swallowing, running my tongue over my teeth. My fangs sliced it, and my own blood tinged my mouth for a few seconds before it healed. I swallowed again, and my fangs shrank, some strange new malleability changing them. My nails shrank too, from claws back into the normal, dirty fingernails I was used to.

Johann's breathing slowed, his heart skipping beats. Blood ran from the corner of his mouth. I had no time to figure out what I was right now.

For the second time in the past few nights, I gathered a human into my arms. This time I wasn't being chased. I was safe, the master of a castle. But I still had to hurry.

Johann was lighter than I remembered, even lighter than Matilda. His scent surrounded me, pine and musk and sweat and traces of leather and herbs and fresh wood . . . it was dizzying. He would taste . . .

No. I wasn't hungry. I didn't need his blood.

You will. Dimresh's final words hissed in my mind.

I ran. Johann flopped in my arms, and I held him in place. I wouldn't let him die. Not like Matilda.

I dashed down steep stairs and then over plush carpets, and finally down familiar hallways. They weren't as dark as I remembered, the black stones shot through with gray rot and green creeping, curled vines that grew in from outside. I raced down the hall and out the broken, rotted door, where milky moonlight illuminated the forest along with the promise of dawn.

I paused for one moment, the rush of my stopped

momentum whipping leaves. The dipping half moon glared in my sensitive eyes like a sun. Milky light stretched over the green and brown of the trees, the shining drips of morning dew, and the faint white curls of mist over the loam.

The forest had always been dark, but I'd never thought it was beautiful before. This was a vampire's world — my world. The one I could now see even more clearly than before.

But I didn't have time for beauty. The sun was close, and Johann was dying. I had taken too long to kill Dimresh. I had failed Johann so many times tonight, but I wouldn't fail him again.

I kept running, the sounds of the forest coming through the drumbeats of my footsteps. Deer hooves struck grass in the distance, and a cougar's claws dug into fallen leaves. Bats whistled overhead after insects, and below me mice and moles dug holes in fresh dirt. Coyotes barked in the distance, greeting the dawn when they would hunt.

And ahead, the village of Penthorn stretched out, quieter than it should be, too many houses and farms lost to time and vampires before me. It appeared over the horizon as I exited the dense growth of the forest, houses laid out in no intelligible pattern, guttering torches illuminating brick roadways between the brewery and the inns and the town center. The river surrounded it, flowing water that roared in my ears.

But the rushing water didn't bring the fear it once had. It was no longer my enemy. And even if it was, Johann needed help I couldn't give.

I cradled him tightly and leaped over the river that would have once weakened me.

I landed effortlessly next to Matilda's house but didn't pause. Johann was still alive. He had to be, and I had to get him help.

Broken houses flashed past me, and crooked streets took me to the square. It was almost morning, and someone must be around. Surely someone was awake. Once I would have known where to take him, remembered where a doctor could be found. Or I could have taken him to Matilda, who had helped me. Now . . .

This had been my village, but I'd lost even the memory of it.

I gritted my teeth. The scent of blood tinged my nostrils, and I realized my fingernails had sharpened again, digging into Johann's cheek.

Someone screamed. I whirled, and a woman's face in the window nearby vanished, her eyes wide and white.

"Help him!" I shouted into the night. No one answered me. "Help!"

Light spilled from a doorway, and a man appeared in its frame. The firelight from inside was blinding. "What's this . . . is that Johann? The hunter?" He took a few steps toward me, and then his eyes went as wide as the woman's in the window. "Hey now!"

I put Johann on the ground, struggling to look normal. No claws. No fangs. I wasn't a thrall. A vampire could hide. I could hide now, couldn't I? "Help him," I said. *"Please."*

The man met my eyes. "Kaiden?" he said. "The . . ." His eyes narrowed, and he took a step back. "You died. The vampire took you."

"He's dying," I said, pointing to Johann. My nails were black and pointed like claws. "Please, help him! Find someone!" The morning mists began to thin. I felt it in my body and heart. The sun was approaching. I needed to get back to safety, to hide and sleep.

To the castle that was now mine.

"You can't be . . . Who are you?" The man stepped forward, fist clenched, his gaze swinging from Johann's form to me. "What happened to him? He said . . ."

Dark anger swirled in my chest, and the words I could use

flashed in my mind. *By my blood . . .*

No. I wasn't like Dimresh. "Please." I gritted my teeth, my fangs jutting as the words twisted into a growl. Johann's heart thudded slower. *"Help him!"*

"Vampire!" the man shouted. He took more steps back, leaving Johann alone on the ground.

"If I wanted to kill you, you'd be dead," I shouted. The sky was pinking, and my eyes burned. Too much light. "Johann is dying. Please . . ." I blinked tearing eyes. "Please help him. I can't."

The man stared at me. I didn't have any time left. I turned and ran from the village and the approaching day, the sound of Johann's heart still beating in my ears.

CHAPTER THIRTY-THREE

A man knelt at an altar, where a stone carving of a woman oversaw a plate of fresh green herbs. There was no scent, no sound, just images, and I knew I was dreaming.

The carving was familiar, like a larger, more detailed version of the one that had lain sodden and forgotten by the side of the road. Stone hands reached out for the plate. At the base of the carving, vines and roots were carved in gnarled patterns, as though the woman had sprung from a tree, and her skin was carved with tiny leaves.

The kneeling man wore robes finer than Dimresh's had been, purple and gold streaks adding color to robes of dark black. His lips moved, words that must mean something, but I couldn't tell what. If they were prayers of magic, they were ineffective.

After a few more words, he looked up at the ceiling, his gaze serene.

A shadow crossed over the kneeling man, and I turned. The first thing I noticed was the man casting it wore a fine silk vest shot through with tassels, and an array of fine silk pants and clothes and a cloak so complicated it must have taken help to put it on.

The second thing was that the man looked just like me.

The dream faded, even as I reached for what it meant. Something deep inside me burned, as though my blood itself was boiling in my veins.

I opened my eyes to my old sleeping spot in the dark rooms beneath the hallways of Dimresh's castle. For a split second, everything, even Johann, felt like a dream.

But when the hunger burned in my stomach, it felt different.

Hunger had dogged my waking ever since I could remember. The overbearing, vicious feeling had been what drove me to get up every night. It was the cruel, animalistic hunger of a thrall. Now it was weak, not the driving force it had once been. I could control it. It took no effort to ignore it.

I stood, letting the scents and sounds of the castle wash over me. Up stone steps and down long hallways, my footsteps silent.

I was hungry, but I didn't need to hunt. And without a need to hunt, without the overpowering craving, there was nothing.

I could go to Johann. I knew his scent better than anything else. But I didn't know what I'd do if he was dead. Or how I would react if I saw him alive.

Vampires need human blood.

Dimresh had to have lied. I didn't need to hunt, but I did need to prove him wrong. Then I could go to Johann and see what happened. I could know it was safe.

Instead of leaving through the hallways, I walked through the main gate of the keep. The heavy wooden doors had been latched shut for years, an iron bar half-sunk into the rotted wood.

How long had it been? What had happened to this keep, years ago? The dream flashed in my mind. Whatever building I'd seen had had been well-kept, almost new.

I turned back, but there was no sign in the entranceway of an altar or any hint of anything resembling one having been here, just the confusing array of beams around the central structural pillar. A warlike keep, not . . . whatever had been in the dream. A temple to Laurel.

I lifted the iron bar. It clanged as it hit the stone floor. The doors creaked, and then one of them swayed and fell sideways, the wood rotted through near the hinge.

I headed out in the forest, leaving the doors to the castle open. I didn't know if I'd be back.

Just like the night before, the forest was bright and full of life. The moon was slightly narrower now, the night itself dimmer. Green leaves were tinged with brown and rustled in a cold wind. I was sure I could hunt even in the light of just the stars in midwinter.

I tracked the scent of deer, noting the small depressions in the leaves, the sharp Vs in the dirt where hooves had pressed into the mud. One small, the rest large. I sped up, but there was none of the excitement I used to feel from the first hunt of the night, the knowledge that the burning hunger would soon be sated. It was just . . . easy.

I came upon the group of deer without a sound, and before the buck of the group had a chance to raise its head, I leaped. Instead of a killing bite, my momentum took me into it with such force that its neck snapped.

A mistake. I would have to adjust how much strength I used. I wasn't a thrall anymore.

I bit down into the twitching animal, my fangs sinking into its veins.

My mouth and throat and stomach burned. I spat out the blood, my stomach twisting, and I rolled onto the ground, fighting not to heave. My insides twisted and ached, my fangs lengthening and my claws scrabbling at the dirt.

Tears welled in my eyes and ran down my cheeks as I vomited up the burning deer blood. Dimresh hadn't lied.

The pain didn't ease quickly, and I spat and heaved. The deer had stiffened by the time I was able to stand. A panther waited in the shadows of the leaves, its eyes glowing and its tail lashing.

I left it to its meal, the one I should have had. It didn't try to attack me. Nothing would.

I was a vampire lord, just as Johann said I would be. Greater than a thrall, with powers I didn't understand and a hunger that could only be sated by human blood.

Why had I wanted this? The hunger would only get worse. I couldn't have Johann before. I could have him even less now.

My steps took me to the edge of the village. Matilda's house sat dark and empty. With my new perfect vision, I could even see into the square, where smart people hurried between buildings, afraid to be caught outside at night. Fools and drunks were the only ones who took their time. One man grabbed another by the shirtfront and pulled him inside a building.

No sign of Johann.

I should leave. If I truly could have nothing but human blood, then going into town was a mistake.

But something deeper than hunger drove me to leap over the river and enter the town, my speed taking me silently through the streets. I lifted my nose to the air, searching for the scent of him, the tinge of pine and the familiar scent of his blood.

I had to at least know.

I found the scent behind the brewery, where I had left him. I darted behind the building, and I was only a shadow to the woman plying her trade down a dark alley. The scent took me away from the town square and the brewery, down houses that held the scents of vegetables and fresh millet and the sounds of snoring.

I paused once. I knew this path. I closed my eyes against the brightness of the moon.

Medicine for your mother. An old man held out a bottle. His bushy mustache twitched. Be ready, boy. It's likely too late. The ague is worse every year. I don't think I'll be seeing you again.

I had hated him then for telling me that my mother was going to die.

I blinked and kept going, past the cracked pipe that jutted out of an abandoned house, leaping over the puddle that always smelled of sewage. When I turned a corner, I saw the hospital.

It had been a barn once, but so long ago that not even my new sense of smell could pick up scents of horses or sheep. Just the scents of decay and rot, mixed with the tang of herbal medicines, a dangerous scent that made me slow.

But underneath it all was the scent of Johann.

I crept to the door of the hospital, hewn into the side of the building. I flattened myself against the wall when I heard footsteps. The enormous barn doors just around the corner swung open.

A cart pulled by a donkey exited the building. The scent of death reached my nose. As the cart passed by, a woman wearing green waved once, a final goodbye, before swinging the barn doors shut once again.

I tensed, but Johann's scent never wavered. It wasn't him.

Open-air windows ringed the building above my head. I jumped straight up, catching the rim with both hands and swinging inside. I landed on my feet in what had once been a hayloft, now a storage area for blankets and bandages.

The scent of hay and herbs mingled with rot and death and blood. I wrinkled my nose, the aroma of blood not enticing enough underneath the many fragrances that spoke of illness.

Was there another plague? Or was it just common that people here got sick?

I blinked in darkness. I had known this once. I'd been here before. I should know it. I was a vampire and had been a thrall, but I'd been human once, just like everyone here.

I peered over the edge of the hayloft, down into the hospital. Many rooms were empty, but an old woman lay in one, white hair covered in a woolen hat. Her lungs rattled as she breathed shallow in sleep. A young man lay in another, his leg covered in a bloody bandage. His gaze passed over me, and he shifted in obvious pain, revealing the leech that fed from his shoulder. A waste of blood.

Once I would have been tempted. Easy prey. But now I just saw weakness, pain that I could do nothing about. These were people I should know. No, they were people I should care for. They were mine.

I blinked. Where had that thought come from? Was that what Dimresh had believed? Was that why vampires killed and ate those in their territory — because they thought people belonged to them?

Was that what it meant to be a vampire lord?

My sharp fingernails dug into the wood of the hayloft. I relaxed them, willing them to go back to normal. I could figure out what I was later. I needed to find Johann. Maybe he could help me.

I leaped across the open space, one hayloft to the next. On this side, I saw the woman in white leaning over a pallet in another room, whispering something to the man who lay there.

Johann.

Something deep weighed my body down. I froze in place until the woman left. Johann looked wretched. His breathing sounded strange, and bruises bloomed on one shoulder and disappeared under a bandage around his chest. But his heart beat strong, and his eyes were clear as he leaned back against the pillows of his sleeping pallet, staring up at the ceiling in quiet contemplation. He looked . . . serene. Like the man in my dream.

I dropped down soundlessly behind him, but he reacted anyway, tensing beneath his tattered woolen blanket. Pride for his hunter training made me smile, or maybe it was just because I was close to him.

"Johann," I said.

He relaxed, tilting his head up farther. I moved around to face him, and he smiled.

It made me so happy to see that smile.

"Kaiden," he said. I loved to hear my name on his lips. "You did it. Look at you. Your eyes . . . they're beautiful."

"I . . ." I swallowed, my fangs pricking the front of my tongue. I willed them to go away, to hide. I hadn't even thought of how I must look. "I couldn't have without you. And you . . ."

I didn't know what to say. Got hurt. Were controlled. Almost died because my magic forced his body to work in ways it shouldn't have. Instead of saying all that, I motioned to him. "I'm sorry."

"You have blood on your shirt front," Johann said. "Deer?"

I didn't answer. I didn't know what to say.

He chuckled. "I guess vampires do waste blood." He pushed himself up onto his elbows. "Don't be sorry, Kaiden. Under your magic, I was still aware of what was going on. Part of me was glad to help you. And without you, I would have died. Your magic was safe, in a way. Protective. And when Dimresh died and his fear spell faded, I could throw off your magic. I didn't mean to scare you."

It sounded impossible. "You . . . you stayed under the spell on purpose?"

He smiled at me again. "I suppose so. It was a comfort against the fear spell. Like I said, without it I would have died. And I trust you, Kaiden. I really do."

I looked away from his deep brown eyes. I wanted to celebrate with him, to revel in our victory. He wasn't angry. He cared about me. He trusted me.

But it didn't feel like a victory anymore. Dimresh's words echoed. *You're making a mistake.*

"Vampires can't drink animal blood," I said.

His smile faltered, his brows furrowing. "What do you

mean?"

"Vampires can't drink animal blood," I repeated. He frowned, and my voice dropped low as I spoke. "I tried. Deer blood made me sick. Dimresh told me, but I didn't believe him, but animal blood burns." I gritted my teeth at the memory, my fangs protruding from my lips. "I'm not hungry now. The hunger is different, weaker. I don't need to eat every night." As I spoke, my fears came to the surface, coloring my words. "But I will need human blood, won't I? And it will be worse." Johann sat up, supporting himself on one arm. "If I don't drink blood, I'll . . . I'll die, won't I? But if I do . . ."

Johann reached out, his hand warm on my arm. I let him touch me, his hand gliding down to take mine. He was weak and fragile, a human, but his touch grounded me as steadily as a tree.

"We'll figure this out," he said. "Just because we beat Dimresh doesn't mean I'll stop helping you. I trust you. I made you a vampire lord, and I intend to see this through. Trust me, please?"

"I do." I held his hand tighter. "I always have."

He took a deep breath and then winced in pain, lying back on the cot. I wished there was something I could do.

"I've sent a messenger to the hunters' barracks," he said. "They'll be here to pick me up and help me recover." Footsteps grew closer, the caretaker of the hospital heading toward Johann's room. I drew back. I was a vampire, not a hungry thrall, but I didn't want to be seen by people who might have once known me. Not with blood on my shirt, not when I didn't know what would happen to me once I got truly hungry.

Johann held my hand tighter. "I know it may be hard for you, if you can't have animal blood. Just . . . can you head to the barracks?" I shook my head as soon as he said it. The thought of going back without Johann, having to defend

myself against accusations and hunters without hurting people with power I barely understood was terrifying. "Then can
you wait for me? Wait at Dimresh's castle. Please, Kaiden?
We'll figure this out together."

"I . . . can wait."

Johann smiled, squeezing my hand once more before letting go. "You're a vampire lord now, Kaiden, but at heart
you're no different, are you?"

"Who are you talking to in there, Johann?" The kindly
voice of the woman came through the door. Before she
opened it, I had flipped back up into the hayloft.

"No one," Johann said. "Just dreaming, I suppose."

"That vampire did a number on you," the woman said. She
knelt down, holding out a foul-smelling bowl of what looked
like tea. "Still in pain?"

"At times," Johann admitted. He drank the concoction, and
it must have tasted as bad as it smelled because he grimaced
when it was gone. "That slop helps."

"Willowbark and poppy," the woman said. "Sorry I don't
have sugar for taste."

Johann chuckled. "I'm guessing it tastes no different than
what I throw at those bloodsuckers."

The woman rolled her eyes, but smiled as she did. "You're
sure we're safe now?"

"Safe from here to the merchant road, at least from the
vampire at the fallen castle," Johann said. He wheezed when
he spoke at full volume. "Soon enough, people here will know
they don't have to be afraid."

"What about the one who left you in the street? The one
Ronaldo chased off?"

I raised an eyebrow. Ronaldo had chased me off, had he?

"You don't have to worry about that one," Johann said.
"There's nothing to fear from him." He gazed up at the ceiling
as he spoke, looking as serene and idealistic as the man in my

dream. "Rickardt will return safely with other hunters, and this town will be free of vampires for a long time."

"I'd love to see the day," the woman said. "My grandmother said that was true in the old days, that people weren't afraid at night." She snorted. "Of course, maybe it was back then there were so many of us to choose from, the risk was lower. It's easy to have hope when you've seen better days."

"Good days, and nights, will come again," Johann said, his voice softening. The medicine she'd given him was doing its work, his heart slowing to a steady rhythm. His gaze searched the hayloft where I hid. "Trust me."

I watched him sleep for a few moments, and for the first time, no insidious hunger made me think of him as prey. He was just . . . Johann. A man I cared for, enjoying the safety of a night's rest.

My night stretched ahead of me, nights into eternity. I would wait for him. And learn.

I had a whole castle to explore.

CHAPTER THIRTY-FOUR

A blond man stared back at me from the finely carved mirror. The man I'd been two months ago, before I had died to Dimresh's fangs. Pale skin, blond hair, finely toned muscles I hadn't truly earned. And normal, human eyes, the irises blue. Beautiful eyes, Johann had said. Standing naked, my ruined, bloody clothes discarded, I didn't hate what I saw.

At least until I smiled and my fangs became obvious. I could hide them with effort, at least. Another trick I could use if I ever hunted humans.

No. I couldn't think of that. This was the second night, and vampires didn't need blood every night. I could ignore the growing hunger.

I had learned another trick last night, too, when I uncovered the mirror. I didn't know why Dimresh had covered it. Maybe because of the strange thing we could do. With a thought, I faded from the mirror, my reflection gone as though I wasn't there at all. Instead I saw only the red and purple tapestries and golden shag carpet of the master bedroom of the castle. The windows on the far wall could swing open to view the forest and the village of Penthorn beyond, but now they were tightly latched, with only a faded quilt hanging over them that had sewn decorations of what the town must have looked like once. I could pick out the reds of brick houses, the greens of rolling farms, and the yellow of the sun over the hills.

More than anything, this castle was a monument to lost history. The lost Empire. And to distract myself from my growing hunger last night after seeing Johann, I had begun digging up whatever I could find.

Most of the tapestries were so old and faded I couldn't make sense of them. Some of the weapons on the weapons racks had carvings and engravings on the steel, but if they'd ever been words, I couldn't read them. Sigils, maybe, of noble houses. Or perhaps just decoration. And the castle itself was clearly a defensive structure. I'd already found trick staircases and small compartments where defenders must have leaped out at attackers.

Hadn't Johann said the Empire was peaceful? I could ask him when he came to visit me.

I swallowed down a surge of hunger at the thought. *No.* I had to stay focused. I couldn't fall prey to hunger, not again. This was different, I told myself. Just hunger, not the unstoppable craving from before, when I was a thrall.

Another kind of craving kindled, though, one I accepted. Thinking of Johann and his strength, his kindness, his well-formed body and strong jaw and strong, muscular legs . . .

My body heated, but this time it was strong, a true fire, and the intensity of it made me gasp. This was the first time I'd felt like this since becoming what I was now, and hope mingled with lust.

I opened my mouth, letting out a wordless sigh. Already naked, I could see my growing desire reflected in the mirror. I turned away, heading toward the plush bed.

I'd stripped it clean of the covers Dimresh had used. I didn't need so much, just a simple blanket. But I appreciated the softness of the feather-filled mattress as I lay down, the sleekness of the velvet coverings over the bed. I hadn't known comfort like this since dying. Maybe ever. Mattresses in Penthorn were usually filled with straw.

I closed my eyes, shutting out the sight of the castle — the beams overhead and the fluttering, ragged tapestries. My body blazed from the inside, like the kiss of moonlight from a full moon, reflected light that glowed and guided instead of burning. "Johann," I said, and lost myself in fantasy.

His touch was soft and strong, his hands on mine. Then on my body. He knelt over me as I lay on my back, stroking me from hip to neck. My body shuddered under his touch. One finger trailed over my neck, up my jaw, sizzling heat and softness. *Life.* He traced it over my lips, my fangs . . .

I moaned on the bed, my fangs poking my lips.

In my fantasy, he trailed his finger down again, over my nipples, and I arched my back. He pressed me down, back onto the bed. "Kaiden," he said. I loved hearing my name on his lips. He trailed his hand down, over my chest, my stomach, lower and lower, and I surged beneath his touch. His hands were so hot around me.

He leaned down, and where his hands had gone his mouth followed. Now they were kisses, licks, up my chest and neck. He held my hand in one of his, and the other stroked me, heat and friction. His kisses traveled up my neck. My jaw.

I opened my mouth, letting out another moan. "Johann," I whispered. His breath was hot against mine. His pulse beat hard in his neck, his scent surrounding me.

He lay down on top of me as our mouths met, his lips molding against mine. His body molded too, chest to chest, hip to hip, now his firm body rubbing against mine instead of his hand. He was as hot as a sunny day, and I gasped, my breath hitching, breaking the kiss. I needed . . . I needed . . . My thoughts began to fray.

He kissed me. His tongue moved against mine.

I didn't want to bite him. I wanted to kiss him, keep kissing him, keep his tongue against mine, help him avoid my long, sharp fangs.

I was gasping now, even when I didn't need air, gasping just to moan, to say his name. "Johann . . . Johann . . ."

I wrapped one hand around his body, pulling him closer. His breath washed over me. "Kaiden," he said, his voice loud in my ears. The kiss broke, and Johann moved closer, guiding me inside him. I wanted it. I wanted *him*.

My moans choked off, and I gritted my teeth. Pleasure I hadn't felt in months began to grow overwhelming.

Johann moaned in my ears, his face against mine, his body jolting as I thrust inside him. "Kaiden," he said, and I couldn't speak. He was so warm, so hot. His body thrummed with life, with what I didn't have, with promise and heat and tightness and . . .

My body shook. "Johann . . ."

He kissed my ear, turning his head. "Kaiden," he whispered.

It wasn't enough; my hand wasn't enough, the fantasy fraying. I turned over onto my side, stroking and thrusting into my hand, into Johann, my fangs slicing my lower lip. "Johann," I begged. I was so close. "Johann, please . . ."

I knew what I needed. So did he.

Johann tilted his head. "Kaiden."

I moaned, thrusting harder and harder. I wanted it. I didn't, but I did.

"Kaiden, please," Johann said.

I couldn't speak. I was so close. My body surged again and again, each time closer and closer to the edge. I thrust so hard, squeezed myself so hard it nearly hurt. I needed this so badly.

"Trust me, Kaiden," he said, his voice hot in my ear. "Trust me."

I couldn't stand it anymore. I bit into his neck, blood hitting my fangs and filling my mouth. "Kaiden!" he said, a bellow of satisfaction.

I cried out as the fantasy splintered into red-soaked pieces, my body shuddering over and over. My fangs sliced down into my own lip, my back teeth clacking together. Spots flashed behind my closed eyes. My release splashed hard into my hand and overflowed onto the mattress in exquisitely pleasurable, almost painful spurts.

I moaned once more. In the fantasy, Johann was fine. I licked up a few spots of blood from his wound, and he put a cloth on his neck. I lay on the bed, succumbing to a release of month's worth of pleasure I couldn't have before. Because Johann had saved me.

My body shuddered one last time, and I opened my eyes. The mirror faced the bed, where I lay naked, my mouth bleeding from where I'd bitten it . . . alone.

I wished I hadn't bitten him, even in my dreams. I wasn't a thrall anymore. I was supposed to be in control. I was supposed to be better.

It was just a fantasy. It could only ever be one. But at least now I could enjoy it to the fullest. Maybe that could be enough.

It would have to be. I had to keep distracting myself from the hunger until Johann came back for me.

I had to trust him.

Another night passed, and I woke hungrier. I had to distract myself immediately.

The true treasures of Dimresh's castle were the books, and it was past time I studied them. I just wished they were easier to read.

I moved over to the shelves, perusing the books within. They'd clearly been written centuries ago, even the smell of ink lost to a scent of dust, paper, and leather. One was less dusty, though, and I picked it from the shelf. I caught a whiff of Dimresh's scent on the leather bindings.

The book I opened entranced me immediately. The first few pages were all illustrations done in colored ink, almost like miniature paintings. The first page showed an enormous castle like the one I sat in now, but illuminated in sunlight and not decrepit and old. *The capital of the Leoren Empire,* read the caption. On the next page, men and women wore clothing of fine silk, just as Dimresh had. But these were dyed in pinks and reds, scarlets and blues, shining in the sun like flowers on a clear day. And on the next, men and women wore robes of mingled greens and yellows, their sleeves trailing on the floor, each robe embroidered on the back with an image of a sprig of laurel leaves. Priests of Holy Laurel, from the days when she'd had power.

I turned the next page too quickly. Part of it frayed, tearing off in my hand. The page was of an altar, a man with the stamp of Holy Laurel on his green robes kneeling in front of a statue of Laurel. Instead of a rain-soaked lump of stone, this showed a woman made of dozens of tiny leaves. One hand was overturned, as though reaching down to pat a child. The piece in my hand showed the base of the statue, carved roots gnarled around her feet.

Just like in my dream.

I must have seen a picture like this before, that's all. Or maybe Matilda had told me once about the ancient statues. Just memories of my life entering my dreams.

I turned the page, but that was all there was in the way of illustrations. The bindings were loose, and the next page almost fell out of the book. *Prayers for Holy Laurel* was the first line, in large, blocky letters. The rest was written in hard-to-read, tiny script.

Prayers for Holy Laurel. Old magic that had once worked. Dimresh must have used this book to figure out what he could do with his twisted magic. The realization sent eagerness and a strange sort of caution through me.

A book from the old Empire, with magic long dead, could still inform vampires now. Could still inform *me* now.

I turned the pages, angry at myself for not being able to

read the tiny looping script. Maybe Johann could. As I flipped them, though, some pages were notched with tiny V-shaped marks — it took me a moment to realize it.

If I tensed my hands, my fingernails lengthened and curved into sharp claws. And the shape matched the marks. Dimresh had marked certain pages.

I might not know how to read script, but I could learn. And until Johann came for me, I had nothing but time.

"*By my blood*," I whispered, reading each word painstakingly from the book. The connected letters were so hard to pull apart. The prayer was supposed to begin with "Laurel grant," but I knew by now that part didn't matter. Spells were selfish. "*Bring light to fill my . . . abed?*"

Nothing happened, the words likely wrong. And I wouldn't want light anyway. The spell I had used with Johann had been darkness, and the words then had just sort of . . . come to me, as though I was flexing a muscle, using instincts I didn't know I possessed. I could follow that gut feeling. But if the intuition was born of being a vampire . . . The last thing I wanted was to do something I couldn't take back. Some magic couldn't be undone, after all. I'd been lucky that the hypnosis could.

The books could tell me what the old priests had once been able to do. But somehow, I knew that wasn't everything I could do.

I desperately wished I knew what I was. What vampires were. But somehow I didn't think the answer was in these books — or any books at all.

CHAPTER THIRTY-FIVE

Each night I learned a little more. And each night I grew hungrier.

I knew craving and hunger intimately, then and now. As a thrall, it had been a beast of its own, something in me that required constant control. Lapse for a moment, and it would sate itself without me being fully aware of what I was doing, as though I was following instincts and habits that had been hammered into me — or instilled in me by the fangs of my master. There had been no pleasure in feeding, and no anticipation of pleasure. It was just a mechanism to survive, an automatic compulsion driven by hunger. It was downing a bottle of wine without tasting it, the way I had near the end of my life.

Hunger as a vampire was both more encompassing and less. It was craving born of the knowledge that I would enjoy what I ate, the phantom taste and mouthfeel of blood that would fill me with life and warmth. It was fantasies of Johann, of his presence and scent, and then of his body and the taste of his blood. It was the scent and taste of a fine wine just out of reach, one that demanded to be savored.

But both were equally torturous. A week had passed, and I was so hungry. Fantasies weren't enough. And worse, sometimes my fantasies were without sex at all, and were just me dreaming of biting Johann. Or even someone else, some faceless, genderless human, where the only fantasy was the blood. I wanted blood. I *needed* human blood.

I learned one thing as the hunger grew. I didn't grow weak

without blood, like I had as a thrall. But my magic did.

I learned a lot over the lonely nights. Spells that would be useful, like turning to mist or bringing darkness, and spells that I would never use — like demands to bring fear, simply a reversed version of a spell priests had once used to bring calm to people in need. There were lots of spells used to bring happiness to people, to help them learn, to help bring love and understanding. These I knew Dimresh had used, and I could use, to turn another's will and control them.

I would never do that. But I did learn that I didn't need to use words to use some spells. I could turn to mist with a thought, just as Dimresh had, as easily as I could lengthen my fangs or turn my nails into diamond-hard claws. Whatever magic I had was part of me, not just something I controlled.

The books talked of priests borrowing magic from Laurel. But vampires, even though we used the same magic, were magic itself. And without blood, my hunger grew as my magic weakened.

On the ninth night, I woke to rain pounding the castle, water dripping from the leaves outside. Each night I woke just a bit earlier, the nights growing longer as winter began. Water dripped in certain places in the castle, almost cold enough to freeze, though not the bedroom where I'd spent my last week and a half.

My stomach gurgled with hunger, and my fangs pricked my lip. I couldn't hide them anymore. I still moved with grace and power as I left the soft bed. The wood creaked beneath my feet.

The scent of damp earth met my nose, along with the sharp scent of mold and mushrooms growing on the wood of the castle shedding spores in the rain. My claws curled against the windowsill.

It was more than rain. I sensed . . . something.

Or maybe I was just hungry. I closed my eyes, focusing on

what I had learned, on thinking rather than feeling the yawning emptiness in my stomach. I was a vampire lord, not a thrall. My thoughts circled back to the question I had struggled with every night.

What was I?

I'd thought becoming a vampire lord would answer my questions, I suppose. Like I would somehow know what I should do. But even Johann had said it. At heart, I was no different.

Which I guessed was a good thing. Except that I was so hungry.

There was something out there. Something I could eat.

No. Think. Dammit. It could be Johann. Or it could be one of the villagers traveling.

Only fools traveled at night. Crossing the river at night was asking to be eaten by thralls. Or vampires like me.

Think. *Focus!*

What was I? Dimresh had said things before he died. Things that were important.

Kill me and you'll never know what you are. What we are.

No. Not that. Before that.

Old blood. Something about how vampires had fallen. And . . . a curse. The curse would kill me like the rest.

Vampires couldn't die of starvation, could they? Or maybe they could. I didn't think not having blood would kill me, but maybe without magic, I would . . . unravel, somehow. And the way not to die would be to . . .

Eat. Drink blood.

No. I slammed my fist on the sill. Even if drinking human blood wouldn't make me mindless as a vampire the way it would as a thrall, I wasn't a murderer. I wasn't like Dimresh. I'd killed him to save Penthorn, hadn't I?

Or had I killed him to make myself better? To stop being a thrall?

Either way, killing wasn't the answer. But I shivered with

revulsion at the thought of animal blood, of the burning in my mouth and throat.

But I was *so* hungry. I had to eat someone. Some*thing*.

Criminals. People who were sick or dying or useless . . .

No. That's what Dimresh had done to me, drinking blood from a drunk who no one would miss. It wasn't my place to judge anyone. And people had missed me. Matilda had.

I sank onto the floor, huddled around my empty stomach. I wasn't a hungry thrall, a slave to my desires. I could resist them. But by doing that, all I could do now was suffer.

A few minutes had passed when I realized that the human life out there was coming closer.

I wasn't sure how I knew. I could sense what felt like a presence in a room, but on a much grander scale. Someone coming into my . . . territory, I supposed. The castle and lands around it were mine. Penthorn was mine.

And now someone was coming toward me.

Hope and dread mingled in my chest. Johann. It had to be. Please, let it be him.

I stood, my reflection catching my eye. I didn't have the magic right now to hide from it, or to hide my fangs and claws. But my eyes were still blue. I was still . . . me.

The clothes I found in the closet were silks and velvets, the finer things up front. There were ripped and shredded clothes in the back, and some things that almost certainly had been taken from victims. I chose a silk shirt and woolen pants, an outfit that didn't match but smelled the least of woodsmoke and the faint tang of fear sweat.

I hadn't left the castle since seeing Johann. I desperately wanted to see him again. I needed him.

I told myself it wasn't for his blood as I leaped out the window onto the slippery wet grass and mud below. It was a three-story leap, but whatever magic or curse made me what I was made it easy. I had been strong as a thrall, but not graceful like this.

I stood, scenting the air, but the rain that was already soaking through my silk shirt masked most scents. I began to run. Clouds covered the moon, but I could still see the trunks of the trees and the branches that I had to maneuver around, the leaves on the ends the orange-red of late autumn.

The creaking of wagon wheels was the first sign of him. The second was voices. Johann. And one other — Thomas.

I slowed, listening.

"Wheel's going to get stuck. And then where will we be? Sitting ducks for a vampire."

"He won't attack us, Thomas," Johann said. His breathing came shallow and hitched. He was still in pain. "Would I be here in this state if I thought he was going to attack?"

"That's why I'm here," Thomas said. A stakeshooter clicked. "You'd be a fool not to take precautions. Especially with this crazy plan."

Crazy plan? That at least sounded like the Johann I knew.

"It'll be fine, Thomas," Johann said. "You'll see."

Voices from a distance weren't enough. I wanted to see him. To scent him. To know he'd come for me.

"Johann!" I called out. Hardly the stealthy approach a vampire should have favored, but I wasn't a regular vampire, was I?

They didn't respond. They were too far — humans couldn't hear as I could, my ears so sharp now I could hear a mouse squeak from dozens of feet away. I ran, my agility closing the distance in mere seconds.

I opened my mouth to call again when another stakeshooter clicked to my right. I froze. I couldn't turn to mist, not as hungry as I was. And Johann and Thomas were just ahead of me on the path.

I turned toward the sound, peering through the dark leaves.

So well hidden she looked almost like Laurel herself, a woman sat nestled among the gnarled roots of a fallen tree, hidden behind a thick curtain of leaves. It would have been the perfect disguise had the curling, reddening leaves of autumn not left one shoulder exposed.

"Master Hunter," I said. "Lesalie." I licked my lips, flicking a glance once more at the road where Johann and Thomas would soon pass by and then back to the woman who may be hunting me. "Does Johann know you're here?"

"Stay there, thrall," she said.

I didn't have to obey her. I was stronger and faster. But she'd almost successfully hidden from me, and caution as well as curiosity made me stay put as she left her hiding spot. Was this part of what Thomas had said was Johann's crazy plan? Didn't he trust me?

She emerged from the overgrowth, her weapon hanging at her side. The wagon creaked along the path, but it would be more than a few minutes at the pace set by the lone horse. It was just her and me, a vampire and a hunter who I knew by looking at her was more experienced and deadlier than Johann. This woman was as much a killer as I was.

"Is it true?" she asked. "You killed Dimresh. The castle is yours now?" She crept closer and held up a lantern. With a twist of her wrist, copper scraped and sparked, and the wick inside caught. Her eyes widened. "It is true, then."

"I am . . . a vampire now," I said. Hunger burned in my stomach like the flame in her lantern. "But I don't know if the castle is mine."

"And what do you want, vampire?" she asked. The light from the flame flickered over the woods, shadows dancing oddly. My eyes watered at the brightness. I could extinguish it with a thought—or at least I could if I had blood.

Blood. That was what I wanted. But I knew it wasn't what she meant.

As a human, I had wanted . . . drink, I suppose. If I'd wanted more, I didn't remember it. As a thrall, I'd wanted this, to be a vampire, not to be a slave to my own desires. And now that I had that . . .

The wagon creaked, the horse snuffling in the distance. Johann's voice came over the wind, tinged with pain. " . . . gets darker and colder every night. But I like the crisp air."

The answer became obvious. "I want to be with Johann," I said. Hunger and desire flared, and I swallowed. Even if I couldn't be with him as I could in my fantasies, I still wanted to be close. He'd given me a second chance. Maybe he could help me.

"And then?" Lesalie asked. Her wrist had relaxed slightly on the stakeshooter. "Johann won't live forever, you know."

But I would. I wondered how old Dimresh had been. Had he been alive during the fall of the Empire? Was Johann right, and vampires had caused its fall? "I don't know," I said. "I'll figure it out, I suppose."

The scent of Johann's blood suddenly reached my nose, and I stiffened. Hunger wrapped me, not like the instinctual compulsion from before, but like a sensual whisper, a promise of luxury. But that wasn't why I broke away and ran.

The growls and snarls of a thrall were loud in my ears, eclipsing the sounds of Johann's heavy breathing and Thomas's curses. I broke from the tree line, where a thrall advanced on Johann, its eyes as black as mine had once been. It growled, mindless and crazed, and leaped for Johann.

He wasn't holding a weapon.

I jumped, and my speed snapped the thrall's neck and threw it skidding into the forest. It wrenched itself to its feet, hissing. It was a man, or had been, and it scented the air once before trying to dart past me toward Johann.

I grabbed it by the neck, and then realized what I was holding.

Not human. But not an animal. I had already killed thralls. I had drank one's blood once as a thrall, a few disgusting sips. But it had never occurred to me until now that they could be my main source of food.

I bit into the thrall's neck, and the blood was as foul as I remembered. It went down thick and tasted of rot and mold. But it stayed down. Hope blossomed in my chest even as the phlegmy, horrid blood of the thrall slid down my throat.

I didn't have to bite anyone. I could survive like this.

The hunger finally died away, leaving only an edge of disappointment. It hadn't been the meal I wanted. But it would sustain me. I wasn't even hungry enough to finish it, and dropped the now-dead thrall to the ground. His eyes weren't black anymore.

My stomach turned, but it wasn't because of the blood. If things had gone differently . . .

"Kaiden," Johann said. I looked up to see his bright smile, which lit up the forest even more than Lesalie's lantern. "How are you?"

Chapter Thirty-Six

Johann walked fearlessly beside me as he stepped into the castle where he'd been puppeted by me and attacked by a vicious vampire. Thomas peered up at the ceiling and then at all four corners, his hand on his weapon the entire time.

Behind the three of us came Lesalie. She held her weapon, too, but if she was suspicious, she was extremely good at hiding it.

"Amazing," Johann said. "I saw it before, but it was almost as if through a cloud. Now it's much clearer. And brighter." He held up a lantern, and I transferred my gaze to the ground where the light wouldn't sear my eyes as badly. "Where did you stay as a thrall?"

I didn't want to see that dark hallway again, and the dingy room I'd stayed in mindlessly for months. "There's nothing important there. But upstairs, there are books. From the old Empire."

Johann's eyes widened.

"Go look over them," Lesalie said. "Stay with the vam . . . with Kaiden."

I couldn't tell if she trusted me or not. But she let Johann, still wheezing and in pain, follow me while she and Thomas stayed downstairs, studying the rusted weapons on the rack.

He seemed to forget his pain when he saw the bookcase. "So many!" He knelt down next to the books, raising one eyebrow. "I see you've studied a few too? The prayer book?"

"It has pictures of the old Empire," I said. "Le . . . oren?"

"Right, the Leoren Empire," Johann said. "Kaiden, this is a

275

treasure trove. Some of the books we've seen before, but so many of these"—he swept his lantern over the bookcase—"are new. They could give us insight into the Empire. Ways to gain back what we've lost." He turned back to me, standing up and wincing slightly when he did. "Did you find anything useful?"

His happiness warmed me. "Nothing about vampires. But the old spells . . . they're similar to what I can do."

"Right. That's what I figured." He flipped through more pages and must have noted my claw marks. "Read a lot, did you?"

"I . . . tried to distract myself," I said. "I was hungry."

Johann nodded, putting the book down. "I'm sorry. I came as fast as I could." He faced me. "I didn't want you to suffer. I'd hoped you would find a thrall wandering around here, but I guess not. I should have been faster."

I shook my head. "The hunger now . . . isn't as bad as before."

"That's good to hear. I'm glad I found one, too. I was sure the thrall would work. Not fully human, but not animal. And if you can drink a vampire as a thrall, it made sense, at least to me."

I nodded, the taste still revolting on my tongue, but I didn't tell him that.

"What would you have done if I'd attacked you and not the thrall?" I asked.

"What would you have done if I hadn't come back?" Johann countered with a smile.

"I . . . I knew you would." The answer eased my fears.

"And I knew you wouldn't," Johann said with certainty. "I trust you, Kaiden. Thomas and Lesalie may not. But I do."

His words made me smile, and this time, fed, I could hide my fangs. I could look normal.

He stepped forward, and the air between us became

charged. The lantern swung in his hand. He placed it on a side table, our shadows dancing together on the far wall. I could smell him, his luscious scent, his willingness. He wanted me. I wanted him. He stepped forward, his eyes searching.

My fantasy in front of me. But every fantasy since that first night had ended in blood. I couldn't risk it. Not now. Maybe not ever.

I stepped away, turning my head. Johann huffed a breath, maybe disappointment. Maybe acceptance.

"Dimresh said a few things," I said, and Johann nodded. "Before he . . . before I killed him. I thought they were lies, but he was right about the . . . human blood."

"What did he say?" Johann's eyes glittered with curiosity.

"Dimresh said the curse would kill me," I said, my words coming fast. "He called me an old blood, and also mentioned something about vampires killing each other when we . . . first fell."

Johann's eyes narrowed. "So. Old blood. Vampires . . . fell. And a curse."

"Does it make sense to you?" I asked.

"Not completely. I've heard the term old blood before, but I thought it meant a vampire who was very old. The idea of curses and vampires falling could mean being turned, and the curse could be the dark magic that does it. Perhaps he referred to when all the vampires were turned at once."

"I'm not old, though," I said. "I was . . . just a thrall."

"Not just a thrall, clearly," Johann said. "There was something about you that even Dimresh didn't catch on to until it was too late for him. And now we'll never know, I suppose."

"Never?"

Johann looked up. "Not never," he said. "Unless you're happy not knowing. This is your castle, after all. You've achieved all you wanted. Do you want to stay here?"

"Here?" I glanced around the room, at the books, the soft

featherbed, the old tapestries that a merchant would likely kill for, and the window that overlooked Penthorn. A castle, and luxuries those in Penthorn would never dream of. I could hunt thralls when I needed food. I could live forever.

And never know why.

"No," I said. "I want . . ."

"What do you want, vampire?" Lesalie had asked. I wanted to see Johann. I had him here. But he was a person, someone I wanted to be with, not . . . mine. Not the way Dimresh had thought he owned the people of Penthorn, this territory.

This castle wasn't mine either.

"I want to know more," I said. "I want to know why I could become a vampire. I want to know what other vampires want. I want to know . . . what Dimresh could have told me if I hadn't killed him."

Johann smiled and put his hand on my shoulder. His touch was like fire, firmer and yet softer and more caring than I remembered.

"I'm glad to hear it," he said. "I'd still like to have you join me as a vampire hunter, you know. A strange one, to be sure, but probably the most effective one. With you, we can make a real difference. Vampires like Lasren, lords we couldn't touch . . . you could change the world. And think of it this way—free meals while putting down thralls."

Like I had once been. I wondered if there was a way to save them. To save vampires.

Old blood and a curse. A mystery for three hundred years. If I fought other vampires, talked to other vampires, maybe I could figure it out. And I could do it with Johann. I wouldn't have him like I did in my fantasies. But it was something.

"I'll do it," I said.

"I knew you would," Johann said with a smile.

ABOUT THE AUTHOR

Ravon Silvius lives in a tiny apartment with two tiny cats in a tiny town in the United States. Despite the cramped living quarters, Ravon enjoys coming up with big ideas for novels, with some plots coming from Ravon's findings as a neuroscience researcher and others coming purely from Ravon's imagination.

www.ingramcontent.com/pod-product-compliance
Lightning Source LLC
Chambersburg PA
CBHW061551170626
46811CB00001B/164

*9 7 8 1 4 8 7 4 3 1 0 2 0 *